I0699679

VILE HOPE

VILE HOPE

JACIE NEHER

Trigger Warnings

this book contains graphic descriptions of self-harm and suicidal thoughts and actions

there are also intense scenes of physical and emotional abuse

To all the kids who grew up scared. This book is for you.

And to my sister, Lily, who beat me with a pillow when she read the ending.

A Summary of Dark Oasis

In case you want to brush up on your knowledge before exploring Dolion and Loralie's past and continuing Clair's pursuit of freedom and peace.

WARNING: THIS SPOILS THE ENTIRETY OF THE PLOT OF DARK OASIS, THE FIRST BOOK IN THE SERIES.

Part one of Dark Oasis took place in 2017. It followed Clair and his grandfather who lived alone in the forest of Devil Oasis. Shortly after Clair turned nineteen, things started changing. His grandfather became fearful of the world around them, and Dolion and Loralie, the twins who haunted the forest, started frequently showing up in Clair's life. For nearly a century, Dolion and Loralie have been attempting to get people the age of nineteen, the age the twins were when they died, to kill themselves. At the start of Dark Oasis, Clair became their next target. They broke Clair's mind and pulled him further into the dark oasis within his own head. It led him to cut himself, to consider killing himself, and to unintentionally end his grandfather's life and burn down his childhood home. Just when Clair seemed hopeless, Julie entered the Oasis and gave Clair someone to be strong for. She was another one of Dolion and Loralie's victims. Julie didn't survive. Clair buried her on Edicius Hill in memory of his first friend.

Part two took place in 2019 and followed Perdu Witherite, Julie's boyfriend. Perdu did not handle Julie's death well, and he struggled with his connection to reality as a result. At the start of Perdu's story, he was nineteen, and therefore he was vulnerable to Dolion and Loralie. The story opened with Perdu leaving Devil Oasis and seemingly escaping Dolion. When Perdu returned to his home not too far from the forest, he unknowingly brought the twins back with him. Dolion had such a strong hold on Perdu's mind that Perdu became nearly obsessed with the darkness. When he went to his siter, Evina, for help, she tried to support him as best as she could, but she was scared for her brother and didn't know what to do. Eventually, Perdu pushed Evina away and isolated himself from her. That was the last time they saw each other. Meanwhile, Clair knew Perdu was in trouble so he left Devil Oasis for the first time in his life in hopes he could help. Clair and Perdu spent the night trying to keep Perdu alive as Dolion guided Perdu's mind to see flashbacks of what the house used to be like when Dolion and Loralie lived there. Clair and Perdu learned a lot about what Dolion and Loralie's lives had been like through letters and items they found in a closet under the stairs. In the end, Dolion's hold on Perdu was too strong, and he convinced him that Evina's life would be better without him. Clair watched the moment Perdu hung himself through a dream.

Throughout the book there were scattered POVs of a woman named Edith, who later started going by Lady when she gave up control of her life to the forest and the curse. Lady left her children, Karl and Edmund, to merge with the lake in 1922. She knew the curse that Dolion and Loralie's death would bring, and she was hoping that making a deal with the land would protect her children. As part of the deal, Karl and Edmund wouldn't age until Dolion and Loralie's death. Lake Halcyon, Lady's lake, provided peace to Clair throughout his story even though he didn't understand why. Lady, his great grandmother, was always watching over him.

Rules of the Curse

1. *The barrier between the twins and a child's mind is broken when the child turns nineteen. Only when the child openly confronts and resists the twins, truly meaning it with all their heart, will the barrier close and the child become safe again.*

2. *In death, the twins will not be capable of interacting with the one they care for most: each other. They will live in eternal hell, able to see and hear each other, but unable to find comfort or conversation in one another.*

3. *The twins hold no power over their target unless the child is in the heart of the Oasis. Nevertheless, the twins are capable of calling their prey and luring them into their trap.*

4. *No killing. In death, the twins will be capable of interacting with the physical world but will not harness the power to murder, only to manipulate the minds of their targets to encourage thoughts of suicide. This is the most powerful form of death; this is the death that must be achieved.*

Prologue

Lady

2022

As the rushing waves of Halcyon and the whipping winds of Devil Oasis sing praises throughout what has become my home, I fall deeper into an unwelcome darkness. Death drips from the branches like blood from a wound as fear swells in the hearts of the living.

And yet, despite the darkness and fear, Clair remains. It would puzzle me if it weren't for the curse; this land was born from it, as were the twins themselves. Clair, too, might have been born from this curse, but I regret to say I'll likely never know. Whether born from it or not, he is a part of it. The desire to change all of this, for better or for worse, burns in him just as it did with Edmund, just as it did with me.

This curse is made of the very destruction of innocents. Thunder rolls in protest as another child enters the borders of the Oasis. And so the cycle begins again, just as it has for generations since the untimely death of the twins, Dolion and Loralie, who haunt the forest. The darkest corners of the forest come alive with sick excitement as the child draws nearer to the center of the land, nearer to her doom. If I had eyes, I would close them; if I were more than a dead woman tied to this lake, I would relish in the power to look away and pretend nothing bad ever happens. But I cannot, just as Clair cannot run. Devil Oasis keeps me watching and will always keep Clair within reach. We are tied to this in ways I hate to admit.

Even as I prepare myself for the death that is to follow, I can feel Clair's heartbeat quicken in anticipation. He can feel it too.

He was once the prey of Devil Oasis, this forest, and the twins, as we all were at one time or another. The pain strikes my heart again as I remember that time, when Clair was no more than just the twins' target, on the run from the darkness they encompass.

It's affected us all. Even my children, Karl and Edmund, whom I tried to keep safe for so long. After the twins were born, they didn't age until the twins died. I thought that would keep them safe, but in the end, it only brought them harm.

Even Dolion and Loralie, the ones who are doing this to us, were once nothing but victims in all of this. Maybe they still are, if you think about it. They were once alive, once only children who were just as afraid and just as lonely as the rest of us, if not more. I had already become part of the lake when the time for their death came, and I felt their pain and misery right along with them. I still bear the emotional scars of the suffering children, who clung to each other through a world that tried to tear them apart...

Part One

Imagine being one. One body, one mind. Everything made sense. But at birth, one became two. No explanation, only fear. We look the same, we think the same. Two bodies, one heart, one soul.

CURSE RULE #1

The barrier between the twins and a child's mind is broken when the child turns nineteen. Only when the child openly confronts and resists the twins, truly meaning it with all their heart, will the barrier close and the child become safe again.

Chapter One

Loralie

1941

Hand in hand. Brother and sister side by side. If Mother sees his hand grasping mine, she will surely beat him. At age three it was fine. Nothing was thought of the twins who clung to each other. By our early teenage years, Mother would threaten us with her fists. Not long after, Dolion would come into our room for the night with a bloody and bruised face. This time it does not matter who sees us. In seconds nothing will matter anyway.

Dolion's fingers wrap tighter around mine. *Are you positive this is what you want?* I hear his voice in my head. I nod, lying. Of course this is not what I want. This is what *he* wants. And I live for him. Besides, when Mother finds our bloody dead bodies, she will know never to shame her children again. Never to force them apart. Never to ridicule their dependency on each other. Doli and I are twins. Born together, now we must die together.

I grab my cold blade from my pocket as he grabs his. With our palms facing the sky, he looks at me and places his blade on my wrist.

I'll see you in the afterlife, sis. There, no one will separate us.

"I love you, Doli," I whisper as I place my blade on his wrist.

Three . . . Two . . . One . . .

I press hard and move quick, and blood begins pouring. He kills me, I kill him. The moments left in our lives turn to seconds, and then it all fades to black.

Dolion

I expected the afterlife to feel whimsical and freeing. I expected it to call our names as we entered. I expected to see my sister and rejoice. I expected freedom. I got defeat.

My wrist burns when I become aware of my surroundings. My head rests on a rough pillow. As my vision clears, I find my feet propped on the arm of a couch. I believe this to be Mother's couch, the one with the light wood trim and floral covers. The scent of lavender reaches my nose. I'm in my mother's living room. Defeat clouds the air surrounding me. Using all the strength I possess, I look to my right to see Loralie lying on the couch beyond the small table. And to my dismay, Jonny is heading right toward me, followed by Emile, cigar in hand. Did we not succeed?

"Looks like not even death wants you," Jonny says, dropping into the chair next to me, the candlelight reflecting off his short dark hair. He may only be sixteen, but he knows he has power over me. "Tell me, Dolion, why did you and your girlfriend do it?"

"I'm not his girlfriend!" Loralie spits, causing our stepbrother to jump even though she's halfway across the room. "Say that one more time, Jonny. Try me."

Jonny narrows his eyes at me. "Stop depending on each other so much and I might believe her."

If I could yell, maybe I would. Maybe Jonny would fear me the way he fears Loralie. I could be the man. I could stand up for her, threaten the others as she does for me. If I could speak, would I?

"Jonny," Emile says, standing by the swinging kitchen door, his slicked black hair shining unnaturally, his squared chin and cheekbones casting those daunting shadows across his face. "They have had quite enough. Do not tire them out before their mother comes home."

Jonny nods and walks into the kitchen, his hands by his sides.

When Mother gets home, I will be in hell.

Loralie, I say, *are you all right?*

"No, Doli, I'm not."

Was that spite in her voice? Surely she is not mad at me. I wanted us to go too. It's not my fault we survived.

The front door slams, quickening my heart rate. Loralie struggles to sit up, preparing for Mother's entrance. I sink deeper into the cushions, staying where I feel safest. Mother sets her path directly for Loralie and grabs her wrist. She examines the wrapped gash before throwing her arm back to her. It lands in the skirt of Loralie's mud-stained cream dress.

"Stupid!" Mother yells, her voice reaching that level that leaves my body aching and my insides shuddering. Loralie looks her square in the eyes. "If you are seen like this, you will never win his approval, Loralie. The party is tonight. What on earth were you thinking?" Her voice echoes through the house, and all the strength I had is instantly sucked out of my body.

"You." Mother points her long, thin finger at me, turning her attention from Loralie. My heart stops beating. "You forced her, didn't you? You forced her to go along with it."

"Mother, he didn't do anything." Loralie pushes herself from the couch to stand, her black hair flowing across her chest, shoulders, and back.

Just make it through this, I try to encourage myself. *When it's over, you can cry.*

"Stop protecting him, Loralie." Mother grabs my arm and yanks me up. "At least sit like a man," she says to me.

"Shut up, Mother!" Loralie yells. "Dolion and I are family. Of course, you have no idea what that word even means, do you? Leave him alone. Dolion did nothing!"

"Don't talk back to me, young lady!" Mother says, her dark hair, usually held in a bun, now swinging freely with her words, her usually creased face pulled tight as her jaw clenches.

"No, *you* don't talk back to *me*."

I take in a sharp breath. Loralie doesn't know when to shut up.

"I'm getting so sick of your annoying, pathetic little picks and nags at us. Quit it!"

In a rage of anger, Mother rushes over to Loralie and grabs her wrist. Loralie gasps at the pain inflicted to her wound. I curl my own wrist into my chest. Loralie's mouth gapes open as she twists and wriggles, trying to ease the pain.

"Go upstairs and prepare for the party tonight," Mother tells Loralie, forcing her voice to be suddenly calm. Leaning in and quieting herself, she says, "I don't care if you care about him or not; the world must never hear of your brother and his pathetic mute self."

I feel the heat rush to my face. If only I could be invisible. Or better yet, not exist at all.

"Get ready for the party. Thank goodness I bought you a dress with long sleeves. Go."

Loralie turns up her nose and stomps up the stairs to our room. Each step is louder than the last.

"I wish you were dead!" Loralie yells from upstairs. "I wish you died instead of Father!"

"I do too!'" Mother yells back at her.

So do I, I think, turning toward Mother.

For a moment, it's like she forgets she's not alone. She sighs, her scowl turning softer, becoming a look of despair. She looked this way right after Father's death too. The way her body threatens to curl in on itself, the way her eyes shimmer as though she may cry—it reminds me of myself. Of the ways *she* has made me feel. In a flicker of an instant, my chest tightens, and my arms want to move to hug her. Her face and her body are devoid of anger; it's been replaced with exhaustion. She's in this mess of a situation, stuck here . . . just like the rest of us.

But when she turns to find me watching her, I am immediately reminded that the flicker of light I saw is only one moment surrounded by endless darkness. When her eyes land on me, I feel her anger and hatred returning.

I've seen that look before. Only once. The first time she hit me.

"You are *not* going to ruin this party," she says.

Shit. How did we fail to die? Jonny's right: not even death wants us. After all, death always wins. It gets what it wants. It refuses what it hates. And once you think you've figured it out, it sends you home to the torture of life when you should've been freed. Death gives you a glimmer of light, but it is, indeed, a very vile hope.

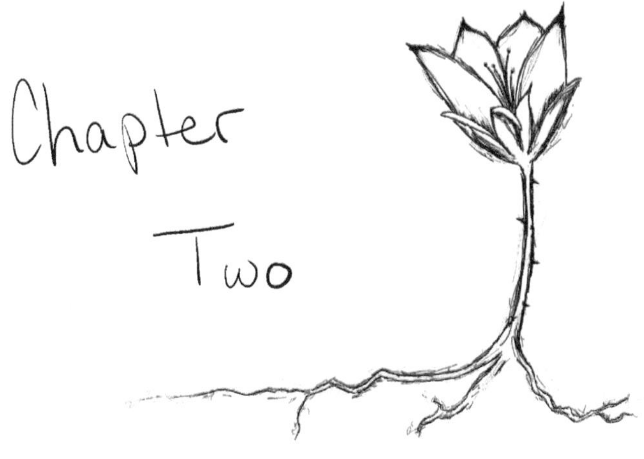

Chapter Two

Clair

2022

H *elp me, Clair. Please.*

I wake up gasping from the dream. The dream I've had nearly every night since Perdu died.

Chapter Three

Dolion

1941

"Dolion." Mother's voice comes from the kitchen as I'm walking past the room to grab my shoes. I was going to get out of the house for a little while, maybe sit on the porch while they prepare for the party. The stress is starting to kill me. "Could you come here for a second, love? I need to talk with you."

I stop at the doorway, my heart clenching around itself as nerves spike through me. She needs to talk to me? I haven't done anything! I swear I haven't! My eyes already burn with tears, and the thought of Mother seeing them scares me even more.

She seems to be in a good mood, I tell myself. *Everything will be fine. Just go in there before her mood changes.*

When I walk into the kitchen, I find Mother standing by the new iron-and-porcelain stove. It was a gift from a neighbor. She stirs something in the pot. I'm sure she's preparing for the party tonight.

I drag my feet along the floor as I walk to her, keeping my eyes on her hands as they stir the food, though she doesn't seem angry right now. I stop a little ways away, waiting for her to tell me why she called.

She sighs, keeping her eyes trained on the dinner before her. In the silence, I find myself ready for this to be over with, for her to tell me what I did wrong so we can move on. She'll tell me how she's disappointed in me, how she knew from the moment I was born I wasn't going to be worth raising. She doesn't seem angry enough to hit me, however. She doesn't even seem mad.

Even though I feel ready for whatever she has to say, I can't help it when my palms sweat and my throat clenches. I try to breathe deep, but it's shaky and shallow. I want to be in my room. *Please say what you have to say so I can leave.*

"You know I love you, Dolion."

That makes my heart shudder more than anything else could have.

Love me?

I nod slowly, not wanting to upset her.

"That's why you have to understand, this is for you. It's to help you become better." She looks away from the stove now, turning to face me. "I don't want to hurt you," she whispers. "But you give me no choice. If tonight doesn't go well, we will lose everything."

I nod again, wishing I could promise her I won't get in the way. I've never left the room when we've had people over before.

"Dolion"—her voice is so soft, so gentle—"you know I care about you."

I nod along with her.

"Yet you insist on disobeying me. I told you to stay away from your sister. We need her. If you feel you must end your own life, then do what is best for you, but you can't take Loralie away from us."

She reaches out for me. And though I want to pull away from her, I find myself allowing her to grab my left hand. She pulls me close, cupping my hand in hers tightly, like she's cradling something of value. I close my eyes, a single tear falling away, and I let myself feel everything. The calm air between me and my mother, the way she holds me, the way she talks so gently. Maybe things really are changing. Maybe Loralie finally got through to her and she understands that she can't treat me the way she has anymore.

"Dolion," she says. "Look at me." I open my eyes slowly, and Mother stares back. She smiles slightly, a sad smile. "I'm so sorry you've made me do this, Dolion. I've told you to stay away from her."

Her hand grips my wrist tightly, rubbing through the fabric and against the split skin of my cut. I flinch at the touch.

Her fingers tighten around me. My body tenses. I'm unable to move, but something deep within me is screaming to run. Something is wrong. Something is very, very wrong.

M-Mother? I know she can't hear me. *What are you doing?*

"Stay away from your sister," Mother says. "That's all you have to do, and I promise you, my son, you will be safe. As long as you do as I tell you."

My hands begin trembling, and my mind continues screaming at me to at least try to escape her grasp, but the part of me that wants to believe she wouldn't ever truly hurt me forces me to stay, just to prove myself right. She would never hurt me beyond what I deserve.

Mother glances down at the stove, then back to my hand. My stomach turns as my heart jolts. She *is* going to hurt me. She wouldn't do this. She wouldn't. Heavy tears fall from my face. Sobs get caught in my throat as I try to pull away from her, my bare feet pushing against the cold tile floor. Why is she doing this?

Loralie! I call out for her. *Loralie, help me! Please!* Tears well in my eyes as I look at my mother, her figure blurring. I shake my head slowly, trying to back away from her. *Please . . .* My mother would never do this to me. Never.

I did nothing. Don't hurt me. I did nothing! I hate myself for not being able to talk, I hate myself for not dying earlier, and I hate myself for believing Mother when she said she loved me. *Please, Mother. Please don't do this to me.*

"I'm so sorry, my son," she whispers.

I close my eyes as my skin connects with the hot iron burner.

Chapter Four

Dolion

The burn is agonizing. It stings and throbs. I resist the urge to cover it and apply pressure. As the foolish boy I am, I cry, warm tears falling down my thin face. I attempt to run up the stairs to our bedroom but am unable to find the steps through my blurred vision and trip. *Get to your room before you completely fall apart*, I tell myself. *Get to safety first.* I continue to run, using my healthy hand to cup and hold the raw one.

"If you even try to show yourself tonight, Dolion, I swear you will lose that hand entirely!" Mother yells from the bottom of the staircase. The loud voice makes me want to curl up in the corner of the hall and close my eyes to try to get away from it all.

That won't help, I remind myself. *She can still reach you there.*

I hate going to the room after moments like this. I know it worries Loralie. I just want to die. Is that too much to ask? I make it to the wooden door of our room and reach out with my healthy hand to wrap my shaking fingers around the cold doorknob, but before I go in, before I cry to Loralie like I have so many times, I picture the way I will look to her. Tears dried to my face as fresh ones trace their path, my mouth quivering, my body shaking, the skin on my palm raw. This would prove that she is right, that I am weak. I can't let her see me like this.

Squeezing my eyes shut in an attempt to block the overwhelming longing to be inside that floods me, I turn away from our bedroom. From my safe place. My arms lose feeling, and my hands tremble violently. My tears become heavy and thick.

Find someplace safe, I tell myself. My feet continue moving down the hall, getting farther and farther away from Loralie, until I find myself inside the small bathroom at the end of the hallway and close the door behind me quickly. With my hand pressed against the wood and the other one curled into my side, I finally let myself break down. My breaths are quick and shallow. Sweat has been collecting in my hairline. Tears fall into my slightly parted mouth. I turn slowly toward the rest of the bathroom, leaning against the door, silently praying Mother doesn't come for me.

My body is weak, detached, and I worry that I won't have enough strength to keep myself up much longer. The bathroom around me feels far away. Everything is in a haze. And when I lift my shaking hand up to my face, my knees go faint at the sight of my mutilated palm. My skin is loose, white, hanging from the few places it's still attached to the living skin. Below that layer of mushy skin shines a splotchy bright red, my raw flesh burning to the point of bringing tears back to my eyes.

Looking at the damage *she* did to me, I hear the sound of my skin sizzling against the metal, I smell the burnt flesh, I see the look in my mother's eyes. The pleasure she got in punishing me. For what? What have I done to deserve this?

What did I do?

I curl in on myself, my body ready to hide away until this is all over. But of course, it will never end.

A new round of throbbing begins, and I pull my hand away from my body, straining to get the burning to stop. But when my eyes land on my injury, a new thought occurs to me.

Never has my skin looked so . . . angry. It looks angry . . . like I feel. Suddenly, I find myself looking almost lovingly at the irritated skin covering my entire palm. Because, in an odd, disturbing way, it almost feels like looking in a mirror. I see my own feelings, the ones that have been shoved down inside me for so long, reflecting back at me through the broken dying flesh.

I pull open the drawer, working hard to get my unsteady hands to search its nearly overflowing contents, until I finally come across what I'm looking for: Emile's cigars. I stole them a while ago but smoked only one before deciding I hated it. I pull one out, my fingers struggling to grip one of the small wooden matches lying at the base of the drawer. Finally, I gain control over the match and light it on fire. When the flame is in front of me, flickering back and forth, my racing heart calms and my hands steady out. But it only lasts a moment. Once the cigar is lit and the flame is out, I begin trembling again. Bringing it up to my lips, I inhale slowly. The smoke fills my mouth and finds its way down my throat, and I pull away as I begin violently coughing, my throat burning a little as the smoke settles inside.

After my coughing fit ends with me sitting on the floor in front of the counter, my stomach tight and a little sore now, I look at the cigar, relieved when I see the little orange embers surrounded by black-and-gray ash. It's still burning.

Pulling up my left sleeve, I find the ashy white skin of my forearm. I close my eyes and breathe in deep, the raspy aftermath of the smoke causing small throbs through my throat. I tell myself I can do it. I can do this to myself.

The doubt starts to flood my mind, and I worry I'm not brave enough to do this. I swallow, trying to tell myself I am. I can do this. I can be in control of the pain this time. It won't be her doing this to me. It won't be Jonny or Emile. It will be me. I will be in control of the pain I feel.

I steady my unstable hand and move it closer to my arm. I can't stop. If I pull away from my arm, I won't go through with this. I know I won't. I choke back my tears and try to be brave.

"Dolion," a ghostly voice whispers, grazing my ear.

My head snaps toward the sound. Loralie stares back at me, her eyes wide and panicked. I blink, and my sister is gone, leaving me staring at the red-and-gold wallpaper Mother insisted on having throughout the house.

My heart beats rapidly, and the shadows move around me as if they have sinister intentions. My eyes dart around the bathroom a couple times, and when I find no one else in here with me, I come to the conclusion that I must be losing it.

I bring my attention back to the cigar and refocus myself.

I watch as it gets closer and closer to my arm. The heat radiating from the end finally starts rubbing against my skin. One of the embers falls from the tip, landing on my arm, burning through my outer skin before sizzling out. Fresh tears spring to my eyes at the small prick of pain. It takes everything within me to keep from pulling the cigar away as the heat gets more intense.

You can do this, Dolion, I tell myself.

My tears are thick as fear swells inside my chest, tightening my muscles and my throat. Finally, I admit defeat and pull away, a sinking, numbing feeling following my failure. The cigar falls away from my fingers as I pull my hands up to my head and let myself sink away from reality, from any place I found that had the potential of feeling safe. Broken and muffled sobs make their way from me as my tears become hot, trailing my face. I stay curled on the hard floor for what feels like an eternity, until I have cried myself to the point of mental numbness, silently staring at the wall, my eyes sticky and burning, thinking of nothing yet everything.

At some point I allow thoughts of the outside world to enter my mind again, and I realize Loralie must be worried about me. Reluctantly, I use the counter to pull my unusually heavy body off the floor and make my way toward my and Loralie's bedroom.

When I finally open the door to the room, Loralie stands up promptly from her bed, relief flooding her face.

"What happened down there, Doli?" she asks with a stern voice. Her face is set hard. So much like Mother. Though I will never tell her that.

As she rushes toward me, the wooden floor squeaks below her feet. Oblivious to the burn on my hand, she continues asking what happened. Looking up at her face, I feel like a selfish fool. She has been crying, and I hadn't noticed. Her pale skin has been drowned out in a series of silent tears.

What happened? I ask her, forgetting about myself for a moment. She pulls her hand out from behind her back to reveal the same burn I have on my own hand.

"It just appeared, Doli. I didn't do anything. It just showed up."

I hold out my own hand, still slightly trembling, for her to see as well. Mine is on my left, hers is on her right. Her burn presents a new level to our relationship. Never before has our physical pain been shared. As I stare at the two wounds, I feel the familiar fear begin to swell in my chest. Who are we?

"Doli, what's happening?"

I shake my head and tell her what happened in the kitchen. And after I get her to calm down and convince her not to go downstairs and kill Mother, we lean against the wall and make ourselves comfortable on the floor under the window. The numbness finally takes over as my body sits still.

Our family is afraid of us. Why? Because of Father's accident? Probably. Because we are different? Probably. But the thing I hate the most is that I'm growing afraid of us as well.

"Pinch me," Loralie says.

Why? It's hard to explain my communication with Loralie. I've tried and failed with others. She is the only one who can hear anything I have to say.

"Pinch me and tell me if you can feel it."

I'll pinch myself instead. My fingers squeeze the skin on my thin arm. I look to her, and she shakes her head. If she couldn't feel it, then we're good, right? I feel a sudden shot of pain on my forearm and look to see Loralie grinning. *What was that for?*

"You didn't do it hard enough." She smiles and giggles.

Well, anything? I ask, hoping for the same results. She shakes her head once again and sighs.

"What's wrong with us?" she asks, staring at the wall. I lean my head back and look toward the door. I wish I could answer her question. I wish I knew why I can hardly hold myself up when she's not around. I wish I knew why I can communicate with her. I wish I knew the answers.

I wish we had died, I tell her. *Then we would be safe, away from everyone.*

"If death wanted us, we would be there already. I'm so thankful I have you. I can't believe how utterly lonely this life has been." She closes her eyes. "It has to get better. That's what they all say." After a short pause, she says, "I don't think it can though."

Loralie, you must get ready for the party, I instruct her. *Given how important tonight is, Mother will lose it if you're not ready on time.*

"You know if they succeed tonight then I will be a married woman come summer. They are tearing us apart. Once I am this man's wife, you will never be allowed to hear from me. They won't allow us to communicate." Loralie sighs and stands. "However, I must put on a show. Act as if I want to be there, hold my head high with pride and dignity."

And most importantly, I add, *forget about me. Just for the night.*

Chapter Five

Loralie

A girl I don't recognize stares back at me through the mirror in our bedroom. She's tall, neatly groomed, and well-dressed. This girl showed up all the time when Doli and I were young. Parties, fancy events, and beautiful clothing were my life. Since then, however, things have changed. Our parties are few, and my dresses aren't as expensive. At least I have a party dress. At least I'm still allowed to go to my mother's events.

Poor Dolion, forced to hide away in our room. Forced to pretend he doesn't exist.

In the past few minutes staring at my reflection, I have grown fond of who I am. On the outside at least. My black curls lay neatly across my shoulders, falling across my chest, nearly reaching my waist, and I can't help but love my perfect hair. Mother got me a new dress for this party; it's the first time in years I've had anything new. The dress fits me wonderfully. It's a muted sage green, the fabric smooth and soft, perfect for twirling. The skirt sends excitement through my heart. When I spin, it flows so perfectly, making me feel magical, making me feel like a child again. I had forgotten what that felt like.

When I stop spinning, I focus my attention back on the mirror and take a moment to admire myself, to take in who I am. For now, my usual cheap stained clothes are only a memory. I take my own breath away. My fingers find their way to the off-white lace wrapping around the skirt, running over the rough texture carefully, making sure to take great care of the material. The fabric wraps tight around my torso, giving way at my breasts. The sleeves are long, falling just over the base of my palms. I wish I could think it was kind of Mother to buy it for me. If her intentions weren't selfish, I may have been able to bring myself to love her at one point. If she wanted nothing but the best for us, maybe I would have trusted her. When I was younger, I might've considered her my mother.

"Mother!" I call for her. "Come tighten the back!"

It wouldn't take much to destroy her, to puncture her heart, to watch her bleed to death, to stab her with my hairpin, made special so it's long enough to hold my hair. She closes the door behind her and walks my way, her steps heavy and loud. The air smells immediately of her lavender, and I clench my fist. This is the only room in the house that doesn't smell like her, and her presence ruins it.

She makes it obvious I am still shunned from her "acceptance" for lashing out earlier. I grab my pin in my left hand, the one that wasn't burned, and think of everything I could do with it. It's long enough to kill her, to push through her chest and reach her heart. Or maybe I'd go for her neck . . .

I hold the hairpin tight in my hand until Mother asks for it. As she takes it from me, she has no idea the dream I wish to carry out with that object. *All in good time*, I tell myself. *Just wait. Someday.*

I have no recollection of how I got my dress on with my raw hand aching every time it is exposed to anything, especially the harsh seams of my dress. The lace felt like death on my wound. At least I look like a goddess.

She pins my hair up nicely, small curls falling loose from the sides. No jewelry is placed on me—that will be a decoration only for the wedding. His family asked this of us. As the bride, I must oblige. My mother repositions me in the mirror to see my reflection clearer.

"The light is working against us, Loralie. But trust me when I say he is going to fall for you. You are beautiful."

I don't respond to her, but inside I feel . . . I think I feel happy. My cheeks flush as—I hate to admit—my excitement grows. Jonny has always told us no one will love either me or Dolion. What if this is my chance? I may get to meet a nice man with a wealthy family. Paradise could be mine. My only problem is Dolion. I could never cut him out of my life, but to save the family name, we cannot be seen together. He cannot be seen at all. He is weak for a man; no one would desire him, and he would only bring the family shame. The Witherites are depending on tonight. This is the night to save our fortune. I must break out of whatever curse Dolion and I are trapped in and bring honor to my family.

"Come downstairs when you are ready, my beautiful daughter. His family, as well as ours, will be here shortly."

I nod at Mother as she exits through the door.

In the peace of the lonely room, I breathe deep and try to calm my heart. Focus on my beauty—that is the best I can do for myself now.

I admire the way my body bends and curves. A woman's body truly is something of treasure; it's no wonder men lust after it so. My beauty will carry me through this coming party, and I will, as always, be better for it in the end.

I smooth the skirt of my dress and straighten the sleeves. There is nothing to be nervous about. I breathe out again, but this time my breath is visible before me. I freeze, suddenly aware that something isn't right.

A voice dripping with a disdain not unlike the dark thoughts that fill my own head slowly rises from the peace and quiet of the room. It breaks through the forgotten corners of my mind until it fills me with a comfort I long ago used to find refuge in.

Child, it hisses.

The calculating voice is cold and desireless. A lost temperament of a world forgotten . . . maybe even unspoken.

Each silent breath from the voice reminds me of the little girl I once was, who wasn't held back, who wasn't silenced, the girl who was allowed to have her own mind. I long for that again, for the freedom I once had. Back then I had nothing to lose, but then Dolion started getting hurt every time I stepped out of line. Mother learned that's the only way to control me.

And even as I fall into the deep comfort of the voice, I remember this is a part of myself I keep hidden for a reason. The wicked and treacherous thoughts that fill my head and heart have no place in my life, at least not if I long to be accepted by the world. And suddenly, the whispers turn into a violent attack on me instead of comfort, reminding me of what I could be and the freedom I've given up. *All to keep Dolion safe.*

Finally, I feel the pull that directs me to the source of the voice, and I turn my head slowly until my eyes come into contact with the very essence of darkness itself. Beyond the window and far past where this house lies, the land that meets the horizon calls to me. There's something about the way the wind swirls like a magnetic pull, something calling me into the depths of the unmarked world where no men dwell.

It's stronger than the temptation of a man, though I'd admit that to no one. The pull and desire to give myself to the empty, desolate land and take refuge forever in its protection nags at my mind. What would happen if—

Dolion knocks on our door, interrupting my thoughts and breaking the pull to the land.

"You don't have to knock, silly. It's your room just as much as mine." Though I try to keep my voice steady, I hear it waver.

I did not want to walk in on you changing. He smiles at me. It's a sad smile. *He is going to love you. You look beautiful.*

"Oh, stop," I tease him, knowing full well he is right, of course. I look amazing. "I must get downstairs. I hear the guests arriving. Are you going to be all right up here?"

I am going to say yes because there is nothing you can do about it anyway.

I nod and look at the cloth wrapped around my hand, around my burn. Mother didn't notice it while she was in here. As long as I keep the cloth on and my long sleeves covering it and my cut, I should be all right.

"I'll see you after, Doli."

Loralie

As I depart my room, I hear the music, played by my uncle and aunt no doubt. They are the most talented in the family. The sounds of people chattering excite me. I had forgotten the thrill of parties.

As I walk down the white staircase—freshly painted by Emile, as is the rest of the house—I see my mother coming toward me. I feel elegant. The sleeves are light and simple, and the dress flows evenly. I feel like a queen, my own goddess, controlling my fate and my destiny. I am also, though, feeling the lack of blood in my head, dizzy and tired. However, for this moment, I must push past my own body's limits. Tonight is about revival.

"Loralie, nearly everyone is here. Charles is here, in the living room. Wait to go speak to him until Emile comes over; he will introduce you. For now, stay put and wait."

As quickly as Mother came, she leaves. Jonny comes over and stands next to me. His three-piece suit, which used to be Father's before he died, barely fits. Hatred fills my body at the sight of Jonny in *Father's* clothes.

He was my father, not yours, I wish to say to him. I wish to grab the suit and rip it off his large body. But I compose myself.

"You look ridiculous," I tell him. Watching his scowl form is always the best part of my day. "Jonny?"

Beads of sweat trace his round jaw and large neck. His red face shakes and quivers every few seconds as his fists close tighter around themselves. I follow his gaze, and a smirk plays on my lips as his girl engages with one of the wealthier gentlemen.

"You told her we're poor, didn't you?" I force down a laugh. "I told you not to."

"Shut up," he grunts. "Or I'll—"

"You'll what, Jon? You think I'm scared of you like Dolion is? Mother and Emile hate you just like they hate us. No amount of bullying us in front of them will change that. You're weak, Jonny."

Emile breaks through the conversing crowd in front of us, heading directly for Jonny and me. Jonny straightens up and turns to face me, attempting to tower over me. I roll my eyes before facing Emile.

"Jonny, what's wrong?" Emile asks, noticing the anguish remaining on his son's face.

I sigh before gesturing toward Jonny's girl. "She left him," I say.

Emile turns back to Jonny. "That's it?" he says through a laugh. "*That's* why you're upset? We all knew she was going to leave you eventually."

Emile makes eye contact with me, and I allow a small giggle to escape. When I look back at Jonny, I find his face has gone completely red, this time flushed with embarrassment. He lowers his head, still attempting to make eye contact with his father, who refuses to look at him.

"Loralie, I'll come get you in a couple minutes. Wait here," Emile's venomous voice says before he disappears into the crowd again. Jonny sulks after him, his head hung low.

I stand and watch the busyness unfold. The house is lit more than we normally keep it, the music gives the false impression of a happy home, and the sound of people's laughter and conversation irritates me. Can't they see this is all at the expense of a young woman's entire life being thrown away? This party, if all goes well, will take everything away from me forever.

If all goes well . . .

Or maybe I could do what I do best and anger Mother and Emile. Maybe I could make sure nothing goes well . . . Maybe . . .

A man standing in the crowd catches my eye. He keeps his distance from everyone else, seeming to be uncomfortable surrounded by so many people. He's tall with dark eyes, even darker hair, and a charming oval-shaped face. There's this look about him. Something tells me he's uncomfortable here.

I smirk. Men are always so much easier when they're uncomfortable.

I grab a pen off the table and make my way over to him. My steps are strong and confident, but I give them the sense of aimless wandering, hoping he'll think I accidentally stumbled upon him. I brush past him, my shoulder barely touching his. At just the right moment, I drop the pen and continue walking toward the window.

"Excuse me, miss?" a deep voice says from behind me.

A light grin flashes across my face before I compose myself into something less victorious and a little more curious. Then I turn around, making my eyes as innocently wide as is believable. I blink twice slowly and wait for him to continue speaking.

"I think . . ." He clears his throat. "I think you dropped this?" He holds the pen out toward me.

"Did I?" My voice is sweet and innocent. "Oh my, thank you." I step forward and reach out for the pen. My hand lingers on his for a moment. He stiffens, and I move my eyes gently up to his before I pull away.

"And what might a gentleman like yourself be doing at a party such as this?"

This man is stirring something inside me: desire. His muscles, his perfect face . . . I run my eyes over him, knowing his body must be beautiful. I fight to compose myself.

"I'm Arron. My brother is Charles," he says in that charming deep voice. "I believe you are Loralie?"

"I am." I smile again. I think he just got even more appealing. Mother and Emile would lose it if . . . Well, not only is this another man, but it's Charles's brother. Picturing the anger on Emile's face is all the encouragement I need.

I place my hand on his arm and lean in, making sure my body presses lightly against his. His warmth covers me, and I find myself craving him.

"I could use your help," I whisper through a smile. "I'm rather . . . unhappy about this arrangement."

"You're not the only one," he mumbles.

"Loralie." Emile's voice breaks through the tension. I push away from Arron immediately. "Where are you?"

"I'm over here," I say. Emile beckons me over to him, and I give Arron one final smile before leaving. Mother and Emile will regret the day they forced me to marry a man against my will.

Emile draws me to the center of the room, grabbing my arm and pulling me toward Charles. I give my stepfather a scowl and pull my arm away from him. He keeps his calm since there are guests in the house. We make our way over to Charles, my long legs carrying me gently and gracefully. So, this is the man I may soon wed. I guess he could be worse. Strong posture, firm jaw, dark hair—he's a decent-looking man. Yet not as handsome as Arron. Charles sees Emile and smiles, nodding in his direction, beckoning us over.

"Ah, Emile," Charles says in greeting. Emile offers my hand to Charles, who takes it gently. "This must be Loralie? I have heard so much about you."

If I were meeting him for something more casual, I think I would approve. If I were meeting him at any other event, for any reason, I fear he would have caught my eye. But here I am meant to like him. I have no option. Winning a man's approval has never been forced upon me before.

His dark eyes look at me, glancing over my body before meeting mine. I dip my head. Yesterday I could've been rude. Yesterday I could've rejected an invitation from any man I desired. Today I must act my age and face the truth. If all goes according to plan, I will be bound to this man for life.

Emile sighs, probably relieved I have chosen to behave.

What would Dolion think of this? I wish he could come to these events with me. The thought of Mother keeping him locked in our room sends shivers crawling on my skin. My gaze shifts to my burn, wrapped and hidden. Poor Dolion. *I promise we will be free together soon,* I think. *We will find a way.*

"Loralie," Emile whispers next to my ear. "Say something. Do not disappoint me."

Avoiding Emile, I look at Charles and play a gentle smirk on my lips.

"It is a pleasure to finally meet you." I make myself cringe. I hate my forced party voice. "I've been waiting for this day for far too long."

This morning, a blade was cutting through my wrist. I wanted out of this. I wanted my brother by my side. This morning, I wanted a way out. Even now, I cannot beg hard enough for death to take us away, because that is what Dolion wants, what he needs, and I love him. Can the world not understand that? Just because others will curse their family and drive them away does not mean Doli and I have to be that way. He is my brother and the only person who understands me.

"Well, I'll let you two be." Emile nudges me toward Charles. *You get a man by making him desire you.* His eyes say the words he cannot. Anger. Emile has no right to tell me what to do. He has no place in my life. "Take care of my daughter, Charles." He winks and laughs.

At his words, the very air in the living room grows darker.

"I'm not your daughter." The hot air escapes my mouth. My left fist clenches as I glare at Emile.

He stops at my voice and turns to mouth something to me. "Shut up and do *not* ruin this."

I lower my head, continuing my long glare at him.

"My *daughter*"—Emile glances at me—"is sorry for her behavior and apologizes in advance for anything else she might, and probably will, say."

It swells—the anger, the hatred, the overwhelming longing to be away from this place. I can feel the break coming, the moment I lose control and let my anger release into the world. It's coming—the day I stop caring who I may hurt or what others think. I have to get out of here. Now.

"Stop it!" The words tumble from my mouth. "I am not *your* daughter," I say, passing Emile and storming out before the anger pulsing like an electrical current shocks my body and sends me off the rails. My feet carry me faster than I had hoped, drawing attention to me throughout the house. Gasps and shouts make their way toward me. For a young lady who has a party thrown entirely for her, I am very ungrateful.

Dolion

Jonny's girlfriend came upstairs a couple minutes ago with someone new. She must have left Jonny. Their giggles and whispers ring through the bedroom door loudly as they hide in the hall away from the rest of the party. Despite what Emile, Mother, Loralie, or even Jonny say, Jonny cared about her. Or maybe he liked being cared about.

Sudden yells echo through the house, followed by the slam of our front door. Of course tonight is falling apart. It's Loralie. I love her, but my sister does not listen to anyone. That may be what I admire most about her. My sister is strong, independent. All I can hope is that she realizes she still needs me, and I need her.

I make my way to our window. Loralie stands behind our house, her hands cradling her face. A smile forms on my lips. An evil smile, a selfish smile. Loralie screwed up, and now she is mine. Mine to hold and mine to stand by. Another, smaller, slam comes from the front door. My smile fades, and my face strains. A man I don't recognize walks around the house and toward her. It's not Charles, the man who threatens to take her from me—I've seen him before. This is someone else.

She hides her face, turning from him and continuing to hold her hands up. *That's it, Loralie, don't let him near you.* Her head snaps up to look at me. She can hear me? She squints and gestures me away. The man says something, and Loralie points up toward me. *Oh, fuck off.* Loralie glares in my direction. The man waves, and Loralie grabs his arm to hold it down. Mother would murder us if she found out someone had seen me. Loralie shakes her head at him. He slowly nods. *Seriously, Loralie. Don't let him fool you.*

She ignores me. Loralie ignores me. She's choosing him over me?

My fists ball up. My left hand burns and screams at me, but I remain quiet. I grab the curtain, but before I can pull it closed, something off in the distance, a long ways away from the house, catches my eye: a single tree, standing all alone in the middle of a large field. That field has been there for as long as I can remember, and never has there been anything even as small as a bush. Something about this tree is like a beacon in the darkness, standing there as a symbol of hope. A very dangerous and vile hope. It calls to me, swirling in agony and despair but thriving nonetheless. It reaches out for me, welcomes me. I close the curtain violently, suddenly desperate to be rid of that tree. When I peek out to get one last glimpse, the tree is gone. I tremble.

I walk over to my bed, collapsing onto the surface. *Just stay with me, Loralie. How hard can that be?* I curl up, wrapping my arms around my knees. Tomorrow is a new day. Maybe I will be remembered then.

Chapter Seven

Loralie

"**A**re you all right?" Arron asks. "Things got kind of stressful in there."

"I'm fine." I keep my eyes on the ground below, straining my mind to hear from Dolion again. But there's nothing. He's quiet now.

"Well, if you want, we can—"

"Listen," I interrupt him. Emile is going to regret ever putting me in this situation. I think it's time he remembers who truly holds the power. I reach out and touch Arron's arm, slowly looking up to meet his eyes. "I don't understand how I'm feeling right now." My eyes flicker to his lips and back. "It's all so . . . overwhelming."

He steps closer to me, and something shifts a little in my stomach.

"Loralie," he says quietly. "I'm not a fool. I know what you're doing."

"So?" I whisper.

"You're supposed to marry my brother." His voice is so soft.

"Indeed, I am." I pull him closer to me. "Surely there's anger between you and your brother, or you wouldn't have let me go this far with you."

"Loralie . . ."

"Speak protests if you must, if it protects your conscience," I whisper, looking up into his eyes. "But I know you want me. Don't you, Arron?"

I breathe in shaky breaths, longing for his comfort. It's been so long since I've felt a man's touch. I know as soon as he touches me, I'll forget about Dolion, just like I always do. I'll forget about Mother and Father. I'll forget about Jonny and Emile. All I'll be aware of is the power I hold over the man I'm under. The power he doesn't realize he so willingly gives.

"Arron," I whisper, placing my hand on his arm, running it up to his shoulder slowly. I feel every muscle tense under my hand.

"Yes?" He chokes over his word.

I smirk. I've already got him right where I want him.

"Give in to me." I press my lips against his ear as I whisper, and his uneven breaths warm my neck.

"We really shouldn't, Loralie."

I hum in response, tucking my hair behind my ear. "Arron," I whisper. "Do you want to help me forget about everything?"

I grab his hand softly in mine, staring up into his eyes. I bring his hand up to my lips, kissing his fingers gently, then the back of his hand, then his wrist. I bite my bottom lip.

"Loralie . . ." His voice is breathy. "What are you doing?"

I shush him before placing his hand on my breast. His breathing quiets. "We're alone, Arron."

"Loralie, we shouldn't. I'm—"

"You said you were unhappy about this marriage too, Arron. Tell me . . ." My hands trail down his chest until my fingers find his waistband. "Do you want to help me ruin it?"

Arron swallows, closes his eyes, and nods slowly. His hand gently squeezes my chest before he breathes out his next words. "What would you like me to do, Loralie?"

I lean in to kiss him and let my hand slip inside his pants.

Dolion

My sister's hands slam into the glass pane between us for the thousandth time, and though I can see that she is shouting and yelling, begging me for help, I can't hear her. Even without her voice, there are sounds of people yelling all around, shouting and using harsh language against one another. Though I can't see them, I can hear them perfectly, their voices echoing through the dense dark forest surrounding me.

I'm curled on the ground, my side pressing into the hard dirt below, tall dry grass rising above me. My hands are clasped over my ears as I strain to block out the sounds. My body shakes. It takes all of my strength to keep my limbs from going limp. I can't make a sound—not even to my sister. When I think of the girl trapped on the other side of the glass, my gut tightens. Is this guilt? Why do I feel guilty? I'm the innocent one.

I feel small, the booming world around me towering tall, the trees disappearing into the sky. I can't get out of this. Something within me tells me this has been happening for longer than I can remember. My life before this hell is lost to me. All I know is this pain. I can't even remember what my sister's voice sounds like. We're trapped in this nightmare, and a little voice inside tells me we'll never be set free.

My eyes open suddenly, and I attempt to sit up in bed, wanting to be sure Loralie is here. But when I try to move, I find my body still, as if the air above me has grown heavy and is pushing down on me, smothering me into the bed. It presses harder against my chest the more I struggle against the weight, and the air passing through me becomes thinner and slips away from me until I can hardly breathe. My lungs burn in a panic and beg for air. I push frantically against the weight, but my body refuses to move. I'm trapped.

Loralie? I attempt to call to her. Is she in the room? Is the party over? *Loralie!*

A figure appears, hovering over me as I lie in my bed.

"Everything's all right, Doli." Her sweet voice breaks through the pounding in my head. "What's happening?"

I can't move! Even as I say it, I feel how false my worries are. My arms and legs thrash around in an attempt to break free of the weight no longer restricting me. Loralie pulls away to avoid getting smacked. The bedding gets tangled in my limbs, and tears fall.

"Dolion," Loralie says, her voice gaining urgency. "You have to stop!"

I can't! Fear coats my words. *Help me, Loralie. Please!*

She attempts to grab my arms, which have fallen by my sides and started shaking, but I involuntarily pull away from her as my arms and legs continue trembling.

"You have to let me help you," she says.

I'm scared, Loralie. I can't control it!

Her eyes lock with mine for a second before she makes an attempt at my arms again, this time her fingers roughly grasping on. She pins them beside me, pressing them into the mattress. Her worried eyes become cruel, and her lips transition into a subtle grin. Her face becomes Mother's. I snap my eyes closed, breathing hard, telling myself it's not real. It's not her. *You're safe.*

I find myself pulling madly against her restraint, but she just tightens her hands around me.

Stop! I beg of her. *Please stop!*

But Loralie doesn't let go of me. The way her fingers tighten around my wrists, the way she tells me I'm fine even though I'm not, causes me to open my eyes slowly, ready to prove to myself it's just Loralie. Loralie would never hurt me. But when my eyes finally focus on her, the fact that Loralie is holding me down instead of Mother or Jonny or Emile breaks something inside of me. I discover, for the first time ever, I'm just as scared of Loralie as I am of everyone else.

I find myself filled with a longing to be free of her. I pull my right leg in toward my chest and push against her, sending her falling to the ground. A loud grunt sounds before she falls quiet, remaining completely still.

I lie still as well for a moment, my mind trying to process everything that just happened. My body is mine to control again, and no weight is pressing down on me. All the fear has been drained, and I'm left with shock. What happened? She grabbed me, and . . . I hurt Loralie.

Loralie.

I fall to the ground next to her limp body, shaking her, begging for her eyes to open. She still has a pulse and breathes steadily. She must be unconscious.

I am sorry, Loralie. Please wake up.

She doesn't. She doesn't shift, she doesn't move. What have I done?

Just wake up!

I didn't mean to hurt her. Does she understand that? I cannot help her. I cannot get help. I cannot do anything. My tears slide off my face and hit the floor. Finally, I sit back and give up. It is hopeless. I am too broken and confused inside. I want my sister. I don't want her to leave me. All I wanted was her comfort, and she was there for me. I hurt her. Loralie. The one person in this world I care about.

I must have once again fallen asleep during my thoughts. I wake up to the sound of harsh shouts.

"Dolion! What have you done?" Mother stands in our doorway, staring directly at me.

Lying in front of me is Loralie, alive but not awake. The sun coming through the window magnifies one area. Of course it is her hand. The white cloth she had covering it has fallen away, revealing the burn.

"You could've damaged her beauty. Think of what would happen if Charles saw. He would refuse her. Is that what you want?"

I think back to last night. I think of that strange man with Loralie, only a few years older than us, waving to me. And smiling. No one smiles these days.

I did nothing, I want to say. I want her to hear me. I want to plead my case. Unfortunately, the only one who could stand up for me is passed out on the floor. This is all my fault.

I look at a drawer where I hid a knife and see myself grabbing it. Shoving it through my chest and bleeding to death.

Please just kill me, I beg my mother. *My only condition is Loralie gets to follow when she is ready.* So that I know she's safe. So that she does not have to suffer the pain of this world without me. Alone.

Chapter Eight

Clair

2022

Dolion turns to me. My heart races as I realize he can see me. He knows I'm here, in this dream. His eyes lock with mine, and I expect to find him smiling, expect the monster to grin at his victory. But instead, Dolion looks at me in a way that seems wrong for him. He looks at me with fear, with sorrow, with pain, and with desperation.

And though he never speaks to me, I know what he wishes to say.

Help me, Clair. Please.

I snap my eyes open. The sound of my thudding heart fills my ears. I clutch the knife next to my bed and calm instantly. It's just a dream—that's all it ever is. That same dream, over and over and over again.

Dolion

1941

At any moment, the acceptance or refusal letter will be here, and our fate will be decided for us. We may be separated by him. Charles. He doesn't get it; Loralie and I cannot survive without each other. We don't have the courage. She is my strength, I am her clarity. We cannot exist alone. I know that, but does Loralie? I look over to her. She's awake now. Only slightly weak. Mother says she hit her head on the floor when she fell. Only Mother tells it differently. She says I pushed her, which I did, but she says I pushed her when she refused to let me burn her and knocked her out so I could finish it off.

All I can hope at this point is for Charles to have found distaste in Loralie. It would be better for both of us to stay together. I walk over to where Loralie sits on the couch, left alone by everyone else. She looks at me, her dark curls falling in front of her face.

"I know it wasn't your fault, Doli."

We haven't talked since she woke up. Her small hands tremble, reaching toward me. I cup her hand in mine and sit by her.

"But what did happen? Why'd you push me off?"

I look at the floor, my eyes following the patterns laid out so neatly across the rug. She wouldn't understand. She knows pain, she knows hurt, but this? She would blame me. How could it make sense?

"Doli?"

Just stop. She looks at me with question in her eyes. *We may be separated. Forever. Please don't waste our remaining time talking about this.*

"Are you scared?"

I don't want to lose you.

"You could never lose me. I'll always be here, just gone for a while."

I don't want that!

"Just calm down. We'll be all right." Loralie squeezes my hand.

Knock, knock, knock come the swift raps on the door. At the sound, the house springs to life. An anxious buzz fills the air as Mother, Emile, and Jonny make their way into the living room. The sounds of hurried footsteps thudding across the wooden floor and my heart beating fast cause my nerves to spike. I can't lose Loralie. I just can't.

Loralie stands as Emile opens the front door, and I follow her. Emile grabs the letter from the man outside and closes the door. I give a gentle squeeze to Loralie's hand, and she returns it. Everyone quiets as Emile opens the envelope. He reads to himself, his oily hair falling in front of his dark eyes, before looking up and facing Loralie.

"You did it," he says. "I can't believe you did it."

Loralie

I did it? Arron and I never told anyone what we did—we weren't gone long, and no one noticed we were together—but still, I can't believe I actually did it.

I won his approval. Actually, the money he thinks my family has won his approval. But still, I'm good enough. Images of a life free of Mother, Emile, Jonny, and Dolion flash through my mind. My stomach turns with shock and nausea as I revel in the images. No Dolion . . . *Freedom.* I spent the night hoping I would get turned down, I spent the party trying to ruin it; this is the part where I am supposed to tell Mother and Emile what I did and finally witness the end of it all. But if I do that . . . I hate the thoughts running through my head. *If I do that, I won't be free of Dolion.* I can't spend forever living in the shadows with him, not when I am capable of achieving so much greater.

My wide eyes turn to face Dolion, who, expectedly so, is frowning hard at the rug. I know I'll be separated from him, but it can't be forever. We're twins. Twins belong together, right?

Mother runs over to me and wraps her aggressive arms around my shoulders, pulling me away from Dolion. He stands there, unable to move, staring at me. I suppose I am his strength, his voice. He will be lost without me. I will miss him, he *is* my brother, but...

"Listen to me, Loralie," Mother starts. "You've won his approval for now, but he can still change his mind. You have to swear he won't find out about our poverty. It would ruin us. Tomorrow our lives will begin to change. You've given us the greatest gift." She goes on. Wear this, do that. Don't trust him, don't talk to him. Look down, be polite. On and on and on.

Dolion, left alone in the corner while everyone else allows their input to flood in, looks into my eyes. He's crying. I take a deep breath and force my eye roll to cease. His head drops. He departs the room, heading upstairs without looking at me.

"Loralie!" Mother snaps at me. "Your brother is fine. Listen to me. You have to pack tonight. I'm not sure what time tomorrow you will be leaving. The letter didn't say, so just be prepared."

I can hear him and his cries. He is in pain.

"Loralie!" Mother says yet again.

"I'm sorry," I say, but it's not to Mother. It's for Dolion. I push Mother out of the way, heading for the stairs. He's up there, and he needs me. "I'm sorry."

Dolion's wails send panic coursing through me. He isn't well. I'm afraid of what his thoughts may be doing to him. I pass Mother, Emile, and Jonny. Jonny grabs my wrist, and I turn around and punch his flat face. "Get off of me," I say.

No one else attempts to make me stay. I run up the stairs and push open our bedroom door, unsure of what I will find. Dolion stands when I enter, guilt and shock plastered on his face. My gaze travels from his eyes down his neck, then across his shoulder, and I follow his arm to his forearm. Now I understand what this separation is going to do to him.

One cut follows another, parallel to the last, falling in a line down his wrist.

"Dolion?" I can barely make out the word.

He falls to the floor, dropping the bloody blade. He doesn't cry. His breathing becomes slow and heavy.

Can't you just tell them you won't go?

I sigh. My feet carry me over to him, and I drop next to him, putting my arm around his limp shoulders.

"I have to do this," I say, trying to sound defeated. "You have to realize Mother won't have it any other way."

She cannot *control our lives any longer. My life is mine, yours is yours. Why doesn't that matter?*

I grab the blade from the floor and hide it under a box, knowing I won't always be around to protect him. The marks on his arm only show his weakness. This will be his life without me—I can't change that. I hug him and hold him tighter. A tear escapes me and rolls onto his shoulder. My brother. My friend. The only one I have ever been able to trust. We will be separated.

A small pain breaks apart the excitement in my chest, and it grows throughout the night. Blood turned excitement into pain and a future into heartbreak.

Chapter Ten

Loralie

Charles himself comes to get me in the morning.

Last night was rough. It's not my fault Dolion's hurting, but I feel like it might be my job to fix it. All around the room is my "family." Mother looks at me with expectation and warning. I am the child who is supposed to bring her wealth, and her eyes tell me I better succeed. Emile is just Emile; he looks evil and chilling, his sharp cheekbones casting their usual shadows across his square face. And Jonny, big, strong, cowardly, and cold. Dolion has not come down.

His absence weighs heavy on me. If only I could see him, tell him I love him and I'm sorry. He was quiet this morning. Wouldn't even show his face when I woke up. I know he's hurting. I am too.

The knock comes. Mother becomes rigid as she positions herself behind me, hands on my shoulders, and Emile answers the door. I search for Dolion, just needing to see him. My eyes travel over to the white

"

staircase, hoping he might come down. But, of course, there's no one there.

Mother begins putting pressure on my shoulders, guiding me toward the open door and my bags sitting on the worn wooden floor by the entrance.

"I haven't said goodbye to him yet," I whisper so only she can hear.

"There are things in life more important than him, Loralie."

My body gives in to her, and I begin walking toward where Charles stands in the doorway. The sun shines in behind him, darkening his sharp features.

I'm never going to see Dolion again, I think, silent tears pricking my eyes at the thought. I scold myself internally. I have to fight my own body to keep from running upstairs to him. *Be a good girl, do as you're told, your life is no longer yours . . . Has it ever been?*

Loralie?

My head whips around, not giving up the search.

Time stands still once I make eye contact with him. For a moment, we stand watching, waiting. Waiting for what? Things to change? He doesn't run to me, doesn't beg me to stay. He just stares, as if he is watching his own life die before him. I suppose, in a way, he is. I am too.

Mother's grip fades away, the birds' chirping in the morning air disappears, and the sunlight is lost behind me. The only thing I'm aware of is the boy I'm leaving behind. *He will be all right*, I tell myself. I study the way his shoulders hunch, the way his hand rests gently on the railing. He's always so gentle. He couldn't harm another being if he wanted to. That's why he needs me.

When my eyes find his, I'm surprised to see he's not crying, he's not breaking inside. He holds his head high, like he's been ready for this day for many years. I smile gently at him, shocked to find that I am the one crying. The tears taste salty on my lips.

Dolion grips the railing tighter as he nods at me, telling me it's all right to leave him behind. I want to nod back, I want to run to him, to hug him, to tell him I love him. All I can force myself to do is glance at the floor beneath my feet before I shuffle toward the door and away forever.

Chapter Eleven

Loralie

I'm pulled from party to party, showcased like some prized animal, introduced to person after person who will never remember my name, nor I theirs. It's like my entire childhood since Father's death all squeezed into a month.

Of all the people I've met, Charles's family are the few I've had nearly no interaction with. I hardly know anyone other than his sister and her husband, who have been at most of the gatherings and events. And Arron. That's not to say they haven't been around. Until we wed, Charles and I have been staying in his parents' home—more like mansion—with some of his family while his mother and father are overseas. They are supposed to be arriving tomorrow, and we'll begin preparing the wedding and the arrangement between families.

My stomach twists as I think about the wedding and especially as I think about Arron. I've never been careful with men, and I've never had reason to worry. However, it's been over a month since my last cycle, and I threw up last night before going to bed. I shake my head and push that thought away as I pull out Dolion's latest letter again. I'm just paranoid. That's all.

I've been receiving letters from Dolion for a couple weeks now, and I write back as quickly as I can without Charles or the others finding out. He isn't doing well. I knew he wouldn't. But I have to try to distance myself from him or I'm only going to grow miserable. I have a job to do; I finally have importance in this world. I can't simply give it up for Dolion. I can't go back to him. That life is over. It's gone. But now, standing with this letter in my hand, I wish I could do more than sneak out to the mailman in the mornings to deliver my letters in secret.

I sit at the desk in my room and pull out a piece of paper, preparing myself to write him back.

Dearest Dolion,

Surely you don't believe this is a decent idea? The things Mother would do to you if she were to catch you sneaking out! No more than a month has passed; you needn't be so cross. I am struggling as well. Many thoughts I wish I hadn't had creep back inside. I do understand your pain, Doli. Don't victimize yourself when you have a sister who is also hurting. You think I want this? Him? Any of it? I never chose to leave. You never chose for me to go. We didn't want this. We are freaks, unnatural and dangerous. It's the world's job to hate us. Don't do anything you'll regret. Just try to survive all of this. Please. For me. I'll do it as well. I love you.

Sincerely,

Loralie

I don't want him to come find me. Mother would hurt him if she were to catch him. But also, a life without Dolion is easier than I prepared for. No one to watch over and protect. No one to fight for, no one to love. It's easier, it hurts less. My burden is lifted. I can finally breathe.

Another child broken . . . Another child lost . . . Another child dead . . .

A broken gasp rings through the cold room as I snap awake. My fingers grip the sweat-soaked sheets until aches spiral through my knuckles, and my heart thuds in my chest as if it, too, wants away from this body. In my dream there was a sickness, a disease that had settled itself into my core. It grew and festered, its dark tendrils of death and ruin beginning to seep out of my body. In this dream there was a voice that guided me and led me away from this sickness. It brought me comfort, helped me escape the growing thing in my stomach. And then it healed the sickness and helped me realize that without all of the destruction and pain of the world, the sickness was no more than a baby boy. Arron's baby boy. *My* baby boy.

My stomach turns again, and I fight my growing panic. My body will be stretched out. My life will no longer be mine.

Charles rolls over in the bed next to me, his hand resting on my chest. He insists I sleep in his bed every night. My body feels heavy, and it seems as though it presses into the mattress, burying itself in the folds of sheets and blankets. I stare at the dark ceiling, the moonlight casting long shadows across the bed and wall, and think about my dream.

That's all it was, a dream.

Even so, the longer I lie here, the more convinced I am there's something rotten growing inside me.

I shake my head and blink away the last of my tears. It doesn't matter if there is a child within me or not; I'll be married soon anyway, and no one will think it more than a child of marriage. Charles's baby.

Will Arron know?

Stop being a fool, Loralie, I think. *There is no baby. It was just a dream.*

I try hard to convince myself even though I know it's a lie.

Chapter Twelve

Dolion

Living in a memory. That's what my life has become.

I hope Loralie is doing better out there, with Charles and his family, discovering what her life is going to be.

I stay in memories of a time that was different, when I had not only Loralie but Father as well. Mother was not the same person she is now, and I had yet to meet Jonny and Emile.

I go downstairs sometimes. Mostly because Mother won't bring up food. She's taken to refusing to speak to me. They all go about their lives as if I'm not here. I never served a purpose to them anyway. Loralie was the one who always mattered; she was the only reason they tolerated me. Loralie wouldn't have it any other way.

My sister always had power over Mother. Mother claimed it was because Loralie was to marry off someday, and there was much to be gained from that, but Loralie knew the truth, and so did I: Mother has always been afraid of Loralie.

Now that Loralie's power over them is gone, I am no one to any of them. Not that I would want to be. I slink through each day, in and out of the shadows, occasionally passing by one of them with less of an impact than driftwood. But mostly I stay in my and Loralie's room, lost in the memories.

Once or twice I went so far into the memories I forgot the past isn't happening now.

Loralie and I would play on this floor. We'd play house, but Loralie would never be the mother, which meant I'd have to, but I never really minded. Loralie would go out to work for the day, and I'd stay home with the children. They could get real whiny at times, and Loralie would tell me to make them shut up when she got home. I'd shush the children and promise them Loralie didn't really hate them, she was just like that sometimes.

"Trust me, I should know." I would sigh and look at all their little faces as I spoke to them. That was before my accident, back when I still had a voice. Loralie didn't know this, but I would always pretend there were ten little children, all following and watching me. I would tell her there were only two to keep her happy. She thought more than two were too much work. "She gets like that with me sometimes, even though I know she loves me more than she could ever love anybody. I'm her brother, you know. My father says that means Loralie and I are important to each other. I think Loralie believes that too. I think she would hurt me a lot more often if she didn't."

The imaginary children would listen to me so intently.

I always let my real life get in the way of imagination. Those poor kids had to suffer through so much complaining from me about my own home life as a child. But as long as Father was around, it really wasn't that bad. I can hardly think of what I actually had to complain about. I remember being unhappy in life, which was foolish of me. That was when things were good, when they were happy.

Another memory breaks through my mind, something I haven't thought about in years. A boy. I saw him around the house a couple times. He never did anything, just stood there watching. When I was little, I didn't fear him, but maybe I should have. He wasn't family, he wasn't someone who was supposed to be in the house, and the others never saw him. He'd just stand there, and when I turned my head away, he would always be gone by the time I looked back.

He wore clothes similar to what my father would wear in the fields, only the boy's clothes felt off, different from what I normally see, as if they were from another time. He always seemed scared, as if I were a ghost to him. I always figured *he* was the ghost though. What else could he have been?

Even so, he never scared me. There was something about him I could relate to. I saw myself in him, and that comforted me more than anything. I never told Loralie about him; he was my little secret, an aspect of my life she couldn't control.

My stomach rumbles suddenly, and the familiar hollow aches climb their way through my chest and into my throat. My head spins with each grumble. I need to eat, but just looking at the bedroom door causes fear to swell inside me.

Get down there quickly and come back. It will all be over soon, I promise myself.

Creeping down the stairs, I overhear Emile's gruff voice. I know that tone. His mocking tone. It sounds different though, not directed toward me, almost foreign, in a way.

"And then he stood there watching her!" Emile says through laughter.

"I don't see any reason to make such a fuss of it, Emile," my mother says. "We've seen it coming for a while now. That son of yours couldn't keep a girl if his life depended on it."

I take a deep breath and prepare to head into the kitchen, hoping to pass behind Mother and Emile without them seeing me. As my feet gently find the floorboards at the base of the stairs, however, something else catches my attention. Jonny sits in the living room in a chair opposite Mother and Emile, his face beet red and tears brimming in his eyes.

I pause, my hand still on the banister.

"I'll do better next time," Jonny says, his voice quiet and hesitant. "I think Molly in town has taken an interest in—"

"Honey, she's interested in the money she thinks we have," Mother says, her hands busy stitching.

Emile's deep chuckle comes from behind a newspaper.

Jonny lowers his head, leaning back slowly in his chair. Something about him, about the way he holds himself, reminds me of myself. Of the way Mother and Emile have made me feel. Even of the way Jonny has made me feel. I try to remind myself to hate him, like Loralie does. He's been so cruel to me, after all. But when he lifts his head slightly, his eyes land on me, and he pauses, his face growing redder.

I pull my gaze away from him and hurry into the kitchen, making sure the door closes softly behind me before I shuffle over to the closet, desperate to get something to eat and return to my room.

As I gather food off the lowest shelf, I hear the kitchen door swing closed behind me. My muscles tense as my arms tighten around the food. I try to quiet my breathing, hoping whoever it is doesn't see me in the shadows. Then the light flickers on, and my heart sinks.

"Were you spying on us?" Jonny's voice, now strong, comes from the other end of the room. "Answer me."

I turn to face him, shaking my head and looking down.

"If you say a word about what you heard to anybody . . ."

There's something about Jonny I've never felt before. I'm not afraid of him anymore, at least not in this moment. I place my food on the counter and reach toward the drawer where Mother keeps my paper, in case she needs me to tell her something, and pull it out. Then I carefully write the words I'm thinking.

You're not worthless, you know.

I give it to him, my hand surprisingly steady. He takes the paper quickly, and his hard face softens as he reads it. He's quiet for a moment before seeming to remember that he is supposed to be angry at me. He forces his face to display hatred.

"You think you know everything, don't you?" He steps closer to me. "I know I'm not worthless. Of course, you'd be an expert on the topic, wouldn't you?"

I reach for my food and prepare to leave the kitchen. Jonny stays unusually silent. As I walk toward the door, brushing past Jonny, he finally says something, his voice quieter than usual. "I'm not like you," he says. "I'm not."

But it almost seems as if he is trying to convince himself more than me.

Chapter Thirteen

Loralie

Arron won't meet my eyes today, and it makes me wonder if he knows.

Surely he doesn't. It's not something even I know for certain. A small knot tightens in my core, and it tells me I'm right. Arron's child is within me.

"Oh, you mustn't be so shy!" Charles's sister thrusts her child into my arms, and I stare at the baby, only a few months old, unsure of what to do with him. He's small. His little hands grasp at my curls, and his eyes are wide as his toothless mouth breaks into a smile. "He likes you!" Her constant enthusiasm makes me fight yet another eye roll.

"Where's Charles?" I ask, keeping my voice as polite as possible. "I haven't seen him yet this morning." He wasn't in bed when I woke up. Waking to the bright sunrays stretched out across the empty bed made me feel at peace this morning. At least I didn't have to deal with the way Charles wakes up and pulls me close to him every fucking morning.

His sister hums as she stares at her child still in my arms. "He must have gone into town early," she says as she picks up her baby and nuzzles her nose against his. "That means we have all day to do whatever we like, doesn't it? Yes, doesn't it?"

I can't stop another slight eye roll this time as she repeatedly talks in that baby voice, making her son laugh.

"I was thinking we could bake cookies." Her voice becomes serious again as she looks at me, cuddling her baby close to her chest now. "When I married Michael, his sister and I spent a day together, and it made me feel so much more welcome. I'd like to be that for you if I can, Loralie."

The fact that this woman is being anything other than overly excited, as I've always known her, makes me pull away slightly as the realization that I don't even know her name settles in. This woman is nothing but blond hair and shimmering dark eyes to me. An annoying member of Charles's family that I am forced to deal with.

"Oh, no need to go out of your way."

"I'm here all day with this little one," she says, smiling at her child.

Suddenly, any desire I had to ask her name vanishes, and I find myself wondering where Arron is, desperate to get away from this woman and her baby.

In the momentary silence, a faint sound I can't place penetrates my mind and thoughts. It's small, the crackling of a fire maybe. And the scent of burning embers swirls in the air. Smoke? Maybe that too. I glance at the fireplace, its hand-carved wood displaying the family's wealth better than the newly tailored clothes they all insist upon wearing.

There is no fire burning in the hearth, however, just the backdrop of blackened bricks and ashy dust.

The smell of smoke persists.

My palm begins burning, but it's a different type of burn than when Mother burned Dolion's hand; that one was consistent unbearable pain. This feels more like heat and tingling, almost satisfying, as if this feeling is something I've been craving.

Slowly, fearfully, I turn my palm over and open my hand. My eyes widen in shock, and I snap my hand closed as a shot of panic springs through my chest. My eyes dart to Charles's sister, but thankfully, her precious baby is holding all of her attention. I chance another look and open my hand, but all that rests on my palm is the recovering burn that appeared when Mother burned Dolion. Nothing abnormal, nothing strange.

Still, every time I close my eyes, I see that awful sight, glowing embers protruding through ash bubbling up out of my skin. My hand was the exact image of a dying fire.

I shiver.

What's happening to me?

Chapter Fourteen

Dolion

My heart skips with excitement and anticipation when I see Loralie's latest letter sitting on the dresser. It seems as though it's been so long since she last wrote, and I can't tear into the envelope fast enough.

When the paper is finally unfolded and her words are laid out before me, I fall into a content stillness.

Dearest Dolion,

Surely you don't believe this is a decent idea? The things Mother would do to you if she were to catch you sneaking out! No more than a month has passed; you needn't be so cross. I am struggling as well. Many thoughts I wish I hadn't had creep back inside. I do understand your pain, Doli. Don't victimize yourself when you have a sister who is also hurting. You think I want this? Him? Any of it? I never chose to leave. You never chose for me to go. We didn't want this. We are freaks, unnatural and dangerous. It's the world's job to hate us. Don't do anything you'll regret. Just try to survive all of this. Please. For me. I'll do it as well. I love you.

Sincerely,

Loralie

My eyes burn as her words blur. The excitement of her letter's arrival has vanished and been replaced with hurt and betrayal. I stare in an uneven focus, drifting in and out of reality. The crinkling paper is rough under my fingers, the edges sharp against my skin.

Don't victimize myself when I have a sister who is also hurting? She's gone! She got to leave this place while I'm stuck here to rot until I die. Who does she think she is? She's free!

I slam her letter onto the desk and pull out a pen and piece of paper. With my head in my hand, I position the ink over the page and wait. She knows I'm the weak one, and she left me alone in this situation. How dare she act as if she has it worse than me when she's at least free of Mother and Emile.

My grip tightens on the pen, and the words sporadically come to me. I begin writing.

Loralie,

I am so sorry. You have had so much faith in me, but you ought to have known from the beginning there is no way I could ever be who you assumed I should have been.

I write out of spite and shame. I know who I am. She doesn't have to tell me I'm pathetic—I already know that.

I continue.

I am weak. I've always been broken easily, especially when you're away.

Especially when Loralie is away. Without her, I am nothing; everyone has made that perfectly clear.

Hot tears fall onto the paper, blurring the word *weak* until it is no longer legible. I crush the paper in my fist and toss it to the side of the room. Without Loralie, I am nothing. Why? Why can't I be strong enough to take care of myself without her?

Because you are worthless, I answer my own question.

But what if I'm not?

The front door slams as someone enters the house. Emile's deep voice greets my mother, who must have just come back from town.

I shake my head. If I were more than worthless . . .

I hold my arm out in front of me. The healing cuts I made sit bright red on my pale skin, and Mother's burn is on my palm. If I were more than worthless, I wouldn't bleed so easily.

I close my eyes and sigh.

A voice stirs in the darkness. *Even your sister bleeds . . .*

Snapping my eyes open, I search the room, but it's empty. Did I drift off for a moment? Maybe I had some sort of flash dream.

Even Loralie bleeds. She may bleed, but Loralie doesn't break.

I lie in my bed and pull the blanket over my curled body. Sinking into the warmth of my mattress, a chill washes over me. I shiver. My breath becomes visible before me, swirling through the curls that hang over my eyes as my fingers shake. I try to bury myself deeper under my blanket.

I crane my neck to see the window of the room. It's still closed. Then why is it suddenly so cold?

I tuck my hands into my chest and wrap the blanket around my shoulders. What is happening?

Closing my eyes, I hope I can fall asleep soon and wake up warm again when this is all over.

My eyes slowly open as a curious feeling begins to settle in my palm. The cold spreads slowly from the burn Mother gave me. Even though my hand is clenched, I can feel the cold seeping across my skin.

Something about it is calming, reassuring, as if I've been craving this since the day I was born.

I slowly turn my shaking hand over and open my palm. Through the dark of the room I see the horror of my hand. I snap my eyes closed, but the image of ice shards and swirling frost won't leave me.

When I collect myself and open my eyes again, my palm is back to normal. In the dark I can't even see the mark Mother left on me.

I turn onto my back and stare at the dark ceiling. What the hell was that? The cold clung to my skin as if I were the freedom it had been longing for, seeping into me, weaving itself into the very essence of my making.

I ask the question Loralie and I have been asking our entire lives: *What is wrong with us?*

No, not *us*.

Now it is just me, alone and afraid.

Chapter Fifteen

Clair

2022

My body is not mine in this dream. I have no control over anything but my thoughts as I continue to watch what takes place in the yard, under the large tree that sits in front of the house.

Perdu is broken. Perdu is hurt by the world, by Dolion, by so much more than anyone other than he could know. He's so broken that he follows Dolion. He follows him far into the dark, so far the light is nothing but a memory. He follows him up the chair that now sits under the tree. He follows him until the rope is around his neck. He follows him until the sun rises and he is left hanging.

Dolion turns to me. My heart races as I realize he can see me. He knows I'm here, in this dream. His eyes lock with mine, and I expect to find him smiling, expect the monster to grin at his victory. But instead, Dolion looks *at me in a way that seems wrong for him. He looks at me with fear, with sorrow, with pain, and with desperation.*

And though he never speaks to me, I know what he wishes to say.

Help me, Clair. Please.

I sit up suddenly and glance around my home. I fell asleep at the table while I was skinning a rabbit. I shake my head and sigh. I've never fallen asleep so easily before. The air is thinner than usual, and the light that still flickers from the fire is muted and dull. A thin layer of ice coats the handle of my door. Something is wrong, and it makes me feel nauseous. I don't know what's happening, but I have to fight the urge to run to Halcyon Lake in the middle of the night just to feel some sort of peace and safety. It's always been a place of comfort for me.

Loralie

1941

I ball up the batter I just spent ages mixing and drop it onto the baking sheet.

"Let's bake together," Charles's sister said. She wanted to make me feel welcome, or so she said. But since she pulled out the butter and eggs, she has done nothing but coo at her baby and tickle the child's tummy. At one point she even dared feed him without leaving the room.

I tighten my hand around the ball of dough as she begins singing to her child. The smell of baked cookies reaches my nose, and I drop the ball I was holding. It's fully baked.

I turn my palm over and stare at my hand again. There is nothing there. I focus all of my anger and direct it to my palm, determined to make my skin catch fire again.

Something is happening to me, and I will figure out what it is. I think about how much I would love to make Charles's sister shut up, how good it would feel to take her enthusiasm away, and a small flame bursts from my palm for only a second before it vanishes. I step back in surprise, bumping the table behind me.

"Are you all right, Loralie?" she asks.

My heart is fluttering, but I attempt to pace my breathing.

"I am," I say without looking at her.

She walks around the table and comes up beside me. I know what she's going to say before she ever does. "Here, hold him. He'll make you feel better."

"I don't want to." I try to keep my voice steady, but the irritation is trying to break through.

"Just take him, Loralie. He's so cute and small—you won't be able to help but smile."

"Listen." I straighten myself to look into her always-cheerful eyes. "I do not wish to hold your baby, and I would appreciate it if you left me alone."

"You needn't be so dramatic." She forces her child into my arms and watches with a smile on her face as I hold him. The irritation that was irking me shifts into something much stronger.

This woman has no respect for me. All she cares about is her stupid child. She can't even see past her own love for him to see that I asked her to leave me alone. Standing here, with her little baby in my arms, I want nothing more than to watch that constant smile fall from the mother's face.

I straighten my back and stare deep into her dark golden eyes. I relish these last few moments of her eyes smiling before her innocence is shattered like glass against a fist. Then I let her baby fall from my arms.

Her smile morphs into terror, and her eyes instantly fill with tears. She shrieks as she rushes to scoop her child up from the floor at my feet.

"I told you I didn't want to hold him," I say.

"What the hell," she whispers, coddling her child. "You could have hurt him."

He cries as she rocks him.

"Trust me, if I wanted to hurt him, he wouldn't be able to cry right now."

A new look of fear flashes across the mother's face as she tucks her baby into her chest.

"Is that a threat?" she asks.

I shrug. "Do you want to find out?"

"Charles!" She calls for her brother.

I smile, my eyes never leaving hers. I hold out my palm, praying a silent prayer this will work. Fire erupts from my hand, casting shadows across the woman's face as her eyes light up in horror.

"Don't tell anyone anything." My voice is quiet but strong. "Or I think you can guess what will happen."

At that moment, Charles enters the kitchen, and I snap my palm shut, causing the fire to disappear.

"Are you all right, Helen?" Charles asks her, rushing to her crying baby's aid. "You called me, did you not?"

"Everything's all right, Charles." She says it with a calm voice, but her eyes never leave mine.

Chapter Seventeen

Dolion

Feet thud on the steps as someone climbs the staircase, and my eyes open at the sound. I hold my breath and listen, praying they'll pass by my room. They reach the landing and shuffle across the floorboards in the hall. The closer they get to my room, the tighter the knot in my chest becomes. I clutch my blanket in my hand and wait. The floorboards creak, and even the walls of the house seem to be shuddering.

Please pass my room, please. I didn't do anything wrong. Please leave me alone.

The seconds stretch until they feel like hours. Finally, the footsteps stop, and my breath freezes. Then comes the sound I've been dreading: the slow knock on my door. A sudden chill runs through me.

I didn't do anything. I didn't.

If I keep quiet, maybe she'll go away. Mother hasn't come to see me in so long, I almost forgot what this fear is like. Almost.

She knocks again and waits. Mother never knocks twice, if she knocks at all.

Then the door slowly opens, and I sink deeper into my bed and cover my head with my blanket.

"Calm down, coward. I just want to talk."

I freeze. Jonny?

I let out the breath I was holding, surprised when I can see it in front of me. Shit. It's getting oddly cold again. I clench my fist, not wanting the ice to return now.

"Come out, Dolion, or I'll give you something to hide from."

I reluctantly obey Jonny, knowing he'll follow through with his threat if I don't do what he wants. I keep my blanket wrapped around me and sit up in the corner of the bed near the wall. Jonny remains standing so he is tall above me.

I keep my hand under the blanket, but I can feel the cold seeping across my skin again.

"What you wrote in the kitchen . . . Why'd you say that to me?"

I stay quiet, feeling dumb. What does he expect from me? It's not like I can say anything, and he knows it.

"Can't you write it down or something?" He pushes his words through his annoyed drawl.

My body is too tense to move and grab paper. I want to shrug or shake my head, but I'm afraid of angering Jonny. So I sit, and Jonny waits.

Eventually he grabs the paper off my dresser. He turns to me and throws it at me, and the paper hits my face. He tosses the pen at me too, but it lands next to me on the bed. Then Jonny takes a seat near my feet and stares at me.

With shaking hands, I reach for the paper and pen. There's nothing on my palm, thank goodness, but the cold sensation is definitely there.

You're not worthless, I write again.

"You already wrote that," Jonny shouts, then immediately whips his head to the door and quiets his voice. "Why did you say that to me? I'm not like you, Dolion."

I shake my head. No, he isn't, not in every way. But I remember the heartbreak and humiliation on Jonny's face when Emile was making fun of him. He is like me where it counts, and that's all that matters right now.

Mother and Emile can be cruel. I reach out to him with the paper in my shaking hand. What am I doing? Loralie would scold me for putting myself in this position.

Jonny reads what I wrote, and for a moment, I think maybe he'll soften up a bit.

But then he scowls and says, "Not to me. They like me."

I nod, giving up. *Sure, Jonny*, I think. *If you have to tell yourself that, go ahead.*

"They do like me, right? It's not like I did anything to them. They have no reason to hate me."

I sigh and focus on the seam of my blanket, noticing as my finger plays with a loose thread that the hem of my blanket is covered in frost. I fold it under itself and risk a glance up at Jonny. He doesn't seem to have noticed anything.

"Do you think they hate me?" Jonny's voice is barely a whisper. Then he looks up and snaps, "Don't answer that."

Jonny sits for a minute. The emotions shifting across his face display the mental battle taking place inside his head. Should he be nice to me or not—I'm sure that's what's going through his mind. After a moment, his eyes settle on their usual hardened glare.

"I don't need you," he says, and then he stands up and leaves the room.

An almost audible silence drifts through the air after Jonny is gone, and I'm left feeling the weight of my childhood crashing around me.

What if everything I've known to be true has been a lie? What if Jonny is more than Emile's cruel son? What if I am more than Loralie's mute brother? What if . . .

My chest tightens at the thought.

What if Loralie isn't who I've made her out to be either?

Chapter Eighteen

Dolion

L oralie,

I am so sorry. You have had so much faith in me, but you ought to have known from the beginning there is no way I could ever be who you assumed I should have been. I am weak. I've always been broken easily, especially when you're away.

I stare at the crumpled start of the letter. I picked it up a few minutes ago from where I threw it and tried to smooth it out. Now I can't stop reading it, over and over. Loralie is gone, and I'm starting to think maybe that's a good thing. It scares me, but the longer I spend away from her, the more I start to question who she actually is and if she can truly be trusted.

If I can't trust Loralie, then I can't trust anyone.

I put my pen to the paper, and without thinking, I continue the letter.

I tried to do this, and I have. I have won the battle inside my head for months now, years even. You act like you know what goes on in my thoughts when I am afraid and alone, but I know you don't. No one does; no one could.

Loralie especially couldn't ever know what I'm feeling and going through. She betrayed me when she left, but maybe she betrayed me while she was here too. I was always forced to hide in her shadow, forced to stay silent even when I had other ways of expressing myself. Loralie wouldn't let me be strong; she had to be the one to do that for me. My chest tightens, and a lump forms in my throat. She couldn't have meant to hurt me that way. She loves me. Loralie *loves me.*

I nod as if reassuring myself. Of course she does. She always has. I know that.

Through the pain, I continue letting my heart spill onto the paper. Never before have I let myself be free with my words. *Write, don't think.*

Please do better than me. I've gotten past the point of saving. The cuts don't do anything for me anymore, and the scars only show me I am a failure.

Sweat and tears pool on my cheeks. My eyes burn from a lack of sleep and overwhelming emotions. My head hurts, and my muscles scream. My body is dying, but a fire is igniting within my heart and mind. I turn my arm to look at the marks carved into my skin. I come alive at the sight. There is hope in the gruesome pain. My body is shaking, but it's no longer from fear.

Selfishly, I want to do this with you. I want us to end our lives together. If I don't end it before I see you again, I may drag you down with me. Don't forget me, Loralie. I won't ever forget or stop loving you. Take care of yourself for me. I'll look for you in the next life.

Our story is over. The end has come and passed. Loralie and I are done; our lives and fates will no longer be intertwined. Loralie is my addiction, not my savior. I'm scared and lonely, but I refuse to be weak anymore. I can't get away from Jonny, Mother, or Emile—at least not yet—but if Loralie believes I'm dead, she won't try to come back for me. She'll move on with her life the way we should have years ago. If she believes I killed myself, maybe she'll let me go and I can live my life in peace.

I sign the letter.

I love you,
Dolion

Chapter Nineteen

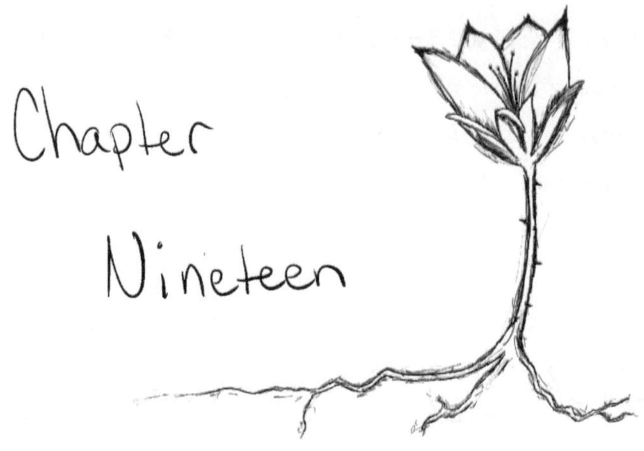

Loralie

Hidden in Arron's room, I practice this new ability I seem to have. I can create fire with just my mind. I can't do it with my other palm, so it must have something to do with the burn Dolion and I have. I wonder if he can do it too. A small pain prods at my heart when I think of him, and I have to remind myself I am better without him.

I still miss him, however. Every so often I do. Especially in moments like this, when he would be the only one I could talk to about something. What would he think of the way I treated Charles's sister? He wouldn't be happy. That's what I have to remember: Dolion kept me from being the person I was meant to be. He held me back, and now that I don't have to live tied to him, imprisoned by his chains, I can be free.

I smile to myself as I think of the pain on the woman's face.

Dolion wouldn't approve of the way I handled the situation. But Dolion isn't here.

"Loralie?" Arron's voice is so smooth compared to his brother's. It's easy to recognize from anywhere. "What are you doing in my room?"

I turn around to face him, looking up at him from my seat on the floor. He is tall and lanky, but those muscles flex in the most perfect way when he's—

I catch myself and move my eyes to the floor. That's how I got into this mess in the first place. I have my own version of his sister's little monster dwelling inside me, and it's his fault.

But his body is so tempting. I've been with Charles so much lately that Arron and I haven't had a chance to be alone for more than just a few seconds. His family is everywhere, and his brother, my betrothed, always has a watchful eye on me. Like he doesn't quite trust me. What is there to lose from being with Arron now?

I reach my hand up to him and wait for his fingers to interlock with mine.

"Tell me what you want from me, Loralie." He sits on the floor next to me as he speaks, his hand grasping mine firmly. "And be honest. I won't play your games any longer."

"At first I wanted to make Mother and Emile angry," I say, letting him play with my fingers as he listens to me.

"You were using me," he mumbles, but he doesn't look at me, keeping his eyes on my fingers as he strokes them.

"Yes, and you knew that. You were using me too." The defense that rises in my voice surprises me.

"So, now what do you want from me?" he asks. "Since your first plan didn't work, what are you doing with me now?"

I find myself wanting to confide in this man in a way I can't with anyone else. He's here with me now, isn't he? I'm engaged to his brother, and he's still sitting on this floor with me, being patient with me.

"I'm pregnant," I say before I can stop myself. "And it's your baby."

He's quiet for a moment. His hand stops stroking mine, but he still doesn't look up. "I know."

"What?" I whisper. "You know?"

He brushes his dark hair from his forehead and finally works up the courage to look at me. He has a childish look to him right now, like there's a world full of wonder and mystery he is just discovering. "I dreamed it, and I woke up knowing it was real." Arron shakes his head and pulls his hand away. "I know how it sounds," he says, his voice quieting. "You just have to believe me."

"I do," I say, though I don't tell him I had the same experience. Something is going on here, something more than any of us know, and it's starting to scare me. "I believe you, Arron."

He looks up at me, and there's a sudden spark that passes between us. It's enthralling and alluring. Arron's lips pull up into a small smirk, and he reaches his hand out to grab mine again. "I don't know what this is, Loralie, but I haven't felt this way in a long time."

His words make me smile, and my body writhes with sudden desire. His head dips down to meet mine, and he kisses me. He is so gentle and kind with his kisses. He's patient, but he's excited. I need more of this man. I can't imagine my life without him anymore, and I smile to myself as I realize I don't have to. I'm marrying his brother; he will forever be in my life, and I could not be more grateful.

I wrap my arms tighter around Arron, and he pulls me close to him. He's breathing heavily, and it makes me grin and look up at him. He strokes my hair and kisses the top of my head.

"Do you still think I'm using you?" I ask him through small giggles.

"I sincerely hope not," he says, then places another kiss on my forehead.

I lay my head back on his chest and stare at his large room. The same deep red wallpaper that lines the rest of the house covers Arron's walls, and his lights make sure not even a small corner of the room is left to darkness. It's warm and welcoming, just like Arron.

"Why didn't you want the party to go well?" My voice is just barely more than a whisper. "You were with me to ruin it. You said you weren't happy about the marriage. Why?"

Arron's chest rises and falls as he breathes deep, his hand running along my bare back as I wait in the stillness of the room for him to reply. When he finally starts speaking, his voice is slow and quiet, like forcing the words out is hard for him.

"I was engaged not that long ago. Her name was Emmeline." He sighs and grabs my hand in his. "I had known her for a long time. I trusted her. Loved her even. I found her in Charles's bed one night. I suppose you could say, as childish as it is, I was after revenge at the party."

I look up at him again and smile. "That's not childish."

"No?"

I shake my head and stretch to kiss him. Then his jaw and his neck. "Not at all."

Chapter Twenty

Clair

2022

But isn't that the point of a dream? *an old voice, ancient with years of heartbreak caught up all in the single sound, asks me.* Isn't the world beyond sleep always out of your control? Free to be twisted and shaped by an outside force because . . . because you have no power over your mind when you've drifted far away.

The source of the voice may be behind me, or maybe above me, or even below me, through the porch and six feet beneath the soil, but my head won't turn to look. I am left completely vulnerable to whoever may be here with me. My body is not mine in this dream. I have no control over anything but my thoughts as I continue to watch what takes place in the yard, under the large tree that sits in front of the house.

Perdu is broken. Perdu is hurt by the world, by Dolion, by so much more than anyone other than he could know. He's so broken that he follows Dolion. He follows him far into the dark, so far the light is nothing but a memory. He follows him up the chair that now sits under the tree. He follows him until the rope is around his neck. He follows him until the sun rises and he is left hanging.

Dolion turns to me. My heart races as I realize he can see me. He knows I'm here, in this dream. His eyes lock with mine, and I expect to find him smiling, expect the monster to grin at his victory. But instead, Dolion looks at me in a way that seems wrong for him. He looks at me with fear, with sorrow, with pain, and with desperation.

And though he never speaks to me, I know what he wishes to say.

Help me, Clair. Please.

My dream used to scare me, but now there is something so alluring about it. Dolion changes with each dream. His eyes become more vibrant, the details in his skin become more vivid, and his voice grows clearer. Each time I dream, I feel as though Dolion is in the room with me, like he's trying to tell me something. When I'm dreaming, I don't hate Dolion. I want to get closer to him, I want to understand him. I want to reach out and touch him, simply to feel the living skin of a soul who died decades ago.

Chapter Twenty-One

Dolion

1941

I 'm sitting in my bed with my palm spread out before me. I focus my mind and my energy on the skin that was burned and try to imagine the ice I saw before. It won't come back.

Can I not control it?

I close my hand and then open it quickly. What do I expect to happen? There was frost on the blanket when Jonny was in here . . . Why? What did I do differently then that I am not doing now?

I wasn't thinking about it then. I just did it.

I look around the room, trying to find anything else for my thoughts to focus on. No matter what I see, only one thought consistently runs through my head: *What the hell is wrong with me? Ice? Why?*

I shake my head and hold my hand in front of me again.

Come on, Dolion. Come on.

A small shiver runs through my hand and wrist, and a spark of hope whips through me. But then it vanishes, and I am left with nothing yet again.

I cover my blanket with my palm and try to cover it with frost again, convinced this time something will happen. But there's nothing.

I really can't control it. Maybe I *am* a monster, just like Mother has always accused me of being. Something really is wrong with me. What happens if they see, if they notice? What would Mother do to me if she found out about this?

Cold spikes in my hand again as I realize I'm scared, but for the first time ever, I'm not scared of someone else . . . I'm scared of myself.

I shiver.

I can see my breath before me.

I shake my head. How come the cold is coming now? What did I do to make this happen?

Out of the corner of my eye, I see ice slowly spreading across the walls, freezing me in my room. Trapping me. I don't understand what the hell is happening.

My eyes land on the dresser in front of me, and I am overwhelmingly grateful for a distraction.

I walk over to it, hoping to leave the ice behind.

When Loralie and I were growing up, we shared a dresser. We didn't have many clothes, so we never struggled with having too little space. The dresser was small and odd. Jonny said that's why Mother gave it to us, because it's like us. Now that Loralie is gone, this dresser has become my desk for writing letters to her. I stuffed all our clothes into the bottom two drawers to make room for writing shortly after my sister left.

Beside the cupboard where I store my writing implements are two small drawers. The top drawer was Loralie's, and the one under it was mine. We slowly collected things that mattered to us and stashed them away from the outside world.

My finger runs along the handle of Loralie's drawer. I really shouldn't open this; I don't know if I can handle the emotions.

Ice spreads across the wood where I touch the dresser, and I pull back sharply. I'm being a wimp right now—that's what Loralie would say. Whatever this ice is, I know it's a part of me. I can feel it stirring in my core like a monster preparing to be awoken. If it's a part of me, it can't hurt me, can it? I try to block it out and keep moving.

I grab the handle and pull the drawer open, an uncomfortable longing to be close to Loralie again controlling me. A longing to find some sort of comfort in this confusing world.

I smile faintly when I see her small mirror and the necklaces she collected over time. She took the other things with her; these she left. My sister and I lived together in this room for nineteen years. Jonny was given the better room, of course. Emile's son is always given the best of everything. Guilt grows in my chest at the image of Jonny, red-faced and crying at the hands of Emile's harsh tongue.

I close my eyes, trying to remind myself he's a bully and doesn't deserve a second thought, much less the guilt that's weighing on me. *I'm not alone in this situation*, I say to myself. *Someone else here understands. Maybe he's only a bully because he's as hurt as I am.*

I shake my head and snap my eyes open. What would Loralie say to that? She would say that those thoughts are exactly what get me bullied by Jonny. If Loralie were here, she would tell me to force those thoughts away.

I think back to the fear I felt when Jonny was in my room and the hem of my blanket was covered in frost.

I sigh and go to close my sister's drawer, reminding myself I need to distance myself from her. But when I shut it, a heavy item knocks around inside. I open it again to see something silver beneath the necklaces and push the jewelry aside, grabbing the object. When I hold it in front of me to see clearly in the light, a pain runs through my chest, and my stomach turns. She told Mother she had lost this. I haven't seen it since Father died.

My breath clouds in front of me.

Loralie and I were young, our faces still so plump and round. Father looks warm and gentle, like he always did. And Mother . . . I forgot who she used to be. Her arm is wrapped tight around Father, hair in a bun and still black, not yet graying. This was the only photograph we had of Father after he died. Everything is so emotionless, unsmiling children and parents, yet the emotions seem to be seeping out of the photograph and weighing heavy in the air. Mother framed it after it was taken and kept it by her bed for such a long time. After the accident, it was nowhere to be found. Father had died, and our photo of him was gone. Why did Loralie take it?

I shiver. The ice is inching closer to me, covering my room. I'm slowly trapping myself inside my own prison as the door ices over. I try to forget about it, hopeful that it will all go away once I'm not afraid anymore. That's the key, isn't it? Fear?

Sitting on my bed, picture still in hand, I remember our lives at this age. They were good. So many happy memories have been forgotten. This picture brings them back. But everything and everyone from that time is gone. Even Mother. She's changed now—Emile made sure of that. I know losing Father broke her. It broke all of us.

Clarity snaps through my mind, bringing focus to the fractured corners of my thoughts. The ice melts away, and suddenly, the world seems upright again. Something about this picture pulls me away from the darkness that has been creeping its way into my heart and mind, and I feel stronger.

I feel capable.

CURSE RULE #2

In death, the twins will not be capable of interacting with the one they care for most: each other. They will live in eternal hell, able to see and hear each other, but unable to find comfort or conversation in one another.

Chapter Twenty-Two

Dolion

A window. A single reflection. A boy who has always been afraid.

The boy looking back at me through the faint reflection of the window displays everything I wish I weren't. He is frail, he is weak, he is wide-eyed and trembling. He is afraid. Of what? Of himself, of his mother, of living, of dying. Everything. I wish I didn't recognize his face. I wish I were a stranger to myself. I wish Loralie were looking back at me.

The reflection mirrors my movements as I grip a small bag in my hand. My focus shifts to the world beyond the glass. It's filled with people and sounds, lights and animals. My heart tightens at the thought of being out in the world. Alone. I attempt to keep myself from curling up in my bed under the covers, hiding away from the outside world I can no longer ignore. I won't stay in this situation any longer. I'm an adult; they can't force me. Not anymore.

I breathe in deep, trying to ease the ache in my chest. But the heavy breath tightens in my throat, forming a lump of fear and dread. I've never gone past the porch without my sister. I've hardly been that far at all since Father's death. Out there, I'll be one small, insignificant person in a sea of chaos. Would that chaos be calmer than the madness within my own thoughts?

Only one way to find out, I tell myself, locking eyes with my timid reflection before I turn away, hopefully exiting my childhood room for good.

My grip on my escape bag tightens until I feel my uneven nails digging into my palm. My shoes shuffle gently across my bedroom floor. As I reach toward the doorknob, fingers nearly coming into contact with the smooth surface, I pause for a moment, attempting to quiet the thoughts swimming through my head.

This is my safe place. My *only* safe place.

I force myself to stand tall as I grab the doorknob and turn, stepping out into the hall, away from whatever ounce of happiness I have left. I don't look back. I struggle to force down every memory of our childhood, everything I am leaving behind.

Closing the door, I make it past the first obstacle, forcing myself outside of my own comfort. Now I just have to make it out of the house without being—

"Dolion."

Caught.

I turn slowly, looking down the stairs at my scowling mother. I hide my hands behind my back so she won't see how violently they have begun shaking. Mother walks up the stairs, each step heavy and loud. When she stomps on the last step, I jump, backing away from her as she crosses over to me.

"Get back to your room," she says, stopping a couple feet away. Still, the smell of her potent lavender reaches me. "Emile and I have a guest coming."

My eyes dart around the simple rug in the hall, avoiding Mother's gaze, but my ears pick up every word she says.

"Look at me when I speak to you," she says, stepping closer. I turn my head away from her again, my hands still trembling and my breathing shallow. The heat rushing to my face becomes overwhelming. The fear. The anger. The rage.

I hate you, I say even though she cannot hear. I clench my fists to steady them, bag still in hand. She steps closer, standing tall. I take a small step back, giving in to my instincts. Giving in to that boy I saw in the window. I cannot be him anymore. I have to be stronger, not only for Loralie, but for myself as well. I owe this to myself.

My heart tightens, nearly choking my breaths as I force myself to stand tall, taller than her. When I don't hunch, I can tower over her. Over most people probably.

Despite the sharp pain in my chest and the growing weakness in my legs, I refuse to let myself turn and run back to my room. I'm an adult; she can't do this to me anymore. Loralie isn't here to protect me. I have to be strong enough to do it myself.

"Go to your room, Dolion." Her voice becomes stronger as I look her in the eyes. Something I haven't done in years.

No.

I start to push past her, heading toward the stairs as her voice rises behind me. For the first time, I am not afraid of her shouts, and her yelling doesn't cause my stomach to lurch. My hands have stopped trembling. I have never felt this tall. I have never felt this alive.

"Dolion Michael, get back here."

Go to hell.

She reaches out and grabs my wrist with her thin fingers, pulling me toward her, attempting to drag me to my room.

"If you don't stay hidden, I'll have to lock you away, and you know how much I hate doing that to you."

My eyes dart frantically to the key she keeps tucked in her waistband. Not again. Not ever again. I am strong enough. I *am*.

I pull my arm away from her and run. I run down the stairs, nearly tripping every couple feet. I run past the living room, through the entrance hall, and out the door. My feet don't stop as I sprint across the porch and beyond the dry grass and dirt.

"Let him go, Annalise," Emile tells my mother behind me. "He is not our problem to deal with anymore."

My legs begin to burn as I keep pushing. I haven't run this much since I was a child. The cool air flowing through my black curls, the sun warming my skin, the smell of fresh air, and a wide-open world all greet me as I take my first steps into a new life. Into freedom. I can't help myself as a large grin spreads on my face until it hurts and tears come to my eyes. Tears of the best kind.

I did it. Me. I am strong enough.

I run until I tire, enjoying the feeling of freedom, of being outside again, even enjoying the burn in my thighs and calves.

I did it.

Chapter Twenty-Three

Loralie

The center of attention—that's me. I fear I could get used to this life. Constantly with new, and important, people, everyone wanting to know about me, who I am, where I came from, and, of course, the attention of an attractive man. I risk a glance at Arron as he guides me up the steps to their home and grin. With his brother standing on the other side of me, he doesn't take the same chance I do and keeps his eyes trained ahead.

Charles, my future husband, steps out before me and opens the door, his head bowing deep as I pass him. My grin grows wider. My stomach has started showing, so I've told everyone I'm pregnant. I said it belongs to Charles, of course, and he's been treating me differently since then.

"So," Arron's mother begins nearly as soon as I make it through the front door, "did you like our cousins?"

No. They were wretched and awful, but my thoughts don't matter. All that matters is my answer. That's the beauty of this place.

"Of course I did." I smile, grinning in a way only Doli could tell is fake. He always knew me too well for anything to be faked. "They had the cutest little laughs." *Annoying*, I correct myself. It's a relief they are distant; I wouldn't be able to listen to them often.

"Have a seat, dear." His mother beckons me. I sit on the sofa with Charles by my side as Arron takes a seat across the room. The smoke from his father's cigar grazes my nostrils. Arron's sister holds her baby close to her, never once taking her eyes off me.

"So, tell me." His mother crosses her legs as she waits for her tea to cool. "What was your childhood like?"

"Mother," Arron says like it's a warning. Charles shoots his brother a disapproving glare.

"What?" His mother's voice drips with disdain like liquid ivy.

"Don't you think we should give her some space? It's been nothing but questions the last few days."

Charles reaches out for my hand and encapsulates it in his. Their father waves his hand through the smoke plumes to continue watching his family argue. I wait for them to finish, knowing it'll be over soon, just like it always is with this family.

"Well, I haven't gotten to ask many questions."

Arron rolls his eyes at his mother's remark. She sets her tea on the small table and flattens her floral-patterned skirt.

"I appreciate the effort, but it's all right. I don't mind answering her question," I say.

What was my childhood like? I think back to my younger days, when Dolion and I would hide in our room, barricading the door until Mother and Emile went to sleep. Some days it was worse. Dolion would always take the worst of it, but every day we were terrified. That never changed. I think back to being confused and afraid of ourselves. We knew we weren't right. We knew no one would explain it to us, but we couldn't help but try to find the answers anyway. Why we were different, why no one loved us. Before we went broke, I guess things were decently good. Mother was happy, at least. That was before Father died.

"My childhood was typical, I guess," I say, lying, of course. "Nothing much happened. Lots of parties, family dinners, and schooling." I shrug.

His mother nods, and Charles smiles approvingly. Arron looks at me like he's trying to figure out a puzzle.

"Any siblings?" Arron asks.

A knot clutches at my chest. Does he know? I know he saw Dolion at the party—he waved to him. I pointed Dolion out because I hadn't wanted Arron to think I was crazy, but I immediately regretted it when I realized what I had done. He can't know—no one can know—about Dolion, or I might lose all of this.

"No," I say, holding my confidence. "Jonny, whom you met at the party, is Emile's son. I have no siblings."

His brow tightens, and his look becomes cloudy. "Can I talk to you for a minute?"

My heart quickens with Arron's words. Dolion could be anyone. Who's to say he is my brother? The room falls silent, and Charles shoots Arron another angry look. I nod and refuse to break eye contact with him, challenging him to confront me. Arron leads me to the kitchen and closes the door.

"Loralie." He faces me. "Why do you keep lying?"

My eyes remain focused on him as I attempt to force him to back out before he regrets it. "What makes you ask that?"

"You're lying about your past. Why?" He steps closer.

Arron isn't afraid of me. I try to stand taller to oppose him, but that doesn't seem to affect him. Why the hell isn't he afraid of me?

"Why should I tell you?"

"Who was that boy in the window? Why wasn't he at the party?"

I gather the courage, pull my shoulders back, and glare at him. "That is not yours to know."

"Stop *lying* to me!" He raises his voice for a moment, slamming his foot to the floor as he steps closer to me.

Instinctively, I swing my arm out to my side to defend Dolion like I have so many times before. This time, instead of a scared little boy, my arm falls against nothing but air. There is no one to protect, no one to comfort when the rages get bad.

Dolion's absence finds the crack in my wall, pouring in and infecting my heart. Three words settle in my mind. The three most unsettling words I have ever thought.

He is gone.

My purpose is gone.

Standing in front of Arron, I suddenly feel more exposed than ever before. I am alone. Dolion is alone. He is hurting. I am hurting. My arms and legs grow heavy as my head spins. Something new stirs within me. A feeling of isolation spreads through my veins, turning my blood cold, igniting a spark deep in the very essence of my being—a spark that reminds me of the love I once had, of the love I gave away.

"I'm sorry, Loralie. I didn't mean to yell."

I drop to my knees, clutching my heart with both my hands. It aches.

"I really am sorry." His pitiful apologies continue.

"I don't mind yelling," I say. "I never have. So stop apologizing."

He nods, backing away from me for a moment. "What's wrong?"

I shake my head, telling him to leave me alone. I'm fine. I will be fine. I might be fine. I'll probably die alone, dead inside, without Dolion.

Arron walks over, placing his hand on my shoulder in comfort. I shove him away.

"Don't touch me," I snap.

"Loralie, what's wrong?"

"I'm alone," I say.

"I'm here," he says.

I laugh, stand, and walk out of the room.

Not for long, I think to myself. *Everyone runs away eventually.*

Chapter Twenty-Four

Dolion

The farther I walk from home, the tighter the knot in my chest grows. I think the world is becoming darker too. Bleaker.

I shiver. Maybe this was a mistake. Where am I even supposed to go?

A small thought nags at me, but I try to ignore it. The more I push it away, the louder it grows.

Loralie.

But I was doing well without her. I thought I didn't need her.

Where else am I going to go? I am alone out here. I have no one.

I sigh with disappointment in myself. I was supposed to be able to do this on my own.

A large black bird flies past me, its massive wings beating the air violently. Taking a step back as it swoops down to the ground, I jump at its loud caw. There's something on the ground where it landed. I take a deep breath and step closer.

The air falls from my lungs, and my eyes widen. Lying on the ground, mangled and bloody, in a mushy mess of tangled limbs, is what I'm guessing is a squirrel. Blood trickles like a steady stream from each place the bird's sharp claws dig into skin, and flesh hangs from his shining black beak.

My stomach turns, and I swallow my vomit.

I stumble backward a couple steps. The bird snaps his head to me, his beady eyes telling me I'm next. I just know I am.

A tear falls down my cheek and trails my neck.

Loralie. I have to find my sister.

I turn around and run. My legs have never moved so fast. My lungs burn with each breath, and the tears streaking my face feel like knives on my skin.

A bird cries loud ahead of me, and panic makes me turn in the other direction. Shadows twisting and bending like they belong to a sinister world make me turn around again. Soon I'm lost and running from everything I see. Terror fills the air with each second I'm left alone in the darkness.

Home. I have to go back home, where I had a warm bed and this nightmare couldn't get to me.

I stop running, my throat raw from the cold air. My chest aches, and my legs are screaming at me in pain. Which way do I go? Where is the house?

I wish I could scream, or cry, or *something*.

Falling to the ground, I accept that I'm lost and alone and give in to the elements. Maybe I'll die here. Maybe that's not a bad thing.

"*Hallo.*"

I pause and hold my breath. Did somebody just say something?

"Ist mit Ihnen alles in Ordnung, mein Herr? Kann ich Ihnen helfen?"

I look up to see the face of a kid, no older than ten, staring at me, watching me curiously. He doesn't speak English.

Chapter Twenty-Five

Loralie

A baby floats in a large lake, staying above the surface as if the water itself is holding the child up. He laughs, playing with the fish that come up to greet him. The sun shines warmly on the child, his innocence and happiness spreading joy to the surrounding world. The sky is brighter the more he smiles, and the sea life leaps a little higher with each laugh. This boy is breathing life into the world around him. He's happy, and so is the rest of the earth.

Then the baby stops smiling, and the sky darkens. He stops laughing, and the fish refuse to come play. Something foul swims in the lake below the baby. Something wicked, something dead.

The baby's gaze meets his mother's eyes. My eyes. I reach out for him, unable to save him or help him. All happiness drains from the child, his face struck with pure fear of the new world he is witnessing.

Hands of a corpse reach above the water and grab my child, dragging him below the surface. My baby disappears, and I'm stuck, held far away from him, restrained from getting him out of this hell and back to the simple life he once had.

My baby will come out of the water one day—something inside tells me so. But he won't come out smiling or giggling. He will come out a man with a permanent frown, a weakened spirit, and a miserable broken soul.

The gray sky, filled with lightning that rips through stormy clouds, looms over the angry waves of the lake. Never again will the fish come to play. Never again will my child laugh.

I wake up, pulled close to Charles just like every night. Unlike Arron, he's not gentle in the way he touches me.

I remember my dream and pull the comforter up to cover my shoulders from the chill of the room. The world tortured Dolion in a way it never tortured me. I see so much more of Dolion in my unborn child than I wish, and that scares me. He will grow up to be weak, to be useless and pathetic, just like the person my brother became.

I shake my head and sigh. It was just a dream, that's all. I need to focus on something other than this baby; it's messing with my mind. I need Arron right now. He'd be a good distraction, someone I actually want to be with, who can help me forget about everything.

I cast a side glance at Charles before sliding my legs off the bed. I'm in a thin nightgown that reaches just above my ankles. My feet settle into slippers, and I shuffle quickly and quietly through the still room and out the doorway. Arron's room isn't too far away, and I reach it rather quickly on my light feet. I don't risk waking the rest of the house by knocking. Instead, I just slip into his room, which is even darker than Charles's since Arron's curtain is drawn and blocks out the light.

I shuffle across his floor as his snores fill the air, hoping to crawl into bed first before I wake him. I won't tell him about the dream; I'll just tell him that I'm scared and lonely.

With my hands in front of me, I search for his bed in the dark. When my fingers finally come into contact with the rough surface of the wooden bed frame, a sudden breeze whips through the air. The curtain ruffles a little at the wind, revealing for a prolonged moment the world outside.

My vision becomes blurred, my body succumbing to a powerful force until my bones and skin are numb. My legs carry me to the window of their own accord, and I draw back the curtain. The window is closed—my mind is working enough to note that. I don't know where the breeze came from.

My hand moves up to the glass of the window, and I slowly and gently knock three times, begging to be let out.

Dolion is out there, and so is something much more powerful than him: the force that has been guiding me this entire time. The land behind our childhood home. For the first time since I left home, I long to be in that land again, to feel its darkness and power drifting through me like I have so many times before.

I shake my head and pull out of the trance that clasped on to my mind. Arron is here, and all I want now is to be close to him. I shuffle across the floorboards, craving his warmth.

"Loralie?" Arron whispers as I slide into bed with him. "Is that you?"

I shush him with a soft kiss and curl into his side.

Chapter Twenty-Six

Loralie

Now that the sun is shining and daylight has broken the horizon, the world outside Arron's window seems different. Last night I could clearly hear the whispers of the darkness calling to me, but this morning there's nothing but a bustling town outside.

"Loralie," Arron's deep morning voice says from his bed. "You have to get back to Charles's room. He's going to wake up any minute."

I shift on my feet, the floorboards beneath me squealing. I'm standing by the window, staring at Arron as he sits up in bed. His dark hair is unusually curly in the morning, and he hasn't shaved yet, which gives him more of a rugged look, like his brother has. I walk over and crawl underneath the covers with him.

"Can't I just stay here with you?" I say, injecting my voice with a fake pout. "Please?"

"Loralie." He kisses me and looks deep into my eyes. "I obviously want you to stay, but Charles can't find out."

"Why? Didn't you want to ruin the marriage? Didn't you want your revenge?"

He grabs my hand and kisses it. Damn, he's so gentle.

"This," he says as he gestures between us, "has become about so much more than revenge. I care about you, Loralie. If Charles were to find out what we've been doing, you would be in so much trouble."

"But then I could be with you more," I argue, not daring to let this go.

"My family has connections in town," he says, his eyes suddenly darkening. "You could end up in the square if Charles found out."

"The square?"

"You'd be hung, Loralie." His voice is a whisper. "Please go to Charles before he wakes up. I'll be here for you, just like I always am, but you can't come to my room like that in the middle of the night anymore."

Arron has been distant the entire day, since our conversation in his room this morning. He won't even look at me. I wonder if he thinks Charles is catching on.

I'd be hung? What type of connections does their family have?

Charles has been by my side more than normal today, and that makes me nervous as well. I should have been more careful; I shouldn't have left Charles's bed in the middle of the night. But when I'm away from

Arron, I feel so empty and alone. Dolion is gone, and without Dolion, Arron is all I have.

I head to my and Charles's room after breakfast, hoping to have some time to myself. The time to think could help me get back in the game, hiding myself and faking everything for everyone. It's not that I don't enjoy being fake. I do. I enjoy being someone else. And this could be my chance at a happy life. I'm so close to finally moving on, to being rid of my family, to being rid of that life, but every time I feel I'm close to freedom, he creeps back into my thoughts. Dolion. He's there nearly constantly, poisoning my mind, altering my thoughts until all I can remember is how much I miss him. How much his absence hurts me. How I don't want to survive without him. Maybe I can't.

One moment can change everything. How fragile are the lives we lead if they can just collapse in mere seconds? Is anything stable? Is anything secure or guaranteed? Maybe we're all just little dots in a timeline that runs completely out of our control. Puppets forced to live through the bidding of the world.

The thoughts pour into me like crashing waves against a current. They fill me up and choke me until I can't breathe. My body grows so weak I struggle to resist the pull, the *need* to lie down, even if it's just for a couple seconds, to feel the comfort of being curled up and tucked away from what life has become for just a little longer.

I curl up in the center of Charles's bed as tears start to fall from my eyes and thoughts of everything overwhelm me all at once.

I think of how much my mother hates me, how much I hate her. Images of Dolion at different stages of life run through my mind, from when he was a child who would smile to the scared man he has become. Arron runs through my thoughts as well. I was so stupid to fall into this mess. Pregnant. A baby, a sickness, squirms within my body. If life touches him, he will end up just as worthless as Dolion. For the first time, I start to feel like maybe I deserve Mother's hate. I curl my arms around my knees and pull my legs into my body, tucking my head into them.

The land behind my mother's house has been messing with my head, hurting me and my child. I have to get to Dolion before it's too late. I'm nothing without him—I realize that now. He's the only one who can help me, who can save *us*.

Chapter Twenty-seven

Clair

2022

*D*olion is winning. It's all so clear to me now. Dolion has always won, and he and Loralie will always win unless something changes. I fight my tense muscles, searching for a way to break free from this invisible prison. If I could just push a little harder, try a little longer, do something better, maybe I could make it to Perdu before it's too late.

But isn't that the point of a dream? *an old voice, ancient with years of heartbreak caught up all in the single sound, asks me.* Isn't the world beyond sleep always out of your control? Free to be twisted and shaped by an outside force because . . . because you have no power over your mind when you've drifted far away.

The source of the voice may be behind me, or maybe above me, or even below me, through the porch and six feet beneath the soil, but my head won't turn to look. I am left completely vulnerable to whoever may be here with me. My body is not mine in this dream. I have no control over anything but my thoughts as I continue to watch what takes place in the yard, under the large tree that sits in front of the house.

Perdu is broken. Perdu is hurt by the world, by Dolion, by so much more than anyone other than he could know. He's so broken that he follows Dolion. He follows him far into the dark, so far the light is nothing but a memory. He follows him up the chair that now sits under the tree. He follows him until the rope is around his neck. He follows him until the sun rises and he is left hanging.

Dolion turns to me. My heart races as I realize he can see me. He knows I'm here, in this dream. His eyes lock with mine, and I expect to find him smiling, expect the monster to grin at his victory. But instead, Dolion looks at me in a way that seems wrong for him. He looks at me with fear, with sorrow, with pain, and with desperation.

And though he never speaks to me, I know what he wishes to say.

Help me, Clair. Please.

Dolion

1941

His name is Karl; he knows enough English to be able to tell me that much. Other than that, I haven't learned much about him. He insisted on following me into town, but I don't really mind; I appreciate the company. I've realized just how thin the soles of my shoes are. The rocks I step on poke at my heels in sharp, quick pains. My pace has slowed from earlier today. Not Karl's though. He must walk into town regularly. Even though the sun has set, I don't think he's tired at all.

Karl, glancing back at me, must see how much I'm struggling. He stops on the side of the road, allowing me to stop for a moment as well. My lungs gasp desperately for air, and my throat burns as the dry dust settles inside my mouth. My legs ache. I fear my bones may snap if they don't rest soon. I know I've rarely left the house, but am I truly this weak?

By the time we begin moving again, my joints are screaming at me to sit down and rest awhile. I can't. I have to find Loralie. Karl moves slower now though. I think he may be worried about me.

We walk along the side of the road, keeping out of sight to avoid unwanted attention. Soon we make it to the market. I'm surprised by the nightlife as a serene, gentle night air settles on the town. People bustle about busily but are calm and patient, going about their lives and chatting with neighbors. Soft lights keep the market in a dim but comforting glow. The smell of dinner from nearby houses fills the block, making my mouth water. This is what I was afraid of? This is the world I have been so scared to see?

So many of these people are smiling or even laughing. No one laughs anymore. Not at my house. A twinge settles into my stomach. Do people really get to live like this?

My feet drag along the cobblestone road as we make our way through the stands of vendors and products. I remind myself that I am lucky to be able to be a part of this now, even though it took me so long to get out into the world.

As we pass one shop with a large window, I choke on the fear that swells in my chest. Loralie's reflection is looking back at me where mine should be. My eyes are trained on hers as she stands there, staring at me. I can't help but feel as if it is actually her staring back. As if Loralie is actually there. Compared to the excitement I expected to have, the fear and dread of seeing her again leave me feeling weak, vulnerable, and confused.

I want to just keep my head down and continue walking, but her hair is knotted, and the look in her eyes is tired and sad. Whatever happened, she is not all right. Two sides of me battle. Part of me wants to reach out to her, to call for her to return home to me. The other part of me is disgusted by her. I'm very aware of my heart darkening again, my thoughts growing depressed, and every ounce of happiness I have gained being strangled out of me.

Then she yells, she screams a villainous scream, and though I can't hear it, I watch the anger spread across her face. She steps closer to me, pounding against the other side of the glass, her desperation controlling her. But the glass won't break for her; she's trapped on the other side, held away from me. When she looks up at me, begging for an answer, to somehow reunite us, I swallow gently and shake my head, telling her to stop. That it's pointless. That we are separated for a reason. A look of what must be hurt crosses her face as she takes a small step back from me. Slowly, the vision of her fades, and I am left staring at my own reflection, but somehow, I can feel her anger, can sense the tension building from wherever she is. And once it's at its strongest, the window before me explodes, shattering, throwing glass in my direction as it breaks.

I cover my head, feeling small burns on my forearms as the glass slices my skin. The window crashing is more than just the shattering glass; it's a quick wind, a flash storm, blowing against my body violently. Once the glass finishes its loud sounds and all has calmed, Karl grabs my arm and pulls, guiding me as we run from the now very loud and very curious crowd.

Chapter Twenty-Nine

Loralie

After crying on Charles's bed for so long my eyes begin to burn, I decide it's time to face everyone outside this room again. My hand presses firmly against the rough wood, but before I can leave the room, I emotionally crumble again, hot tears gathering under my chin. Why am I like this? Why do I need Dolion? Why do I feel so . . . so empty without him? What the *hell* is wrong with me? My body takes control, and before I can think better of it, my fist slams into the door before me, and a sharp pain runs from my fingers to my elbow. I press my forehead against the wood directly above my hand and close my eyes, the remaining tears spilling over and falling to the floor.

"What's wrong with us, Doli?" I whisper, wishing he could be here with me to ease the unbearable pain forming in my chest. Loneliness. That's what this is. "I miss you." My words quiver as ugly sobs begin to rack my body. My knees suddenly lose all strength, begging me to sit, to give my body a rest. I obey. What's the point in remaining strong when there's no one left to be strong for?

On the uncomfortable wooden floor in front of the door, I curl in on myself, wrapping my arms tightly around my knees and pressing my legs against my chest. I am alone. Somehow, the room seems to get larger and larger until I am drowning in the absence of my brother and the emptiness in my heart.

So here I sit, losing myself to the darkness around me, forgetting who I am, where I come from, and why I ever thought I could matter. Because none of it matters without him.

My heart beats faster. My tears grow so hot they nearly burn. The blood in my veins turns to fire. The heat, the anger within, is becoming too much for me. I lean my head forward, cupping my wet face in my hands, crying and softly cursing myself. No yelling. They will hear yelling. I can feel the scream, however. I can feel it bubbling inside me, wanting to be released like the heat that grows within. I put my hands in my hair, pulling at my black roots until my scalp burns. It feels good. But it's only the beginning. I need to release. I must finally accept my fate. My makeup runs, staining my dress. I feel worn, I feel crazy. I need my brother. I need to protect him. I need him to comfort me. I need him. Does the world not understand that?

I look up to the ceiling-high windows opposite me, the night leaving the room in near darkness. Only the dim light of the stars casts a small glow in through the window.

He's out there somewhere, alone, just like I am. I blink a couple times, clearing away the heavy tears enough to see the stars in the sky. He's out there.

"Please," I whisper. "I need you, Dolion. Please . . . Please." My voice breaks through the last words, and I find myself unable to speak any longer—or more accurately, not *wanting* to speak. Somehow, silence makes me feel closer to the boy I've been torn from.

An emptiness takes over, draining my tears, my face raw and burning from all the crying. The air of the room is cool on my damp cheeks. My eyelashes are stuck together as teardrops catch in them. Is this my fault? Did I let them take me away? Did I try hard enough? Does he . . . Does he blame me?

I shake my head. He loves me. He would never blame me.

I'm about to close my eyes again when suddenly they get caught on the window in front of the night sky, where, if I were standing, I could see my own reflection. But someone else stands there, reflected in the glass. My heart pulses violently as a wave of relief floods over me. I turn around swiftly, scanning the room for him, a sick and vile hope coursing through me. For a second, I think I'm not alone anymore. However, I'm met with nothing but darkness. The room is empty, just like it always is. I turn back to the window, more cautious this time. With my palms pressed flat against the floor, I lean forward, trying to stop myself from jumping up and running to the boy in the window.

Dolion stands in the window, small and shriveled, yet he looks taller somehow. Like he's grown up since last I saw him. And I know, in this moment, the pain I feel in my chest is my heart breaking, desperation taking control of me, my descent into madness. I stand, my feet carrying me swiftly across the large room until my palms are pressed against the window. I can't push through. I can't get to him.

"Dolion!" I yell, my voice breaking until my throat burns. "I can't get to you!" I ball my hands into fists and slam them against the glass. "I need you!" It comes out as an unnatural, panicked shriek. "Please!" My curls fall in my eyes as I try to break the window. I have to get to him. I need him. He needs me.

All my brother does is stare at me, watching with what must be pity as I turn into something unlike myself. When my eyes meet his, he slowly lowers his head, shaking it gently, telling me to stop. And for some reason, I obey him, just staring at the boy I long to hold again. It's as if he's further away now than he ever has been. I can't talk to him, I can't reach him, but I am forced to see him, to look upon the one I cannot have. It's like my mind is taunting me. This is all in my mind, right? No. Something tells me this really is my brother looking back at me.

Then he begins to fade into the night, causing a painful panic to rise in my chest. He can't leave me! He can't go away! Who am I without him? I begin hitting the window again, the glass rattling under me but never breaking. How can it possibly hold under my anger? I yell, releasing a scream so wretched it scares even me. And then he disappears completely, leaving only my reflection in his place.

First come the tears, then the rage. The scream comes out like a roar. I need him. How dare they take him from me. Before I know what's happening, the small stool that was sitting next to me is hurled through the window, turning my own reflection into thousands of tiny shards. I stare for a moment, unable to believe I just destroyed Charles's window.

The door bursts open, followed by Arron. "Loralie? Are you all right? What happened?"

I can still see Dolion, just slightly in the nighttime sky. It's his eyes, his voice. He's out there somewhere. Closer than I thought. "I miss you . . ." I whisper.

"Who?" Arron says. I turn to face him, letting Dolion's eyes fade into the stars. "Who do you miss?"

I shake my head and close the door, making sure only he can hear me. "Why do you keep pushing this?"

"Because I care about you." Arron walks over to the window, breaking off the sharp edges of the glass. "Your twin. That's who that boy in the window was, right?"

My eyes widen. "N-no. He could've been anyone."

"He looks exactly like you, Loralie. Just change a few details, and you two are the same person."

"The same person," I hear again, but this time it's a woman's voice. *"How can that be?"*

"Not the same person; they each have their own traits. But put them together and you'll find they are a force to be reckoned with. I promise you, as long as you love these kids, everything will be all right."

"Did you hear that?" I ask Arron. "It's gone now, but . . . did you?"

He shakes his head. I sit down at the base of the door, similar to the way Dolion and I would sit together.

"Fine," I say, giving in. "You want to know the truth?"

Arron nods, sitting next to me.

"He is my twin. But he's mute. I'm supposed to be ashamed of him, but no matter how hard I try, I can't. I love him." It feels so good to admit to someone that I care. "This is the first time we have ever been separated like this, and I think I'm going crazy."

I wait for him to say something. He stares at the window for a while, eyes narrow and dark. Before the silence is broken, he slides his arm around my shoulders, holding me in a way I've never been held.

"I'm sorry you were taken away from your happiness."

I sigh. I wasn't happy. How could I have been? Did he not hear me? I had to hide my brother. I had to act ashamed of him. And though Dolion will never admit it, I know it hurt him. I guess I may have been happier then. Happier than what? Than this paradise I get to be a part of now? It can only be paradise if I feel . . . sane. I don't. I feel crazy. I'm broken and hurt. I'm lost.

"I don't know that I was happy," I say. In a moment of stupidity, I allow myself to open up to him. I pull up my sleeves, which I have intentionally worn long since the party. The healing cut, the one Dolion gave me, is revealed, as well as the scar on my hand. "Dolion and I tried to kill ourselves."

Arron takes a deep breath, his gaze remaining on my arm. "And that?" He points to my palm.

"I was cooking." I shrug it off and lie, suddenly feeling ashamed of who I am. "It was a foolish mistake."

He nods slowly, taking my left hand. I look up at him, his eyes brown and strong. Holding my gaze, he tightens his grip on my hand. I'm surprised when he leans in, touching his lips gently to mine. He doesn't give me more than a second, though I want him to stay with me for longer. Then he stands, nudging me forward slightly to open the door, and is gone.

Chapter Thirty

Dolion

The mumble of the townsfolk continues behind us as we come to a stop. I bend over, gasping for breath as my lungs burn. Karl stops beside me, breathing steady, but still he waits for me. I think I like him. I think I want him to be my friend. Should I feel bad for that? What about Loralie?

The unexpected fear I had of her in the window returns. Why was I so scared of her? How come the thought of being scared of her scares me? A sharp pain stabs at my temple, after a second reducing to a consistent dull ache just behind my right eye. I close my eyes, slowing my breathing and calming down. I love Loralie.

You love her, I say to myself, reassuring my love for my sister. *You always have and you always will.*

Yes, but… A voice somewhere in my mind fights back. *She is a monster, growing into a demon.*

I will always love her, no matter how dark she becomes, I assure myself. *No matter how dark . . .*

I shake my head gently and open my eyes. Karl stands next to me, watching me with worry. He must not be used to someone as out of shape as I am. I stand, giving him a small smile to let him know I am all right. He nods and smiles back before pointing to my arms. I look down to find them smeared with blood from the glass of the window. Loralie hurt me. Did she mean to?

She's becoming darker every day, the voice in my head says.

She's still my sister. I nod, content with my comeback and ready to be done arguing with this voice in my head. But I can't get over the feeling that the voice is actually me. My own fears and my own thoughts.

I examine the small cuts covering my forearms given to me by the glass. After pulling a few shards of glass out, I attempt to cover my raw burning arms with my coat.

We need to keep moving. We need to head farther into the city. That's where Loralie will be. I pull one of Loralie's letters from my bag and hand it to Karl, pointing at the return address. She gave me her location; it's time to follow it.

Loralie

"What the hell is wrong with you?" Arron's father yells at me, a puff from his last drag lingering in the air. Arron's mother scolds him with her eyes for yelling at the mother of her grandchild. "Do you know how much glass costs these days?"

"I told you we should have left her." His sister's voice becomes unbearably whiny.

I back away from them, not because they're yelling, but because I want to do the same. I want to yell, to slit their throats with my words and show them how it feels. But I can't. I won't be allowed to stay if I behave that way. I bite down on my tongue when his father calls me a "poor orphan." I told them about my father's death earlier.

"Just stop!" Arron gets involved. "She made a mistake. Allow her to make it right, and let's move on."

Charles glares at Arron with that look he always has these days: anger.

His parents think for a moment before deciding. "Fine. She and her family will pay for it. End of discussion." They all leave the room, leaving me alone with Arron.

"I really am sorry about them," he says to me. "Just ignore them. It's going to be all right."

I nod before saying, "Arron, I think I'd really like to be alone for a little while." I don't wait for a response. I walk past him, brushing his shoulder as I pass by.

I find myself hiding in a closet, my room too cold with the wind blowing in. I can't show my face for a while. The pain and agony of embarrassment is too much to take. Sitting in the corner, hiding behind a crate, I cradle my legs and cry. This is who I have become. This is who I am. Weak, pitiful, and slowly fading.

Chapter Thirty-One

Dolion

With each step I take toward her, I can feel her darkness, her rage, her anger. I hate the feeling, but sometimes loving someone is worth the pain they put you through, right?

Whatever happens, I know I will find her. I will. Even if I have to risk everything. Loralie is the disease I cannot escape, the plague no one can cure. Even if I were to succeed in getting away from her, she would forever haunt my mind. My thoughts would always be with her, always worrying about her. If I don't give in to the pull and find her, my obsessive need to be near her won't ever go away. I know I'm not processing my feelings about Loralie correctly right now, but I don't care. If she needs me, I have to find her, no matter what. I lost everything, and now I need to get it back.

Or maybe you gained everything when you lost her.

Loralie and I face the world together. That's how it's always been; that's how it always will be.

She is your prison. She is your shackles and your chains. She is the darkness, and you are the light.

When we were still at home, I believed it was our destiny to die together. That was when my life was her life. We are different now. We have changed. Do I want to die any longer? Not if death isn't our only way out.

"Here." Karl points toward a large house on the street corner.

Clouds swarm over my heart, and I'm left with nothing but a brokenness so deep it stings. It's a feeling I have known my whole life. A feeling I have always run from. A feeling I am now willingly accepting for my sister. That pain comes from Loralie. She is definitely here.

The cold feeling begins to spread through my palm, but I do everything I can to push it away.

Not now, I tell myself.

Oddly enough, an intense longing to see her, the darkness, my monster, takes over. I have to see her. Now.

Chapter Thirty-Two

Dolion

I breathe in deep, fist shaking as I reach out to the door. I knock three times, sharp and fast. The door opens, and my far-fetched hopes that Loralie would answer are destroyed. It is a woman, however, middle-aged and tired. She lifts one eyebrow, waiting for me to be the first to speak. Sweat begins to form on my forehead. I hold out my hand, hoping she will take it and buy me some time to think. Her look grows darker.

In the living room, just past her shoulder, a few people sit around conversing. My heart drops when I don't see Loralie among the group. Is it possible Karl led me to the wrong place? No, Loralie is here. I can feel her.

"Wait here," the woman's shockingly low voice says.

I wait. Maybe this is dumb. Maybe it's a trap. A man who looks a lot like Charles, just many years older, comes to the door. I did it, then?

Loralie is here! I look into the living room again, but there's still no sign of her.

"See? I told you, he looks exactly like Charles's bride." The woman stands behind the man in the doorway as she talks to him.

The man grunts deeply, a large puff of smoke exiting his mouth. He shoos her off and turns to face me, his face now barely visible between the thick cloud. For a second, he waits for me to speak. I stay silent, and he finally grows impatient and begins the conversation.

"You know the girl, don't you?"

I nod.

"We aren't in the mood for any trouble, kid. Go away."

I avoid eye contact with the man in front of me, looking past him into the house. I can feel his dull gaze on me as I scan for the curly black hair of my sister.

In an instant, every fear, every worry, every doubt I have ever had about Loralie vanishes when I see her. She walks into the living room, timid and withdrawn from everyone else. I have never seen her so awkward. Something about her is so different than she used to be. She sits down on the sofa gently, a teacup clasped in her hands.

My heart stops once I notice what's changed about my sister. Her dress is looser than what she normally wears, giving way to her large, round stomach. She's pregnant? Loralie is pregnant.

At the sight of her, all my confusion disappears and my questions are answered. It doesn't matter if I am afraid of her. It doesn't matter if she is a monster. What matters is that she is my sister. She needs me. I have to get to her.

The man turns around, looking at Loralie. He turns back to me and he says, "Don't you look at her like that."

I don't care. I study her, trying to decide if I should call for her attention.

"I won't warn you again. Leave."

Loralie! I say, hoping she can hear me. Her arms tense, and her eyes widen as she scans the room. She's searching for me.

"Dolion?" she says, her voice breaking. Everyone, including the man in front of me, looks at her. He gestures to the others in the living room to stop her. They turn Loralie away from me.

Loralie! I'm at the front door! Turn around! They keep her faced away. At first she struggles, then slowly calms down.

The large man shoves me into the road. An icy chill rips through me. *Not now. Not now.*

"Leave us alone, and do not complicate this marriage." The man closes the door. I get up, aching with every step, but still I find the door again. I pound, one fist after the other. My joints are stiff, and my body aches.

Loralie! I shout. *I know you can hear me.*

"Dolion!" I hear her muffled yell come from inside. "Let me go. I know he's out there. Please!"

Let go of my sister! I pound until the same man opens the door, and I fall inside, landing on the floor by his feet. He grabs me by my hair and pulls me up.

"Stop whatever you're doing," he says through his teeth. The strong smell of smoke makes me gag. "You are making her crazy."

I'm too weak to fight back. All I can do is hang from his grip. But I can't stop. I have to know she's safe. *Loralie, are you all right? Please answer me. Are you safe here?*

"There he is again!" she shrieks. "Let go of me!"

She kicks the lady holding her in the gut. The others try to hold her down, but they have no idea how strong Loralie is, what she is capable of. There is a thud. The back of my head stings. Then it's all black.

Loralie

"Dolion?" Arron's family holds me down. I'm unable to control what is happening. I kick them, bite at them, and snap in their faces. I thrash my arms around, trying to break free. He's here. I know he's here. I have to see him and make sure he is all right. He wouldn't have come if something wasn't wrong. He needs me.

"What's going on?" Arron says as he walks in.

"She just lost it, started going crazy. We had to hold her down to keep her from harming herself," his mother says.

"Liar!" I spit. "I'm not crazy. I wouldn't hurt myself."

"Then what is this?" His father holds up my arm, and my sleeve falls to reveal the scar from the mark Dolion made on my wrist. My eyes narrow at him, his grip bruising my forearm.

"Let her go," Arron says.

"Stay out of this," Charles snaps at Arron.

"Or you'll do what, Charles? Hmm?" The look in Arron's eyes is darker than anything I've seen in him before. "Sleep with Emmeline? Oh, wait."

Arron's sister and brother-in-law drop me to the floor, and I stand and run toward the front door. I know he's out there; I heard him. He needs me. I'm met in the hallway by Charles's strong body. He grabs my wrists, and I struggle to break free.

"Let her go, Charles." Arron grabs me and pulls me away from his brother. Charles surprisingly doesn't fight back. He just stares at us, eyeing the way I cling to Arron.

"Leave us alone," Arron mutters before turning around to face everyone else. "All of you. Now."

His family nods. Charles shoots Arron one last threatening glare before leaving the room.

When it's just me and Arron in the living room, he starts shushing my cries and my panic. "It's all right," he whispers. "Tell me what's wrong. Did they do something to you?"

"I heard him," I cry. "He's out there. He spoke to me."

"You just miss him," he says. "It can't be any more than that."

"He said he was at the front door." I attempt to break free of Arron's solid grasp.

"I need you to calm down. If you can do that, we can look outside. How does that sound?"

I nod, feeling like a child in his presence. I take deep breaths, in and out, calming my heart. His grip on me loosens as he leads me to the door. We open it and look around. The street is empty other than the market owners running errands through town. I thought he would be out here. Emptiness overwhelms me, and I sink to my knees.

"I . . ." I start. "I wanted him to be here. I wanted to see him. A-am I really just . . . insane?"

"You aren't insane," he tells me. "You were taken from your family, from everything you knew. You have a right to miss them." He kneels down and whispers his next words. "I believe you, Loralie." He brushes my hair out of my eyes and looks at me. I really want to kiss him. "I'm sorry about my family. They're awful sometimes."

I shake my head. Dolion isn't coming. He wouldn't be here, wouldn't know how to find me in the city. We never spent enough time here to know our way around. I don't even know how to get back home. I wish I had the ability to run away, back to Dolion, but I would get lost. I don't know my way anywhere but here.

I put my hand in Arron's, and he helps me up, allowing me to put my weight on him as we make our way to a couch. He's here. Strong and comforting. I rub my now-large stomach after I'm sitting on the couch and sigh.

"What's wrong with me?" I ask, wanting him to convince me nothing is, that I'm perfect just the way I am.

"Nothing." He gives me a shy smile. "This is part of who you are."

If I have to marry a man, why can't it be Arron?

I lift my eyes to meet his, and he looks back at me, a small smile on his face. He feels the same as I do—I'm sure of it.

His hand sits on my leg. My trembling hand reaches out and finds a resting place over his.

"I think I love you," he whispers.

And with those five words, my entire life falls apart.

Chapter Thirty-Three

Clair

2022

Screams and warnings I am so desperate to cry out are trapped within me, never once making it through whatever barrier seems to keep me from the same world as Perdu.

Dolion is winning. It's all so clear to me now. Dolion has always won, and he and Loralie will always win unless something changes. I fight my tense muscles, searching for a way to break free from this invisible prison. If I could just push a little harder, try a little longer, do something better, maybe I could make it to Perdu before it's too late.

But isn't that the point . . . *An old voice, ancient with years of heartbreak caught up all in the single sound, drifts in and out of my mind. . . . world beyond sleep . . . control? Free to be—*

Clair! *a different voice interrupts. This new voice is panicked and desperate and scared. It's Dolion.*

I don't know what's happening, but something feels wrong.

My body is not mine in this dream. I have no control over anything but my thoughts as I continue to watch what takes place in the yard, under the large tree that sits in front of the house.

Perdu is broken. Perdu is hurt by the world, by Dolion, by so much more than anyone other than he could know. He's so broken that he follows Dolion. He follows him far into the dark, so far the light is nothing but a memory. He follows him up the chair that now sits under the tree. He follows him until the rope is around his neck. He follows him until the sun rises and he is left hanging.

Dolion turns to me. My heart races as I realize he can see me. He knows I'm here, in this dream. His eyes lock with mine, and I expect to find him smiling, expect the monster to grin at his victory. But instead, Dolion looks at me in a way that seems wrong for him. He looks at me with fear, with sorrow, with pain, and with desperation.

And though he never speaks to me, I know what he wishes to say.

Help me, Clair. Please.

This time I awake drenched in sweat and out of breath. I sit up in my bed and squint my eyes, attempting to see into the dark shack. The dream has changed. I rub my palm over my eyes and curl back under my blanket. The air is much colder than normal.

I wish my dream would go away. It used to only happen once every few months, but lately it's been nearly every night, and each time it gets more urgent than the last. More desperate.

I shudder as I think of Dolion's words.

Help me, Clair. Please.

Loralie

1941

I awake with a start, gasping, clutching the bedding surrounding me, tears burning my eyes. In my dreams, Arron replaced Dolion. I grew old, until I was shriveled and small, and forgot my brother had ever been there, forgot Arron wasn't the only one I had ever loved. Dolion was alone. The world hated him, spat on him, turned him away. Dolion died of loneliness because Arron kept me from him.

I turn in the darkness to find Arron lying next to me on his back, breathing deep. An overwhelming sense of anger washes through me at the sight of him. Arron killed Dolion. I watched it happen over time, until Dolion died alone and afraid. Because of him.

"I think I love you." Arron said those words, and that brought me back to reality. Arron is not the man I have been dreaming of my entire life;

he's not even someone I can trust. Why? Because being with him means I can't be with Dolion. Dolion, the only person I will ever truly love.

My hands begin to shake, and the movement grows more violent as I release the bedding and bring my hands close to my chest, folding them in front of me. Mucus gathers in the back of my throat, and I sit up hacking, tears running down my face even harder from the lack of air.

"Loralie?" Arron mumbles.

The sound of his voice causes a pulse of fire to shoot through my veins, heating my face, and I clench my shaking hands. The sight of Dolion dying comes back to me. I turn slowly to Arron, my head pounding.

"What happened?" he asks. "Are you all right?"

When my eyes connect with his, the darkness of the night making his eyes look gray in the moonlight from the window, I hear Dolion's plea for help loud enough to make my ears bleed. But it doesn't hurt my ears; it punctures my heart as I stare at the man who made me forget Dolion. Who killed Dolion.

"Loralie?" Arron asks again, a hint of fear dripping off the tip of my name as it exits his mouth. I soak in the sound. "Why are you looking at me like that? L-Loralie?"

I allow a smirk to cross my face, reminding myself I am in control of this situation here. I don't have to let Arron do this to us. I can stop it. I get onto my knees slowly, the blanket falling away from my body, uncovering my bare legs. I lean onto my palms, my smirk tightening as I crawl toward him. He grins back, reaching his hands out for my hips as I straddle him.

Arron leans back against the wall before he speaks. "So, you don't hate me after last night?"

I smile, running my hand along his chest until I'm at his neck. I pause for a moment, imagining gripping it, digging my nails into his flesh until he isn't a problem any longer. Instead, I force my hand to pass by his vulnerable skin and find his hair, gripping it tightly to keep my fingers from moving to his throat again.

"I am the one who asked you into bed with me," I say, forcing my voice to sound soft and as sweet as I can.

He smiles again, a small chuckle coming with it.

My heart tightens as I stare at him, keeping the effortless smile plastered to my lips.

"I missed you while I was asleep." He hums, his voice faltering slightly when I pull on his dark hair. "Do I really snore though?" His voice is softer now, reacting to my hands as they travel down his chest again and to his sides.

"I'm not known for my honesty," I say, keeping the air in my voice as my face softens. I bite my lip as my hands find his wrists.

"It's the middle of the night," he says. "Do you not want to sleep?"

"I'm not tired." I pull his hands above his head and hold both his wrists in my right hand.

"I let you take control earlier, but I told you, I'm not comfortable with you always—"

"Just calm down," I say, my smile falling entirely as I lean toward him. He doesn't speak again as my lips connect with his. I push my knees deeper into the mattress on either side of him as I grab his wrists again and pull his arms down to his sides. Then, making sure he's focused on my lips and not his arms, I lift my right knee and pin his wrist into the mattress under it. Then I do the same on his left side until the full force of my weight is on his trapped wrists. His muffled voice comes from below me, his body tenses as I'm sure pain pulses through his arms. I pull away from him slightly, missing the feeling of his soft skin between my teeth.

"What are you doing?" he asks, his voice rough.

"Trust me," I whisper, leaning forward again until my lips find his. He's trembling. Am I scaring him? The thought causes adrenaline to travel through me, attempting to drive my actions until I've finally gotten rid of him. Until I can step back and stare at his lifeless body tangled in his blankets. Then, only then, will I be able to find Dolion and finally be happy. But I have to take my time. I have to get him fully under my control so he won't be able to fight back. He's much bigger than me.

The adrenaline quickly turns to an electricity shocking my body and causing abrupt reactions. I have to keep myself from suffocating him, snapping his neck, doing anything that would finally end this. I am, however, out of my own control. The darkness swelling within me causes excitement to shock me again, and, like an impulsive reaction, I bite his lip until the silvery taste of blood fills my mouth. He jerks back from under me, a muffled cry coming from somewhere deep in his throat. I pull back, putting my full weight on his wrists.

To my surprise, tears are now falling down my face, and the image of the man in front of me blurs. I reach for his throat, wrapping my hand around him tightly. He gasps before a broken, gurgled yell fills the room, quickly turning into smaller cries for help.

"You're so pathetic," I tell him. Watching him cry in pain under me makes something within me come to life. An obsessive need to see his end, to see all of their ends, to find my brother and promise no one will ever hurt him again. I am not afraid to do what I have to in order to be his protector again. I'm not afraid to get rid of the threats. If I would've killed Mother long ago, Dolion would be happier. I would be happier. I didn't, but I will never make that mistake again.

"Please," he chokes out. "Please don't hurt me."

"You hurt Dolion," I say. "You hurt me."

A soft warm light breaks through the darkness to my right. I turn to find Arron's father and mother, horror spreading across their faces.

I'm in the warm living room, seated on a deep red velvet couch. My hands absently run over the fabric. Arron's parents and sister and Charles are all staring at me, keeping their guard up. His father has a shotgun in one hand and a cigar in the other.

"Young lady?" Arron's father says. "I asked you a question."

"I'm sorry?" I say, looking up from the intricate carpet.

He sighs, bringing his cigar to his mouth, savoring the moment before returning back to me. "Tell us what happened." The smoke exiting his mouth and nose as he speaks makes it hard for me to take him seriously. "Why did you attack Arron?"

"Did he take advantage of you?" Charles asks, his hateful glare never leaving his brother.

I straighten my posture as I sit, forcing my eyes to Arron's father's gaze, then back to the smoke that continuously follows him around.

"He did not," I tell them, challenging their patience. If they lose this marriage, their family could lose much more than simply me. They could lose the wealth the world presumes I have. How far are they willing to go?

"You realize we could have you hung for this, right, little girl?"

Arron's mother elbows her husband after he speaks. "She's just a girl, Andrew," she says. "And she's carrying a child."

"She attacked our son," he growls, growing impatient. "And if Arron didn't force her, she's been having an affair right under our roof. The baby might not even be Charles's. Then the baby would be just as rotten as she is."

"Let me speak with her." Arron turns, and his eyes meet mine, the glow of the fire casting sickly shadows across his face.

After a moment of convincing, his parents back off, standing in the shadows of the room to watch as Arron sits next to me on the couch. I stare ahead of me, keeping still, holding my head high. I've done nothing wrong. He will not make me feel as though I have.

He lowers his voice, dipping his head toward mine until his forehead rests just above my ear, and to my surprise, he asks, "Are you all right?"

I press my lips together, folding my hands in my lap. Charles stands only feet away from us, his hands twitching uncomfortably.

"Loralie?" Arron whispers.

"Stop acting like you care," I tell him.

"I do care."

"You don't know me. You will never know me." My voice catches in my throat.

"Let me help you. Let me be your support in whatever is going on. You haven't been the same since you heard your brother. I'm worried about you." He reaches his hand out to mine, cupping my palm in his. His hand feels so cozy, so comforting. After all this, he still cares about me? He still wants to be with me? My cheeks grow warm at the thought of it all, of a man caring for me. Even when my darkness shows, he still wants to be there. Could this possibly be real?

I turn my head, softening my gaze as I stare into his calm brown eyes. I smile gently at him, my lips tightening as he smiles back.

"We're going to be all right, Loralie. We will get you through this."

"Why are you being nice to me?" I ask him. "Why are you not afraid of me?"

"I understand pain," he says. "I understand separation."

"Separation?" I ask, not sure what he is talking about.

"Your brother. I can only imagine how painful it is to be away from him."

Dolion.

When I realize what has happened to me, I pull my hand harshly away from his and look at him, mouth slightly agape. In these past few minutes, after Arron calmed me down, I forgot about the one person I am nothing without. Dolion slipped my mind. I was so focused on Arron that my mind wandered far away from Dolion. Far enough to forget, even for a moment, that he ever existed at all. Just like my dream.

A man to fill his place. A man to take over. A man to push him out. If I stay with Arron, I will lose Dolion forever. I look to Arron. The anger and the fear turn to heat in my face, flushing my skin.

"You cannot do this," I say, my voice low and steady. "You will not push him out."

"Loralie?" The question shows clearly in his eyes.

"Stop pushing him out!" I am supposed to protect him, to watch over him. A hole grows in my heart at my next thought. *I pushed him out. I left him.*

"Loralie, what are you talking about?"

"Let me go," I tell him. "Or I will force my own way out."

"What does that mean?" he asks.

"It means finally embracing who I am. Finally letting my darkness show."

Arron turns on the couch so he is facing me. His eyes hold mine with intensity. "If you would like to leave, you may." He reaches for my hand, but I pull away, avoiding touch with the man taking Dolion's place in my heart. "I will not force you to stay."

"I will," Charles says, stepping closer to us. "We need her."

"We're hurting her," Arron argues back. "If she wants to go, it is her right—"

"She has no rights as far as I am concerned." Arron's father looks at the smoking end of the cigar between his fingers as he speaks. "Do you, little girl?"

My head snaps in his direction. Making direct eye contact with him, I stand. I walk toward Arron's father, take his cigar from his hand, and throw it to the ground.

"Look at *me* when you address me," I tell him. Arron's mother quickly rushes to pick up the cigar before a fire ignites on the rug. "And I *am* leaving, and there is absolutely nothing you can do to stop me."

I walk toward the door with strong, confident steps. As expected, Arron's father reaches out and grabs me by the wrist. I turn around with a tight fist and punch him in the face, knuckles connecting with his nose. Arron's father stumbles back as others in the house come to his aid, holding me down. I fight against them, but Charles and his brother-in-law are too strong for me. My arms eventually give in as I am pinned against the wall.

Arron tries to force them to let me go. He tells them I won't hurt anyone any more.

"He's wrong," I say out of anger and spite. "When I get the chance, I will hunt down every one of you and make you pay for what you've done to me."

"Alert the square," his father says. "She's to be hung tonight."

Chapter Thirty-Five

Loralie

"You think you can control me?" I say through a clenched jaw, still pinned against the wall, my back pressed into the striped floral wallpaper. "No one can control me."

They look at me, their faces blank, staring, unmoving as I speak. Like the perfect fools they are.

"I gave up everything . . . *everything*!" My voice cracks, hurting my throat. "I've gone through hell because I thought . . . I thought that maybe someone would love me." I push against the men holding me one more time before I find Arron's eyes. He looks at me with tears. I am already loved; Dolion loves me—he always has. And they all took me from him.

"Let her go," Arron says, his voice quiet but firm. "Give her one more chance."

"She's dangerous, Arron," his father says.

"Then give *me* one more chance. Please."

His father breathes slowly, triggering an abrupt cough before he finally nods at them to let me go. I fall to the ground and scramble to my feet. Arron walks over to me, a desperate look in his eyes.

"Please," Arron says quietly, reaching a hand out for mine. He takes it, and for a moment, I remain still, processing my thoughts. What do I want? Do I want to stay here with him? Do I want to live life like this? It doesn't matter what I want. Dolion needs me.

"You . . ." I say to Arron, pulling my hand from his for the final time, making myself taller than him and leveling our eyes. "You tried to push Dolion out. You tried to make me forget him." I laugh and lower my head, feeling a comforting sense of anger and power flood over me. "I never cared about you. And now . . ." I tilt my head. "I'll make sure you never care about me again." My arm reaches out, and before I can stop myself, my fingers are gripping his neck, digging deeper into his skin. I threaten Arron's life when anyone tries to stop me. Soon they are all too afraid to try anything. My heart races at the situation, giving me the first feeling of freedom I've felt in so long. True freedom.

Loralie!

I hear it! His voice.

Loralie, where are you?

He's here. He's close.

My hands relax. Arron falls to the floor, and I make a break for the door. Before I can escape, I am snatched by two strong men—their faces I cannot see—and pulled elsewhere.

"Dolion!" I yell. "I know you're here. I'll find you!"

"Loralie." Arron's damaged voice comes from the living room. The hurt and shock strung through him make me feel as though I still have the control, and when my eyes meet his pained ones from across the room, I grin before he can turn away.

Despite my struggles, I am pulled to the center of the block, my feet dragging along in large pools created from the rain. Arron and his family watch, waiting for my death, wanting to be rid of their newfound fear.

Let them fear me; I don't care. It's healthy to fear those who are a danger to you.

I'm pulled onto a wooden stage. The crowd—rapidly forming below—begins waiting for them to pull the lever. For them to end a young woman's life. I'm carrying a child, and they're on the edge of their seats, waiting to see my lungs give out.

"Hope this makes you *happy*!" I shout over them, rainwater spitting from my mouth. The tears that now roll down my cheeks are hot. They burn with every trail they make, carrying my anger. Someone whose face is covered in a cloth bag is pulled up next to me, but I ignore it. "You should all know *you* are the monsters. What are you afraid of? Are you afraid of this?"

Flames erupt from my palm, and I break the man's hold for a moment, reaching my fire out toward the crowd. The heat from my hand calms me as it spreads across my face and my body, like it's wrapping me in its protection. Everyone turns to avoid my eye contact. Children are pulled away and locked in homes. Men cower from me. Their fear makes me feel taller. This is what they all deserve.

"Fear me!"

As the man regains his grip on my arms, my hand tenses, and I prepare to turn and light him on fire for daring to touch me again. But something stops me before I get to hear this man's screams. A quiet voice sounds in my head.

Don't do anything you'll regret, Loralie.

I look over instantly, my long wet curls hitting my face.

"Doli?" My eyes find his small smile as the bag is pulled off his head. I pull away from the man holding me, wrapping my arms around him as my flame flickers out. I'm safe. Finally, whatever happens to me, I'm safe. I'll be all right.

"You have no idea what this has done to me," I whisper. Now my tears are cold. They no longer burn, and it's a relief. We are pulled apart. I struggle, fighting against the man.

Dolion looks at me, and his eyes meet mine for the first time since the house. *It's all right, Loralie. Let them. We'll be together soon enough.*

I listen to him. As I find my place, facing everyone with a noose hanging before me, Dolion grabs my hand.

This time's for real, he says.

Dolion

Fire. Loralie has fire . . . I have ice. What does that mean? Why are we like this?

With Loralie next to me, I feel the rot that she is growing inside of me again. Her darkness. I know now, with her beside me, her hand in mine, I will never outrun Loralie. She will always consume me, infect me, and intoxicate me. I will never be free of her, because the fear of being separated hurts so much more than the despair of being with her. Loralie completes me, and I complete her. No matter how much I long to be free of her, the calmness that settles within tells me I'll never let myself truly get that far away.

They count down to our deaths, shouting the numbers so loud my ears ring. Loralie gives my hand a gentle squeeze. "I want to die holding your hand, Doli."

I promise you. I lift our hands. *You will.*

The wind whips through my curls, which have grown so long they now fall in front of my eyes. I try to flick my head back to move my hair. It doesn't work.

Loralie grips my hand tight until my knuckles ache. She's scared. I can feel her fear pulsing through her fingers and scorching mine. I should be afraid, but I'm finding it hard to care about anything other than the discomfort of my grown-out hair.

Loralie would always cut it for me, but she hasn't been around in so long. I didn't even notice it was so long until now, standing here with her. I should be scared to die—I know I should. It's the end of everything I know and the beginning of life's greatest question. But there are things I fear more than death, and being forced to spend a life trapped by Loralie's corruption is the biggest one. I'd rather die right now than have to continue living with her in my life.

Still, the safety and comfort I feel from being able to hold my sister again confuse me. I hate her, but I can't help but love her.

At least I suppressed the ice that was so desperate to erupt from inside me at Charles's house. At least I did something right. I can be proud of myself for that.

Ages pass, and still we are on the platform, waiting for our deaths. Lightning rips through the sky, illuminating my sister's sunken face and wide eyes. She grasps my hand tighter as the time finally comes. All I can hear is my breathing as the guard pulls the lever. The feeling of everything falling out from under me as I fall is so familiar it stings.

My world slips away. My hope slips away. Everything that used to matter disappears until I am left hanging.

But before I can die, something jolts, and I fall to the ground. My hands and knees catch my body. I look up to see Loralie in the same position I am, her dress now muddy from the dirt. Before I can figure out what happened, Loralie's dirty wet hand reaches out for mine. I take it, and she pulls me forward, running from the people. Shouts sound over the rain falling into the mud below. We duck around people, dodging a few hands reaching toward us. Others run in fear.

As if it weren't chaotic enough, lightning strikes close to the ground, causing an even bigger panic to erupt. We are followed only by one. The rest are too afraid of the weather. When we get far enough from the crowd, Loralie stops and turns around, clutching my hand tighter.

"Stay away!" She holds out a large stick that was leaning against the wall next to us. "Stay away, or I swear I'll—"

It's the boy. Karl. His face is small, and he looks at Loralie, cowering from her.

Stop, Loralie, I say. *That's Karl. He's my friend.*

She looks at me like I just told her I killed a man.

"You have a friend?" Loralie asks.

Yeah. I shrug, a small smirk forming on my face. *Why so surprised?*

"And you are smiling?" she asks again, a small unsure smile appearing on her face as well.

I've changed.

"Dolion, that's . . . that's great." Even as she says it, her eyes fill with a look of betrayal, and she takes a small step away from me.

Karl holds out his knife, showing us that he got us down. He smiles with pride, and his missing front tooth reminds me just how young he actually is. Something about him seems . . . wiser than other kids his age.

"So . . ." Loralie looks to me. "What now?"

I shake my head. I don't know. We could go anywhere, do anything. No one will tell us what to do. We can just be . . . us. Her fingers hesitantly reach for my hand again, and I realize for the first time in our lives, we are whoever we want to be. I smile, pushing away the darkness boiling within, the fear of who Loralie could become, and breathe deep. It's all going to be all right.

Chapter Thirty-Seven

Dolion

Karl is taking us to his grandfather's house. He says he'll let us stay there for a while.

Loralie reaches for my hand as we walk. She holds on to me like I'm the only thing keeping her going right now. We all walk in silence, images of everything that has happened no doubt flickering through everyone's mind. We may be silent on the outside, but I don't think our thoughts will ever quiet again. Memories will torture us for all eternity. I flinch as the image of Loralie threatening everyone with her fire resurfaces. I should be afraid of her fire, should be confused and wonder what happened to her. I clench my fist as the cold starts to seep through my skin. I am not afraid because I know her fire is exactly what my ice is: a relic of our abuse. I don't tell my sister about my ice; she's so dark I'm afraid I may need a defense against her someday. She can't know I hold that type of power too or she'll attempt to strip it from me.

Loralie squeezes my hand, and I can feel her gaze on me. I shake my head and give in to the pull of her eyes. I can't believe she's pregnant. She's going to give birth soon. I want to ask her about it, but I can't bring myself to speak. She's going to be a mother. I pity the child.

"What happens now?" she asks when my eyes meet hers. A small tear falls down her cheek and chin. I shake my head again in response. "I'm scared, Doli."

She clasps my hand with her other hand so that I'm captured between both of hers. My sister leans on me as we walk. Her presence weighs on me, and that voice in my mind won't stop reminding me how this is all her fault. We wouldn't be in this damned situation if she hadn't been so selfish. There is darkness in Loralie—I've seen it my entire life—and she keeps sucking me into it with her. I'm afraid I'll never be truly free of her. I'm afraid I'll end up just like her: cold, heartless, the villain of the story that's being told.

"What happened back there?"

She asks the question so fucking innocently, like she isn't the reason we had to go through that. And who the hell knows what horrors Karl had to go through to get us out, all because of my sister. Then she has the nerve to grab my hand like she's the scared one, like she's the one who was forced to go through fucking hell.

I shake my head and fight the urge to push her off of me.

Our home begins to creep up on us. At first it's a small dot in the distance, then it slowly grows larger and larger. I keep reminding myself we have to walk past it to get to Karl's grandfather's house. I knew this was going to happen, but coming so close to everything that is familiar hurts. I long to run to the house, past the tree in the yard and up the front steps. I long to throw the door open and run upstairs to my room, to bury myself in the familiar scents of my blankets and hide from the unknown. But the thought of what waits inside for me keeps me moving my feet forward as I walk past the house. Mother is inside, and so is Emile.

Loralie grips my hand tighter.

As we walk past the house, she looks at me in a way that scares me. She looks at me with hope. She looks at me like I'm going to save her from this nightmare.

A while later, we finally make it to Karl's grandfather's house. Loralie is looking at least a little better than she was before. Karl introduces us to his grandfather, who seems to be nice. He has bright eyes and a kind smile. Maybe here things will be different. Maybe Loralie can recover from whatever happened to her and we can find some type of normal life to live. I'm hoping that means we'll be free of whatever shadows follow Loralie around.

"*Hallo, kind,*" Karl's grandfather says, speaking the same language as Karl.

I nod.

We are welcomed in. The home is small and practical. Its wooden walls make for a dark atmosphere. It has a peaceful feeling. A feeling of love. It's cozy and warm. The lights are dim, but it's easy to see. We are led to a small room with a table set with bread and fish.

Fish? I ask Loralie. She shrugs. I continuously eye the meat, sliced and cooked, ready to eat. Loralie nudges me.

Loralie

I have to fight to keep myself from reaching for the fish Dolion pointed out. How long has it been since I've eaten? The hunger pains desperately climb up my chest and throat.

In the corner sits a small cradle, and little cries come from that direction. I've heard cries like that before. Small cries from a human too small to defend himself. A baby. My heart tightens at the thought of what's growing inside me. I place my hand on my stomach, and Dolion looks over at me, watching me with a look of caution and sadness.

Are you all right? He gestures toward my stomach. I nod.

The grandfather ushers us over to meet the small baby, and when I see him, my heart drops. The child has a birthmark covering half of his mouth. I look at Dolion with wide eyes, hoping he understands. This poor baby will be shunned. Isn't that what happened to Dolion? He couldn't speak, therefore he was different, and everyone was afraid.

The grandfather picks the baby up and rocks him gently. I don't understand much of what's being said. Karl is excited, talking about many things. The grandfather waits his turn and then speaks calmly to the child. Karl then nods and sits at the table.

We get to eat the fish after all. Biting into it is like finally giving in to my darkest obsession. Never before have I tasted something with such rich and exploding flavors.

Dinner is calm and quiet. Occasionally someone will speak, nod, or look up, but mostly, everyone enjoys what they have in front of them. The baby laughs whenever something falls on the floor. I'm convinced the grandfather drops things just to make his grandson laugh.

I find myself slightly jealous, wishing I had grown up this way. I did for many years until it changed. Our father was gone, and Emile came. He changed Mother, and everything just broke. Lives, hearts, and vocal cords. It was all my fault. I look at my brother. He's becoming a man now—he even has small hairs on his chin. He's growing, becoming stronger and braver. Just weeks ago his shoulders and back were constantly crushing him, folding over him, making him appear small and broken, but now he holds himself higher.

If even Dolion is getting stronger, how come I'm not?

I grip Dolion's hand suddenly and squeeze so hard he pushes me off of him. Then I cry, a painful cry that causes the small baby to start crying as well. Karl picks up his little brother and rocks him.

Loralie? Dolion asks, now aware that something is wrong. *What's happening? Are you all right?*

I bend over in the chair I'm in, hold my stomach, and cry out as waves of sharp pain pulse from my back to my lower stomach.

"It's coming," I say through strained breaths. "Fuck, Dolion, the baby is coming!"

Chapter Thirty-Eight

Clair

2022

This is a dream. Somehow, I know it's a dream, but it feels so lifelike, so real. I stand in a dark corner on the front porch of Witherite House, and I'm forced to stare at the sight unfolding before me. My feet are rooted to the wooden floorboards, my eyes trained on it against my will. Screams and warnings I am so desperate to cry out are trapped within me, never once making it through whatever barrier seems to keep me from the same world as Perdu.

Dolion will never win. It's all so clear to me now. Or at least I used to think it was. Something is changing in Devil Oasis, and this dream is changing with it. Dolion will never win, and he and Loralie will always be stuck in this cycle unless something changes.

This is more than just a dream! *Dolion yells at me.* Listen to me, Clair!

I fight my mind, attempting to keep from falling back into the same pattern I'm always trapped in. But I have no control. After all, isn't that the point of a dream?

Isn't the world beyond sleep always out of your control? *an old voice, ancient with years of heartbreak caught up all in the single sound, asks me.* Free to be twisted and shaped by an outside force because . . . because you have no power over your mind when you've drifted far away.

The source of the voice may be behind me, or maybe above me, or even below me, through the porch and six feet beneath the soil, but my head won't turn to look. I am left completely vulnerable to whoever may be here with me. My body is not mine in this dream. I have no control over anything but my thoughts as I continue to watch what takes place in the yard, under the large tree that sits in front of the house.

Perdu is broken. Perdu is hurt by the world, by Dolion, by so much more than anyone other than he could know. He's so broken that he follows Dolion. He follows him far into the dark, so far the light is nothing but a memory. He follows him up the chair that now sits under the tree. He follows him until the rope is around his neck. He follows him until the sun rises and he is left hanging.

Dolion turns to me. My heart races as I realize he can see me. He knows I'm here, in this dream. His eyes lock with mine, and I expect to find him smiling, expect the monster to grin at his victory. But instead, Dolion looks at me in a way that seems wrong for him. He looks at me with fear, with sorrow, with pain, and with desperation.

And though he never speaks to me, I know what he wishes to say. It's what he always says.

Help me, Clair. Please.

Loralie

1941

My body is finally free. The sickness that was stirring inside me now rests in Dolion's arms as he rocks him back and forth. I am finally free.

Dolion reaches the baby out to me, but I reject him and turn away. Then the baby starts crying, which makes Karl's little brother cry, and I slam my hands over my ears and try to ignore the screeching sounds.

Hush now, it's all right. Dolion's voice sounds in my mind as he tries to calm the baby.

"He can't hear you," I mutter to my brother.

Ignore her, Dolion continues. *She's just a little cranky.*

I roll my eyes.

This is all Arron's fault. He's the one who infected me with the child to begin with. Now that it's out of my body, it's even more impossible to ignore, at least with Dolion obsessing over it so much and forgetting about me. The baby takes Dolion's attention from me, and I'm left alone and forgotten. After everything I've done for Dolion, he betrays me for the thing that I hate now more than ever.

This baby is ruining our lives. When Dolion is asleep, I have to get rid of him, but where would I take him? Everything is too far away to travel at night with a baby. Only one place is close enough. We may not get along, but I'm her daughter. Surely she'll help me if I truly need it.

After everyone calms down from the excitement of the evening, they prepare for a long night of baby cries and little sleep. I stay in Karl's bed—he offered it to me before I gave birth—and Karl sleeps on the fading sienna-brown rug with my brother. Everyone in Karl's family shares this one room. The baby sleeps in his corner cradle, and the other two have small wooden beds lined with blankets. Dolion forces me to sleep with my baby in my arms. He says it'll help me feel closer to the child.

The night is long. I lie awake thinking of everything that's happened. The longer I think, the less I believe there's a way out, and that scares me. A tear escapes my eye. How did I end up in this mess?

As long as I have my brother, I know I'll be all right, but this baby is stealing even Dolion from me. I try to breathe deep and keep myself from panicking.

The baby's breath is loud as he sleeps, and it keeps me up late into the night. The thought of this child slowly closes in on me like he's a cage I'll never escape, and soon I'm suffocated in my own mind and desperate for a way out.

Dolion

A small sound wakes me. Karl's home is dark, and not even the moonlight helps me see more than a faint outline of the room I'm sleeping in. Footsteps creak across the floorboards as someone scuttles by where I lie on the rug before crawling into Karl's bed.

It must be Loralie.

My heart tightens in my chest as I realize what I've done. I left her baby, *my* nephew, solely in her care for the entire night. Loralie isn't all right—there's something wrong in her head. I should have known better than to leave him in her care.

What have I done?

What did she do to him?

Is he dead? Did she leave him somewhere alone to starve?

My fingers fidget with the hem of my shirt, and I wait for my sister to fall back asleep before checking for the baby. He's not in her arms.

Fuck Loralie.

Loralie

Someone gently nudges my shoulder. Morning is here, yet the sun is not. The darkness is so present it's nearly overwhelming. Karl puts one finger over his lips and gestures for me to follow him. I look where Dolion was sleeping to find an empty rug. I search the small room quickly, but he isn't here. I've just found him—I won't lose him again. If I do, I swear I will kill myself. Karl runs to the door, holding out his hand, directing me through the opening. When I get outside, I find Dolion with Karl's grandfather. I sigh. *Thank goodness.*

I put my hand on Dolion's shoulder, letting him know I am here, but he shrugs me off and won't look at me. He and the others stare off into the horizon. I follow their gaze, looking just past a few trees and hills, to the most glorious sunrise. The sun is peeking over the horizon, and the sky gradually becomes pink and purple with hints of a crisp orange. A gentle breeze flies through my hair, the grass rustles, and the sky brightens with each second's passing. Everything feels still—the life, the air, the moment.

"Ein Sonnenaufgang wie dieser bedeutet, dass jemand, der es sonst nicht getan hätte, die Nacht hier überlebt hat," the grandfather says. I can't understand him, but whatever he said, he said it with importance, from experience.

"Dolion," I whisper to my brother. He turns away from me. Betrayal slices through my chest. "Dolion? Is something the matter?"

He snaps his head to me, his eyes burning deep into mine. They're red and puffy, as if he got little to no sleep last night. Then he clenches his fist, shakes his head, and starts down the steps that lead off of the porch to get away from me.

The baby cries quietly as the grandfather rocks him.

What did I do to make him mad at me? My heart chokes itself as I make to chase after my brother. Dolion misses a step and collides with the ground. He hits his head and becomes quiet and still.

"Dolion!" I run down the steps after him. My knees hit the ground, tearing my dress and scraping my skin. I put my head on his chest. He's still breathing. "Dolion, wake up!" I can't force him to consciousness. "Help me!" I say, looking up to the grandfather. "Please help me! Help him!"

He grunts, looking at me like a helpless dog. Karl runs over, checking for a pulse. The grandfather refuses to help.

"Ich sehe Gefahr in diesem Jungen. Ich sehe Dunkelheit. Ich sehe eine Zukunft voll Ärger." His words sound threatening. He sounds spiteful and vengeful. "Danger." He points to Dolion. His English is shaky. "His life is danger to others."

"Help me!" I say. "Do *not* make me lose my brother."

He just stares.

"Fine, I'll take care of him. I will save him. Just leave me alone." Don't trust anyone. If you don't trust them, you will already be one step ahead.

The grandfather reaches out his hand to Karl, turning to walk back inside the house. In an act of . . . anger? Maybe. He kicks Dolion's arm as he walks by.

I stare at his retreating back for a second in shock. Then my skin heats, and I narrow my gaze on him.

"Do not touch *my brother*."

The scream I've been holding in for years bursts through the barrier I once built. I grab a metal rod sitting by the stairs. Using all my strength, I swing it toward Karl's grandfather. The yell comes out of me, pushing me to swing my hardest. He turns around just in time for me to see the look of terror plastered on his face before I crash the metal rod into his skull.

It's the same look I saw when I was four. I back away, watching as blood begins trickling down the wooden steps. The baby cries louder, and Karl looks at me like I'm coming for him next.

I stare back at him, trying to suppress a small smirk. What would happen if I just let myself feel? What would happen if I let the darkness in instead of fighting so hard to escape it? Karl is afraid of me. His grandfather, his guardian, is lying with a cracked skull, dead. Because of me. A rush of excitement runs through me. A rush of power. This is who I'm meant to be. If I give in to this darkness, I won't have to be afraid anymore.

I gaze deep into Karl's tear-filled eyes. *I am Loralie, and you* should *fear me.* Everyone has always been afraid of me, no matter what I do. Maybe I should finally give them an actual reason to be afraid. It's time I stop being afraid of myself. It's time I accept who I am. I am a murderer, I am dangerous, and I will *always* be the villain. No matter how hard I try to be good. And for the first time in my life, I realize that I will be all right. No matter who loves me, no matter who hates me. As long as I accept myself. And as long as I have my brother.

The boy looks at his grandfather, reaching out an arm to see if he is alive. He looks at Dolion, then back at me. Fear glistens in the tears that fill the boy's eyes. His hands begin trembling as he attempts to remain strong. He looks at his brother, small and crying, arms and legs thrashing. He shakes his head slowly before leveling his eyes with mine.

"Ich hätte dich sterben lassen sollen," he says quietly, and then he runs off into the sunrise. I look at the small baby, his birthmark wrinkled from the cries. He's so similar to the baby I got rid of just last night, but something about this baby makes me happy in a way my baby didn't. I want to be happy. My arms extend, picking up the child and cradling him. He's so much better than the other baby. This baby and Dolion may be the only people to ever care about me again. No one wants a monster, and now my secrets are out.

Dolion

The sun is warm and bright, and the wind blows gently, rocking the tree above me back and forth. It's the only tree out here, surrounded by an endless field of dry grass. My head is throbbing, but the sounds of the nearby lake comfort me. What happened? Where's Karl?

Loralie? Wherever she is, she's humming. I've never heard her sing before.

My sister walks over to me, the breeze blowing against her hair and dress, and the tall grass brushes against her skirt. There's something in her arms, and she seems happy.

"We're here, Doli." She smiles, looking around at the land that has been calling to us for so long. "We're here."

Loralie, what are you holding? What did she do? Who did she hurt? I fucking knew this would happen.

She kneels down, revealing Karl's little brother. The baby with the mark. Anger fills me—anger toward so many different things, all because of Loralie. She abandoned her own child just to take someone else's?

Loralie! I push myself off the ground, looking instantly at the small patches of blood on the hem of her skirt. The baby has the same blood on his blanket. Damn it. We never should have gone to their home. *What did you do?*

"What makes you think I did something?" she says in a sweet voice. Her finger pokes the baby's nose.

There's a reason everyone hates us. Where is the baby's family, Loralie?

"It was an accident, Doli. You have to understand that."

I let my head fall into my hands. She can't do this anymore. She can't ruin our lives anymore. I never should have gone to look for her. I should have run while I could still get away.

She rocks the baby and shows him the lake.

Why would you take another child when you didn't even want your own?

"This one is better." She holds him up so I can see.

That makes no sense! I let my voice rise to a level I hate. *Can't you see how confusing that is? How much it just doesn't make any sense?*

She continues humming as she rocks the small child again.

Dolion

"All I wanted was to protect you," she says. "That's all I've ever wanted."

Yes, but you've changed since Father died, Loralie. And not in a good way.

"It was my fault," she says, referring to Father's death, to the accident. "Don't you remember what happened? How I failed you?"

Yes, I remember. I remember the way she laughed as we played in the water, her excitement when she found a shiny rock, our father yelling, telling us to get out of the rapid stream. I remember the fear of realizing we were stuck in a harsh current and how Father came to get us. I remember Loralie's screams. I remember being pulled underwater by the force, unable to breathe, feeling trapped and paralyzed by fear until I passed out. I remember the worst part of it all: waking up, unable to speak, finding out my father hadn't survived the water.

Loralie. I sigh. *It's not your fault.*

"Doli, I . . ." She takes a deep breath, fiddling with the baby's small hand. "I pushed you under the water."

She actually wants to talk about Father's death. We've never done that before. Suddenly, nothing else matters other than this moment. My body is weak, like all the energy has been drained from me. I stare at my sister, the girl I've grown up with, spent my entire life with, and wait for her to continue. We're finally facing what happened.

"I fell on you when I lost my balance in the water. You went under, and I panicked. Father came to help, but you were caught on something. We couldn't get you out. After trying for a few seconds, Father went under, and he found you. He came back for air telling me that you had a net or something tangled around your neck. Then it happened. You reached out and grabbed Father's leg. You pulled him under, Dolion. With much more strength than you alone could have possessed at four years old."

I stare at my feet as they kick the ground gently.

"There's more," she says.

I shake my head but don't speak.

"Listen. When it happened, it was like a mistake in time or something. I was underneath with you, in your body. I knew you weren't conscious, but I could hear your heartbeat as well as mine. We were together, Dolion. I could hear you counting down to the pull. I was there, with you, listening to your instructions. We did it together, and I don't think either one of us could control it."

I don't let myself look away from Loralie. Right now I'm not completely sure I can trust her. She isn't the same girl I grew up with.

That voice in the back of my mind shows up again. *You know what she says is true. You and your sister murdered your father.*

But I don't remember that happening.

"There's something more going on here, Dolion. With our lives, I mean. More than we've ever realized."

My hands tremble, but I hide them. I look at Loralie and finally say something. *What do you think it is?*

"I don't know." She looks around like she's afraid someone is listening. Then she whispers, "I'm scared, Doli. I'm so scared."

"Dolion!"

A sharp yell comes from behind us, causing us both to jump. We turn to see Karl, anger ignited in his eyes.

"Monsters!" he calls out.

He was my first and only friend. And now, because of Loralie, he hates me just like everyone else does. I hate myself for coming back to Loralie, but at this point, I know I'll never escape her. She's all I have left in this world, and as much as I despise it, I need her.

If not for us, Father wouldn't have died, Mother would still be happy, and Karl would still have his family. How many more lives will we ruin before this all ends?

The baby cries when he hears Karl's voice. Karl's eyes widen as he looks for his brother, and Loralie tucks the baby into her chest as if she's sending a message to Karl: you can't have him.

Karl grabs a large stick and runs at Loralie, yelling angry nonsense. Loralie shushes the baby as she ducks away from Karl as though this is nothing but a slight inconvenience to her.

Karl plants his feet and turns to face Loralie, preparing to bring the stick down on her.

I will never be able to leave my sister. I will never be able to escape her darkness because, for some fucked-up reason, I still love her. I take a step forward and stand between Karl and Loralie, taking the blow for my stupid, selfish, arrogant, somehow still amazing sister. The hit sends my hands flying to my chest as I curl up on the ground. Pressure on the wounded area causes shooting pains to spike up both my arms. I lie flat on the ground, watching my chest slowly rise and fall. My breaths wheeze. Above me, Karl extends his arms toward Loralie and the baby. She holds him tighter and shakes her head.

Give him the child, Loralie, I say. *He's all he has left. We took everything else.*

Loralie looks down at me like I just murdered her, hurt and shock painted across her face.

"I thought you cared about him too," she says slowly.

I do, and I care about you, Loralie. Let him go. Please.

She shakes her head and looks at me through tear-filled eyes.

Loralie . . . for me.

She sighs and slowly hands over the child with shaking arms. His cries silence when he is in his brother's arms again. Even the baby's life is worse with us.

The way it breaks Loralie to give up the baby angers and confuses me. She so willingly abandoned her own child. *I* was up the rest of the night trying to find the baby Loralie birthed but couldn't care for. *Me.* Not her. Yet she clings to Karl's brother like this child is her own. Loralie is sick; her mind is breaking.

Karl holds his little brother, whispering, "Du bist jetzt sicher, ich hab dich. Du bist sicher."

My only friend turns his back on me, but not before his eyes connect with mine. He shakes his head sadly and turns away from me forever.

With his little brother in his arms, he takes peaceful steps back in the direction of their home. *It's not fair that this is happening to me. Loralie's the one who hurt him, not me. Can't Karl see that? I don't deserve this. I don't.*

I reach my hand out and grab Karl's wrist, pulling at him. He yells, pushing away. I look up, and the next thing I see is the bottom of his shoe coming right for me. I fall back, and my grip comes undone.

Loralie

I kneel beside my brother as Karl runs away with the baby. Dolion's face looks about as messed up as I'm sure he feels. Blood runs from his nose, prominent against his pale skin. I love this boy so much. I love that he is my family. I love that he fought for me. I will always love him, no matter how broken he is and always will be. His love for me, his fight for me, makes him worth every second I have spent and will continue to spend taking care of him.

I pull my sleeve over my hand and wipe the blood from his face. "It's going to be all right," I say. "We mean nothing to him now. We don't have to worry about it."

That's not true. We will always be the people who murdered his grandfather. Always. We can't get rid of that, Loralie. Stop acting like every problem you create can just disappear.

"This isn't my fault, so don't blame me for this. He didn't know me. *I* wasn't his friend." The look in his eyes makes me wish I could take it back. "I'm hurting too. But look how beautiful this place is. We can stay, go, find a new home—whatever *we* want. We finally have freedom, Doli."

Loralie . . . Dolion's voice is quiet as he looks at me. *Please tell me you regret killing Karl's grandfather. Please tell me there's still hope for you.*

"That's the beauty of it, Dolion! I *am* dark. I *am* evil. And I'm all right with that. It's freeing. Sometimes I even find it hard to regret killing Father."

I smile. A real smile. A happy smile. A demented smile. A *me* smile.

Chapter Forty-Two

Dolion

Hatred burns through me, boiling through my core and making its way to the surface. She doesn't regret killing Father?

Who are you, Loralie?

"I'm finally me." She looks at me long and hard, studying my face with great care. "Give in to it, Dolion. Become what the curse wants. It will set you free."

The curse?

Father is dead because of us.

"He got to leave this wretched world. Can't you see that he is better off? We did him a favor."

Is that seriously how you feel? I ask her.

Please say no, I think. *That's all I need. For you to say you're sorry, you don't know what came over you. That there's still good in you.*

She slowly shakes her head. "I can't betray the truth, Dolion. I love you, and I want us to be happy. Trust me."

No, Loralie. I can't trust you. I want a life. I want to be happy. I want to laugh, and I want to spend forever with you, away from this darkness that has corrupted you. Can't you see that?

"I love you, Dolion. I pray to whoever the fuck is watching over us that you love me as well." Loralie lifts her hand, staring at her burn scar, a reminder of the pain we share. "There's something wrong with us, or so we've always thought. But what if we're the special ones? Why can't our curses be a gift?"

Because you are the curse. And you are definitely not *a gift.* I want to feel regret. I want to feel bad and apologize to the only one who's ever been there for me. But this isn't her. She's changed. I've changed. We are different people now. I cannot save her from what she has become.

Loralie

If a person's lifetime could be explained in a book, I would read it front to back. If someone's purpose had a clear definition, everyone would be better off. How do you find who you are meant to become? How do you harness the answers to life's greatest questions? If anyone has the answers, they will die before they get to share them. Because life doesn't want us to figure it out. If we were meant to know, we would. Unless it's up to us to find. Unless the unknown is part of the journey.

"I need you, Dolion," I say, barely making out a whisper. Maybe I am the curse. Hell, I've known I am the curse since the day of the accident. It was my fault. *Everything* is my fault.

I— He pauses before continuing. *I don't need you. I hate who I am when I am with you. The truth is, I hate you. I hate who you are, who you have become, and who I fear you will be.*

"So, you're afraid of me," I say. "Just like everyone else."

I don't want to be.

"You're nothing without me," I say, attempting to control the panic and rage building within. "You are weak and pathetic, and you will always be alone. You need me."

Dolion shakes his head. *No, I am the strong one now.* Tears form in my brother's eyes, causing me to fear his next words. *You need to leave me. Forever.*

My breaths shorten as I stare into the eyes of the only person I have ever loved.

Chapter Forty-Three

Dolion

I swallow hard, staring at the girl who was once my best friend. She corrupts me, she controls me, she owns me, and I am sick of it. I am sick of her hurting others, and I am sick of her hurting me.

You need to leave me. I do my best to stand up tall, to maintain eye contact with her, to show her I am done depending and relying on her. *Forever.*

I have no doubt she loves me, and I know I love her, but when I am with her, I feel myself becoming the very monster that I hate, slipping into her cruel dark ways.

Loralie stares at me, unmoving. The expression displayed across her face is so painful that I can't force myself to look at her. Loralie breaks. Her hands fall to her sides as her body and mind accept defeat.

It's over. Us. Our lives together. It's all over.

"All I want is for you to be all right, Dolion."

Please leave.

She nods, turning slowly away from me. I resist everything within me longing to call to her and tell her this was a mistake. I do need her, I do. I feel myself panic. I fight against myself as anger and fear rush through me, attempting to drive me toward her, to wrap my arms around her and return home to her. But I have no home left in her anymore. If I want to save myself from the darkness that has devoured her, I have to do this. I have to watch her walk away.

You know the truth, Dolion. You know who she is. The voice in my head returns.

Who are you? I ask the voice, tears blurring the vision of my retreating sister.

I'm you, it says. *I'm the light, the good. You let me in when Loralie—the darkness—was too far away to stop you. I'm here for you. I can help you.*

Loralie has good in her too, I argue.

Loralie has love, and only love for you. Love is not goodness, Dolion. It is simply a motivation for her evil.

Loralie is *evil,* I admit, allowing the truth to settle within me.

She will do anything for you, Dolion. Even murder.

Karl's grandfather, I say knowingly. *She's not going to stop, is she?*

No. She will keep killing. She will continue to rip families apart.

I look at Loralie, the greatest of all pain settling in my chest. I know what I have to do.

Loralie

Now that I face away from him, now that he can't see me, I cry. The tears are silent but very real. I don't want to leave him, but he's right: I can't keep hurting him anymore.

I turn back to look at my brother one last time. His eyes don't smile like they used to when we were kids. His body is broken, along with his heart. I know I didn't protect him like I should have. I see the future we could have had, alone but together. We are in the rain, but we are smiling. We've aged quite a bit, but we are happy. We have a little shelter, a home. We tell each other stories and never stop playing games. Dolion and I are happy. And no one ever beats him or shuns him again. I am always there to protect him, and he will protect me. I see it in his face now. I know he longs for that future. But as I turn away from him, leaving him with only the wind and the lake, I see that future fade. When I can no longer see his face, the visions of us are gone. We are not happy. We are not together. Everything is gone.

The journey is laid out before me. Somehow, I will find peace without Dolion. I have to. It may be a long road, it may take years of my life, but finding that peace, that final comfort, will be worth it in the end.

An unexpected but familiar feeling settles against my skin. I look down to see his hand in mine, and my heart fills with relief. I look up at him and smile. He came for me. He still loves me.

I'm sorry, sis, he says. *Don't ever forget that I love you.*

Dolion's face shifts, his expression morphing. He goes from a gentle but determined look to rage, then to regret all in the span of a second.

No . . . I hear him say, panicked. *No, Loralie, I'm sorry.*

I look down. How did I not see it? How did I not feel it? The dagger forced through my heart, blood staining my ruined gown. My body drains of strength instantly, and Dolion guides me to the ground.

I-I'm sorry. Please! I hear his whimpers.

It's not long before his voice begins fading away as his sobs continue. I stare at the sky, confused but not scared. I think my brother just killed me. I think I'm dying right now.

I'm sorry, Loralie. I'm so, so sorry.

I feel him hold my head against his chest. I feel his tears falling onto my face. His words continue, but I can't understand them anymore. I'm not afraid, I'm not in pain, I'm just . . . happy. Happy to be with him. I don't blame him. I could never blame him for putting an end to this misery.

Dolion

Madness corrupts us all. I know that now. Blood and guts and bodies—this is what fills our world, and it's inevitable that we will be driven to insanity. A girl becomes a woman pressured with expectations, and a boy becomes a man with the heaviest burdens. I thought I could be free of my sister's darkness, but with her body limp in my hands and her blood sprayed across my shirt and face, I have never felt closer to the wickedness that was my sister.

Everything I hated about her seeps into me through the blood that stains my skin. It's a darkness so invasive it could never be forced out. And for the first time in my life, I stop fighting it; instead, I revel in how close it makes me feel to Loralie.

I wipe the tears from my eyes and look at the scar on my palm, my reminder of my sister. I find her hand and lock our fingers together for the last time. She was my comfort, my fire during a harsh winter's night.

She was my ghost, and I was the skeleton in her closet, locked away from the world. Her presence haunted me. Her absence haunted me. She made me feel like a god, ruling over my heart and hers. I'll never forget her cries, her screams, and her crazy demon eyes. I'll never forget how terrifying she was. I'll never forget that side of her, the side the world saw. I'll also smile when I think of her laugh, her reaffirming words, the way she always saw value in my life. She showed her fears only to me; I saw her weaknesses and her desires. I had a gift greater than anything else: I knew the real Loralie. I knew that underneath the horrific creature was someone who just needed love. Loralie was the good and the bad. She was dark but . . . amazing.

Her darkness stirs inside me, wrapping around my heart and my mind. My sister was the goddess of death, evil represented by a beautiful face. Killing her was what the world needed; she would've gone on to hurt countless more if someone hadn't stopped it. I want to feel sad, to cry out and grieve for her, but an old longing has taken over my mind again.

The desire to be dead. And to be with my sister again for all eternity.

Her darkness is my darkness. Where she goes I will follow.

I lay her head down gently and give her hand one final squeeze before letting go. It drops to the ground, caressed carefully by the dirt. I use all the strength I have left to stand.

This is when I have a choice. This is when I get to decide *my* fate. But I know whether I die or survive these feelings crashing through me, I will spend eternity chasing after the sister I once had. Because she is Loralie and I am Dolion.

From the day Loralie and I were born, I was poisoned with a feeling too powerful to keep me sane without her. That poison was love for Loralie. I will always love her, and I will always follow her—even if it means leaving behind all of my happiness, all of my hope, and all of my future. I belong with Loralie. The only way to mend the rip in our relationship is to find her, to fight for her, to give in to her darkness and let it consume me.

A chill runs through my palm, and I force it to the back of my mind, finding it much easier to suppress the fear and growing ice than before. I smirk to myself. Maybe I'm actually getting better at this. I tighten my fist and keep my hand steady at my side. I know now that I will die with this secret. A secret even Loralie didn't know about me. That makes my smirk widen.

The lake is calming. Maybe I'm just imagining it, but it's as though there is a peace here I haven't felt in years. There is a gentle breeze that cools my skin and eases my panic. I step close to the lake, and the water rushes over my bare feet. I think I'm going to miss this world, the way the muddy dirt feels between my toes and the sound of the water filled with life. Loralie and I used to play here when we were little. That's what I miss most of all: the way she'd laugh when Father would splash her and the way I always had a friend in her.

I step farther into the water.

I used to dream of drowning. There's something so peaceful and tragic about the thought of my lifeless body floating far below the surface, my last moments spent in a hidden world of death and corruption.

I guess now I'll get to live out that fantasy.

My head goes under, and I let my breath go.

Chapter Forty-Five

Clair

2022

*D*olion has infected Perdu's mind far beyond repair. He's found *Perdu's weakest point and uses it to tear him to shreds over and over again.*

This is a dream. Somehow, I know it's a dream, but it feels so lifelike, so real. I stand in a dark corner on the front porch of Witherite House, and I'm forced to stare at the sight unfolding before me. My feet are rooted to the wooden floorboards, my eyes trained on it against my will. Screams and warnings I am so desperate to cry out are trapped within me, never once making it through whatever barrier seems to keep me from the same world as Perdu.

Dolion is winning. It's all so clear to me now. Dolion has always won, and he and Loralie will always win unless something changes. I fight my tense muscles, searching for a way to break free from this invisible prison. If I could just push a little harder, try a little longer, do something better, maybe I could make it to Perdu before it's too late.

But isn't that the point of a dream? *an old voice, ancient with years of heartbreak caught up all in the single sound, asks me.* Isn't the world beyond sleep always out of your control? Free to be twisted and shaped by an outside force because . . . because you have no power over your mind when you've drifted far away.

The source of the voice may be behind me, or maybe above me, or even below me, through the porch and six feet beneath the soil, but my head won't turn to look. I am left completely vulnerable to whoever may be here with me. My body is not mine in this dream. I have no control over anything but my thoughts as I continue to watch what takes place in the yard, under the large tree that sits in front of the house.

Perdu is broken. Perdu is hurt by the world, by Dolion, by so much more than anyone other than he could know. He's so broken that he follows Dolion. He follows him far into the dark, so far the light is nothing but a memory. He follows him up the chair that now sits under the tree. He follows him until the rope is around his neck. He follows him until the sun rises and he is left hanging.

Dolion turns to me. My heart races as I realize he can see me. He knows I'm here, in this dream. His eyes lock with mine, and I expect to find him smiling, expect the monster to grin at his victory. But instead, Dolion looks at me in a way that seems wrong for him. He looks at me with fear, with sorrow, with pain, and with desperation.

Dolion never speaks to me, and I can't figure out what he wishes to say.

My eyes open.

Part Two

Starting over doesn't always mean quitting. Victory doesn't always mean success. Evina doesn't always mean life, but Loralie always means death.

CURSE RULE #3

The twins hold no power over their target unless the child is in the heart of the Oasis. Nevertheless, the twins are capable of calling their prey and luring them into their trap.

Chapter Forty- Six

Lady

2022

Dolion's head went under, and he let his breath go. That's how it went.

Eighty-one years ago, Dolion killed his sister and then ended his own life in my lake. If I could have shed tears, I would have drowned in them by the time his torture and pain ended. I felt every twist of his panicking body, every thought that screamed in his mind, begging for a breath of fresh air. The Oasis itself seemed to hold its foul breath as it waited for the second twin to die.

Above, my waters stayed still, a peaceful cover-up for the terrors that ripped through my depths. I felt his silent cries crash against the floor of the lake, and the pain and hatred that filled him killed more than one of my fish as it shocked me like electricity. Dolion, just a boy, was so angry in his final moments it created death, as Dolion does best. He was angry at his sister for making him end up here, but more than anything, he was angry at himself for still loving her, for still needing her.

That day changed Dolion, and I'm afraid he'll never be able to be who he once was. Dolion welcomed Loralie's darkness within himself; for her, he became the darkness he has always been so afraid of. He was too scared to live a life without her, but he was brave enough to keep her from hurting anyone else.

I care about Dolion. I became one with the lake when Dolion was born, so I had to watch him grow up, had to watch his mother hurt him. And I couldn't do a thing about it. His mother made me so sick, all I wanted to do when Dolion was a small child was hug him and promise everything would be all right one day. But of course, it didn't end well for him, because he's Dolion Witherite. A boy cursed to darkness and death.

I didn't want Dolion to die, but I knew I had to let him. Using my energy to keep him away from my lake wouldn't have helped him at all. With Loralie dead, Dolion wouldn't have survived very long, just like Loralie wouldn't have survived if Dolion had died first. And that type of death, that of a broken heart, would have been far more painful than any of the darkness that occurred beneath the surface of my water.

Dolion changed when he was in my depths. His light was hidden.

Loralie was born a monster.

Dolion became a monster for her.

Evina

"Then tell me what you want from me!" Dad yells at Mom.

"I want to understand," she says, finally lowering her voice. "My son killed himself. I want to know what I did wrong."

Their bedroom door shuts again as Mom begins sobbing. I come out of hiding behind the couch in the common room just outside their bedroom. I know I shouldn't listen, but it hurts to be upstairs . . . alone.

"He wasn't a child anymore," Dad's deep voice says as gently as he knows how. "It's killing me to watch you do this to yourself, Sarah."

My heart aches at his words, knowing exactly how he feels. Three years. It's been three years of this. Three years of silent dinners, of lonely nights, of Mom crying as she cooks, of Mom and Dad's never-ending fights. Soon I'm afraid there will be nothing left of who we were when Perdu was still alive.

"I was supposed to be there. I was supposed to protect him." Mom's voice is small. "If I had loved him more, if I had spent more time with him . . ."

"Sarah, you have to stop." Dad grows stern again. "You still have a child, and she needs you. She and I lost Perdu too. Please remember that."

Their bedroom door opens once again, and I hide, wiping the tears off my cheeks as I kneel behind the couch.

"I just want to understand what happened to him," Mom says in a quiet voice, nearly a whisper.

Me too, Mom. Me too.

Dad leans back in his seat as his hands rub his eyes, and a loud sigh escapes him.

"Are you leaving the table already?" Mom asks him, finally looking up from her soup. "We just started dinner."

"I have work to do," he grumbles, standing and pushing his seat toward the table. Before he leaves the room, he kisses the top of Mom's graying head gently.

She closes her eyes at his contact and breathes in deep, waiting for him to go. As his quiet footsteps fade into the living room, Mom opens her eyes again, and a single tear escapes her.

"Are you okay, Mom?" I ask.

"I'm tired," she says. "It was a long afternoon."

I nod. They don't know I came home from babysitting the neighbors early. She doesn't know I heard everything. She doesn't know I understand how she feels.

We sit in silence most of dinner. When I finish, I gather the dishes from the table and take them to the sink to begin washing.

"Please let me, Evina," Mom says, reaching her trembling hand toward the plate I'm holding. "I would just like to be alone."

I back away from the sink and watch her muster up the strength to turn on the water.

"I was thinking maybe we could go for a walk later," I say. Getting out could do her good. She's holed up in her room all the time. I never get to see her anymore.

"Not today, Evina."

Not today, not ever.

I open my mouth to speak but snap it closed when I think better of it. She can't get out of her own head and see for even just a second that I'm here for her and so is Dad. I stare at the back of her head, her hair gathered in a low ponytail, as she scrubs the plate. She doesn't even see that I'm hurting too, does she? I clench my fist. My palm is sweaty. After Perdu died, he became all that matters to her.

The walls of the house press in on me, squeezing what little air I have left out of my lungs. The doors and windows are all closed. We're trapped inside a box that refuses to open. Heat floods my face, and the air is so thick I can't breathe.

My eyes land on the back door, which is closed for some reason. There's no fresh air. I can already feel my lungs collapsing and giving in to the suffocation. My hands shake, and my eyes fill with tears. I turn the handle of the back door, but it's locked. My pulse thuds in my ears.

"Mom, why is this door locked?" I rattle the handle and pull on it. "It's supposed to be open. This door is always open."

My chest hurts with each shallow breath.

"I don't know," Mom mumbles.

I pull on the door one more time before turning and running to the kitchen window. I pull it open, and fresh air floods the room like an ocean wave. I'm lightheaded, but I'm safe now. The cool air seeps into my body as if curing a disease.

"The door is supposed to be open," I say again through heavy breaths. She doesn't respond, so I shake my head and leave the kitchen.

I step out onto the front porch and look around the farm. Breathing in the cool air, I shiver as it reaches my lungs. My heart doesn't weigh on me the same when I am in the sunlight and out in the open air. Birds whistle and hop from tree to tree, just as busy as the chickens are, flapping their wings inside their coop. The large tree in our front yard towers over me the closer I get, and when I'm finally in its shadow, a chill runs down my spine. I lift my hand and stroke the rough bark. My fingers graze the familiar texture, clouding my thoughts with memories I can't, and don't want to, escape.

"I miss you, Perdu," I whisper as the leaves above blow in the wind.

A wet nose presses against my knee, and I smile at Marie, Perdu's Saint Bernard. Her fur is covered in dirt, and small twigs and leaves are intertwined on her brown-and-white back. I'm sure she was rolling around in the sun. She licks my leg as the breeze gets caught in the skirt of my sundress. I kneel beside her and pet behind her ear. "You understand how I feel, don't you?"

She stops panting to whine for a second before resuming.

I sigh. "Maybe I'm not being fair to Mom."

My light pink skirt rests on the ground like it was laid out intentionally, making me feel lighter, maybe even a little special. This is what I love about skirts and dresses. Marie nudges my arm when I stop petting her.

If Perdu were here, what would he tell me? He would tell me Mom needs help and that she isn't strong enough to be okay on her own. But I'm not either. I need help too, but nobody seems to see that. Mom is slipping away from me and Dad, and if something doesn't change, we will lose her completely.

Goose bumps creep up my spine, and my muscles stiffen. It's happening again. Not again. My heart flutters as a chilling presence overtakes me. A heavy must settles in the air, the birds stop singing, and everything falls eerily silent. Marie tenses her head and bares her teeth. She senses it too, this feeling that never seems to go away, not since the night Perdu died. The doctor said they could be panic attacks, though he says he's never seen anything like it. The layer of security I have peels back, and I feel exposed to the elements. My mind is opened, my senses are heightened. It's as though someone is watching me.

"Evina?" The familiar voice snaps me out of the trance.

Marie crouches in front of me and growls.

"It's okay, girl," I whisper to her. "There's nothing to worry about."

I look up and smile at my friend, who just approached.

"It would appear Marie still doesn't like me." Her lips tighten as she takes a seat next to me. Despite Marie's size, she crawls into my lap, and the hatred in her eyes never ceases.

"It takes a while for her to come around, after my brother and all," I say.

"I see."

I'm glad to see her. She's the only friend I've had since Perdu, and besides Marie, she's the only one who doesn't make me feel invisible. She's been there for me for years now.

"Why did you come by, Loralie?" I ask her, stroking Marie's head gently to calm her down.

"Oh." Loralie grins, her blue eyes glimmering in an unsettling way. "Just making sure you are all right."

Chapter Forty-Seven

Loralie is beautiful but pale. Her black hair is darker than empty space, and her eyes are . . . chilling. She doesn't act like most people either. She has a free spirit about her. One most of us spend our lives chasing.

I guess that's what I like about her.

"My family is falling apart," I whisper.

Loralie nods and smooths down her purple dress. Her skirt is long, unlike mine, and reaches the ground.

"Mom acts as though she's blind to everyone but herself and Perdu. I used to think she was just coping and she needed time, but now I'm wondering if it's true, if she really isn't aware of anything else. Of me or of Dad. And all Dad cares about is Mom. He's trying to help her, but I think he's really just frustrated with her and wishes she could get better."

I wouldn't have made it through these past few years if I weren't able to talk to Loralie. She's always so patient and kind to me. She's heard the story of Perdu's death a thousand times without complaints and has never been annoyed with my anxiety or tears.

Loralie reaches her hand out for mine and gives me a sad smile. "You've been through a lot," she says. "Losing a brother is . . . Well, I can imagine it wouldn't be easy."

"Do you have any siblings?" I ask her. I know very little about Loralie, but that's never seemed to matter. I guess I've been a little self-absorbed these past few years, always so eager to talk but never to listen.

Loralie shrugs, then shakes her head. "No," she says, wiping something off the sleeve of her dress. "I'm alone."

That's another thing about Loralie that's strange. She always wears the same clothes, a purple dress that looks like it cost a fortune about a hundred years ago.

"I'm sorry," I say.

Loralie gives my hand a squeeze, her long shiny fingernails brushing against my skin. "There's no need to apologize." She smiles at me. It's a sad smile, but soft and kind. "You know, maybe if you could give your mother a conclusion, she would begin to get better."

"A conclusion?"

Marie has settled into my lap and calmed some. She's licking my hand, but every time Loralie moves, Marie snaps her attention back to her.

"Mm-hmm," Loralie hums. "Maybe if she knew what happened to your brother, *why* he died, what made him do it. Maybe then she could come to terms with it all."

Why Perdu left us.

"Do you think that would work?"

Loralie shrugs, like it was just an idea but doesn't matter to her either way. "I'm just trying to help," she says. "I must go. I'll see you soon, Evina."

"Yeah, okay." I would stand and hug her, but Marie won't get off my lap.

Instead, I watch Loralie walk off, her steps so graceful she almost looks as though she is floating. When she is out of sight, Marie springs off my lap and smothers my face in kisses like she is excited to see me.

I fall back onto the grass, giggling and kicking my legs. Her tongue tickles my face, and I push her away, but she won't stop until I'm tired and worn out. My dress is muddy from her paws and from the ground below. I brush it off when I stand and make my way back to the house as Marie trails behind me.

Chapter Forty-Eight

A *conclusion.*

I can't get Loralie's words out of my head. What if she's right? If I can give Mom a reason to be ready to move on, if she can know what happened to Perdu, would that help her at all?

I zip up my coat and tuck my blanket around my feet. The sun has gone down now, and the air filtering in from my open window has that sharp spring chill to it. Marie is lying on my bed in front of me, her head on my lap. She's calmed down from earlier and now even seems sleepy.

"Do you think Loralie is right, Marie?"

She looks up at me with her big puppy eyes. Her face is as droopy as ever, but she looks content to be here.

"You're right, I wouldn't know where to start. Where would I get the answers?"

I stare at the blanket wrapped around me, and a shudder runs through my chest. I turn my head and look at the drawer in my nightstand.

"I know where . . ." I whisper through small trembles before breathing in the fresh air. That drawer has haunted me for so long now. The constant knowledge of what it contains burns a hole deep into my mind. "I can do this."

When I work up the courage to leave my warm bed and stand in front of the drawer, my heart beats just a little faster. I wrap my hand around the small knob. The drawer sticks inside the nightstand, but after a couple small tugs, it slides out. My cold, stiff fingers grab the folded and creased paper.

Back in the comfort of my bed, I stare at the paper sitting in my shaking hands. It's been a few months since I've worked up the courage to open it, but whenever I read the note, it's like I can feel him with me, sitting with me and talking to me. But when the note ends, he dies all over again and I am left alone.

The warmth from the blanket keeps me from moving more than just a few inches. Brown wisps from my fine hair fly in front of my face, and the breeze causes bumps to ripple across my pale skin.

Evina,

I am sorry for what I have decided. I know what this will do to you. Have faith. I've seen you grow in so many ways I never could. You have strength I don't and never had. Please never forget that I do love you. Tomorrow is a new day. I won't live to see the sunrise, but I know you will. I cannot resist the call to end my life. It is too late for me, but it isn't too late for you. You must stay strong and keep yourself safe.

Dolion and Devil Oasis. If you need something to blame for this, blame him and that place. Never step foot in there, Evina. You won't ever be the same once you enter that forsaken land. Once again, tomorrow is a new day. Stand tall, own it, and don't let anyone beat you down. I believe in you. I love you.

-Perdu

Mom knocks on my bedroom door, and I jump, hiding Perdu's note under my blanket.

"Evina, it's cold." Her voice comes through the door, but she doesn't open it.

"Sarah," Dad starts, ready to pick an argument with her again. "Leave her alone. You know she needs it open."

"Why?" Mom asks, sighing with the word. She doesn't sound frustrated, only sad and slightly confused. She genuinely doesn't understand, does she? I roll my eyes and shake my head.

"Let's go to bed, Sarah. I think you're tired." They shuffle across the floor and down the stairs, and I'm left alone with Perdu's note again.

Dolion and Devil Oasis. If you need something to blame for this, blame him and that place.

"Devil Oasis . . ." I look out the window, the cream curtains blowing in the breeze. Past the farmland, before the horizon, a forest stretches far into the distance. Devil Oasis. "What happened to him in there, Marie?"

She's curled up at the foot of my bed, fast asleep.

"He changed after Julie's disappearance. He became . . . distant." I reach and pat the dog's head. "Do you remember how he changed after she was gone? He was so shut in, and he hardly talked to anyone at all. Mom was sick with worry. I think I was more angry at him. I felt like he'd abandoned me. I was so selfish then, wasn't I, Marie?"

She lifts her sleepy head to look at me. Her eyes are dark and wide.

"I'm going." I brace myself as if Marie is going to challenge me. "To Devil Oasis, I mean. I'm going to find out what happened to my brother."

The forest is dark against the starry night sky through the window. A wind rustles through the trees, and even from this distance, I can see them shift.

A knot forms in my chest. Something in there took my brother from me. What if it wants me too?

Chapter Forty-Nine

"Evina!" Dad calls through our home. "Come to the table. Mom and I would like to talk to you."

I smirk to myself, walking through the tall grass as the sunset lights my path. Dad's voice continues to shout throughout our two-story farmhouse. The farther I get, the faster his shouts fade away.

My purple lips spread across my face, dimples showing in my pink cheeks. My breath visible before me causes a shiver, and I wrap the long sweater around my arms and clutch the flashlight tight in my hand.

I feel so free—no walls or doors or windows, only the open air. Nothing to trap me or smother me, nothing to suffocate me. I'm free. And I won't be alone as long as I have Marie with me. She presses against my leg as she walks, her tail wagging, and there's a small jump to her step.

Only one hour from the house rests the place responsible for Perdu's end. Haunting, remorseful, and breathtaking. Devil Oasis. My eyes graze the lake, stretching far beyond my range of vision. Rolling hills and rocky roads, rushing streams with singing birds. There's a buzzing energy here that feels not unlike the gentle hum of doom. But it's beautiful. Full of life and grace. Three years ago, after my first and last venture to the entrance of this land, Perdu lectured me when I dared say this place was beautiful. He told me darkness hid within the shadow of beauty.

My overprotective brother convinced my parents not to allow me to enter the forest. I've always been the young one, and they've always watched out for me, but now it's up to me to be the one to watch out for them.

"They need us, Marie." I shiver. "Mom and Dad need us to be brave."

Now, at the edge of the "forbidden" forest, I hold my breath. Perdu may be right about this place, or he may be wrong, but I need to do this. For Mom, for Dad, and for Perdu.

I inhale, exhale, and step through the gate.

A small dirt path unfolds before me as nerves spike through my chest. My boots prevent my ankles from twisting on the uneven trail, but my focus is on the way the wind has stopped howling despite growing stronger and the intense paranoia that crawls up my spine.

"Evina." Her voice is as smooth as ever. "What are you doing out here? It's almost dark."

"Loralie?" I turn to face her. Her hair almost seems to float around her in the wind. Something feels different about my friend. Even still, a weight falls from shoulders at the familiar face. "What are you doing here?"

Loralie takes a step to me, and Marie growls but doesn't attack. "You walked by my house. I got worried and followed. Don't tell me you're here looking for your brother."

My feet shift. "He's dead."

"Dead doesn't mean gone."

"He's dead, Loralie." A sudden irritation builds inside me. "So, you didn't think I could handle this on my own? I'm not a kid. I don't need someone to watch out for me."

"Would you care for a friend's company?" she asks, holding her pale bony hand out to me. She then takes another step forward and places her hand on my shoulder. "You don't have to do this alone," she whispers.

Marie tucks herself closer to my side as I scan the unknown world of the dark forest.

The lonelier you are, the larger the world is and the colder the shadows are. Flowers die without sunlight, but the rays can scorch the skin off your body. With or without someone, that does not define loneliness. But turning to an empty chair for help when you're bleeding out will beat the feeling into you further. Do I need Loralie with me?

The wind whistles through the trees, and my heart trembles.

With or without Loralie, the image of Perdu walking through these exact trees hours from his death will haunt me. I think of how understanding she's been to me since his death. How supportive and caring.

"Okay, thanks for coming, Loralie." I smile at her and grab her hand as Marie places herself between me and Loralie.

Clair

She's his sister. *His* sister.

I always knew this day would come, didn't I? Evina, like Perdu, is a Witherite. Of course she would end up here.

I look back at the lake as I disappear into the trees, away from its comforting shores. It hurts more and more every time I have to leave Halcyon. I shake my head and start running through the forest. Now is not the time to dwell on painful thoughts. That horrible tug at the back of my heart grows stronger. Sometimes being able to sense the children's presence in the Oasis is awful. And this time I can sense the familiar blood. Another Witherite has come to die.

Hatred burns through me at the thought of the fucking nightmare my life has become. Death after death. I despise the thoughts that say I want to give up, the ones that say I am tired of fighting this never-ending fight. But as long as children are dying, I know I will forever be tied to this.

My reoccurring dream runs through my mind again. There's something so odd about it. About the way it feels as though Dolion is trying to tell me something. There's more to the dream than I realize—I know that—I just can't figure out what it is.

I push myself to run faster. She's somewhere in the Oasis. If I can get near the entrance, I might be able to find her before the twins do. *Hopefully.*

I slam my feet into the earth in a rapid attempt to stop when I reach the darkest part of the forest. The part that stands between me and where I'm guessing Evina is.

Shit.

The thought of whispers from the dead flash through my mind as a chill rips through me, reigniting childhood fears. I could run through the cemetery and get to her faster, or I could go around like I always do and stay where I know I'm safe.

"You can't let your fear control you." Despite my attempt to encourage myself, fear spikes through my heart and keeps my body frozen in place. Fuck this. Fuck everything.

Run, Clair. *Run!*

I keep my eyes trained straight ahead of me, not daring to look at the graves as I sprint. My childhood nightmares flash through my mind, the one's with the ghosts who would drag me below the earth and the hands that would grab at my ankles. I force myself to keep running, afraid fear will hold me in place if I stop.

Chapter Fifty

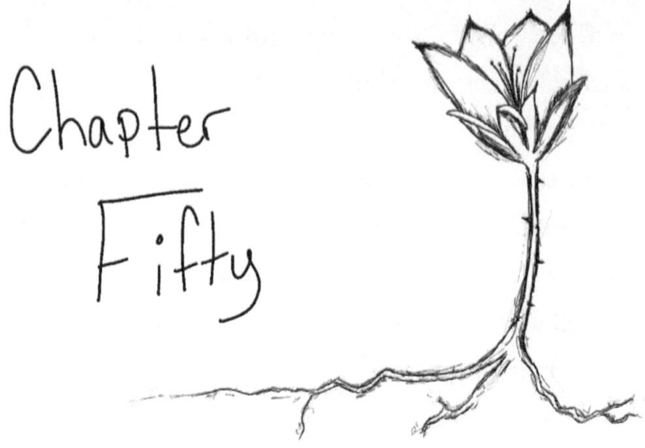

Lady

The curse can feel Evina as she enters the darkness, and it grows excited. Each breath of the earth is patient, and the wind ceases to exist as the clouds swirl restlessly in the sky, almost bending toward the entrance of the land . . . waiting . . . watching . . .

Because today is the day familiar blood returns to the Oasis.

Devil Oasis remembers the way Witherite blood felt years ago when Perdu died, and years before that when Dolion and Loralie died. Now the youngest Witherite has entered the land, and her presence excites something within the curse. The familiar blood. The blood of a family chained to the darkness.

Family.

It's all rooted so strongly to family. My family, their family. No one is safe. The Oasis loves familiar blood.

It has claimed so many lives in my family, and I've been forced to watch every one of them, creating violent storms within my waters. I knew this would come, and I was scared, so I did the only thing I could, did the best I could with what I had to work with: I left my children in hopes that I could survive my mother's sickness, the illness that eventually spread to my mind as well. I became the lake, hoping I would never turn into the mother that mine became. Karl and Edmund needed me. And so I made sure I would always be here to watch over them.

Because my family can never escape. We are bound to this.

I tried to keep my children from falling prey to this nightmare. I made a deal with the Oasis that I had hoped would distance them. As part of the deal, my children's ages were frozen in time for nineteen years. When Dolion and Loralie were born, my children stopped aging, and only when the twins died did they resume. I wanted to keep that barrier of age between them all, hoping an inevitable bond wouldn't form. But children of the curse will always be drawn toward one another.

I failed, like I have failed so many people. And now familiar blood walks naïvely into a trap. Whether dead or alive, Evina Samantha Rose Witherite will never be free of this lush and dangerous land. That's the torture that occurs as a child of the curse. Darkness will never flee.

Evina

"Trust me, Evina." Loralie squeezes my hand. I brought up going to the lake, and since then she's been acting strange. "Don't go there."

"Mom and Dad talked about it—that's why we came here three years ago. To see it. They said the water is crystal clear and the sun shines off it the way it would shine off diamonds."

"Evina." Loralie turns and grabs my shoulders, looking deep into my eyes. "Do you trust me?"

I nod, my body stiff from shock.

"Then *don't* go near the lake."

"Why?"

She gives me a warning glance before continuing down the narrow path. She walks with grace, flawlessly navigating the uneven terrain in heels. Why is she always in heels?

Suddenly, she stops, her skirt swaying around her ankles like it's trying to move forward without her. She's staring straight ahead. A look full of fear, pain, and hope traces every inch of her face. Her hand falls away from mine the way I imagine the hand of a freshly dead body would fall away from its forgotten lover.

"Loralie, what's happening?"

She's staring straight ahead, like she was just confronted by her past.

"Loralie?"

I follow her gaze into the dark trees, which give off a deep blue hue as a shadowy figure disappears into the shadows. I pull my sleeves down over my hands and fold my arms across my chest. There's someone else here? Perdu mentioned someone . . . Dolion, he said in his note. Could it be him?

"No . . ." Loralie whispers once the figure is gone. "Please, no." She reaches her hand out in the direction of the now-empty forest. Then she runs after whoever it was. Her dress flows behind her, and her black curls tangle in the breeze.

The light from my flashlight chases after her, but she vanishes behind a tree.

Marie and I are alone.

I walk under the tallest trees I have ever seen as I try to follow Loralie.

This place, Devil Oasis, is visible from Perdu's old bedroom window. I've seen it multiple times, yet the trees, and everything else, have never seemed this large, magnificent, or terrifying.

Trees loom on either side, leaning over and mocking me. They once seemed beautiful, but now they are possessed by something darker than I can imagine. They want me. I feel their nonexistent eyes watching my every move, hunting me, haunting me. The tall grass blows together, a chorus with a powerful leader, all swaying to the same melody. The winds speak to me, calling me by names I've never heard yet somehow know. A chill runs up my spine.

Stretching the stitches of my sweater, I close it tighter around me. My feet start to ache after a while. My fingers are icy and cold. The leaves on the trees are coming into bloom, and it is beautiful, yet even that strikes fear inside. The farther I walk, the farther I fear I am getting from Loralie.

Shouts and screams echo through my mind, memories of a morning I will never forget. I try to force myself to block them out. An image flickers its way in and out of my mind, like an old TV screen with a bad connection. I shut my eyes and focus on my breathing, just like the doctor told me. Breathe in, breathe out. The image of his hanging body flashes again. Breathe in, breathe out.

It's just my mind messing with me, that's all.

Moans and cries rise into earshot, and this time they aren't memories. They are real. The voice lacks force behind the sounds, giving it a light and airy filter, mixed with dead prerecorded wails. I know I'm supposed to follow. I can feel Loralie pushing me along. Her presence is here. My surroundings have escaped me. I am lost and alone.

Help me, Evina. Loralie's whispers ring in my head. What's happening? *It's almost too late. Find me.*

Tick, tick, tick . . .

I swear I hear a timer now, ticking and counting down. Down to what? My heart beats with each tick. When one increases, the other follows. I'm filled with adrenaline, searching and hoping to see Loralie. I have to find her. What is this? A game of hide-and-seek? My feet rush in one direction only to turn another, never staying on one path, never allowing me the time to look. A light mist rolls over the treetops, flowing down the sides and through the branches. When the drops brush my skin, I shiver, rubbing the exposed place for warmth.

Tick, tick, tick . . .

The timer continues, each tick faster than the last. My heart thumps, shortening my breaths. My fingers find their way to my head, running through my hair and pulling on the loosened strands.

"Loralie!" I call. The mist has filled the forest, blurring my vision. All depth in the world I perceive is gone. Unwinding my fingers from my hair, I extend my arm, reaching to find a solid object to lean against. "I can't find you. What happens if I can't help you?"

Help, Evina. There is no other option.

My hand lands on a tree. The rough bark beneath my fingers brings me peace. When my body is pressed against the tree to prevent a fall, I take a moment to breathe, the mist entering and exiting my mouth. My head spins, and the wind picks up.

Tick, tick, tick . . .

"I can't do this!" I say, closing my eyes tight.

You have to find the strength. You have to.

I take a long breath and force my eyes back open. The world around me is white, misty, windy, and cold. Loralie is not here. I can't do this. I can't find her. Each time the timer speeds up, I panic more. I'm too afraid to leave the tree and search. I can't see, and the wind is too strong.

"You have to help me!" I shout.

Tick, tick—

Nothing? The timer has stopped. I don't see her anywhere.

"Loralie?"

Chapter Fifty - One

The timer, my heartbeat, the moans—every sound stops, and silence rings through my head like an alarm. Every movement is heavy, slow, but airy. If I hold my breath long enough, I think I could float above the trees. I feel separated from myself, watching from the outside in. Judging and hating what I see.

Moonlight reflects off the rolling mist, casting a glow around the forest and rendering my flashlight useless against the shine of the moon. I can see the trees thrashing in the wind, and I know my feet crunch on pine needles and sticks, but not a sound reaches my ears. I can't hear any of it. There's only a distant cry and the sound of someone coughing through their tears. The wails are tired, panicked, and desperate. The sound grows as I walk, coming from behind a tree ten feet ahead. Slowly, the sound of a crackling fire begins to form, but I don't see any flames. From where I stand, I see the shoulder of whoever is crying on the other side. They shake with each sob.

A small feeling prickles at the back of my spine. My heart rate increases. The air becomes heavy.

Not now, panic attack. Even as I think it, I have a feeling this is not a panic attack. It's something different. Something worse.

I reach the tree and prepare myself for whoever is on the other side.

"Hello?" I place my hand on the tree for support and turn to face the crouched figure hiding in the shadows. A boy nearing manhood sits there, hiding his face from me, shriveling more with each cry. My eyes study him for a moment before lighting up in terror. I know him.

"Perdu!" I rush to him, clutching the weak figure close to me. I have to be imagining this. Am I going crazy? But I can hold him, I can feel him, his warm body and trembling limbs. So many things I want to say cause a battle in my mind so chaotic I can't get anything out.

I love you.

I miss you.

I'm sorry, Perdu. I'm so, so sorry.

Deep red gashes line his wrists. The sight of my brother's open skin makes my stomach turn. The images of the pulsing and spitting blood leave stains in my memory. His arms are covered in never-ending red rivers, and his mouth hangs open like he doesn't have the strength to keep it closed. Something tells me this isn't real, but I don't want to believe it. I want to believe I am holding my brother again.

"Are you okay?" I whisper. "What happened to you?"

His body falls limp in my arms. He is still breathing, but he's too weak to carry on alone.

"Evina." Loralie comes into view. Purple dress, black hair, pale skin. Her majestic appearance changed by one feature: tears trickling down her face. I follow Loralie's eyes to Perdu's tired body, fallen and bruised. She cries . . . for him? "I cry for you, Evina." She reads my thoughts. My eyes meet hers. She reaches her hand out. "I know what happened to your brother. I can show you."

I look one last time into Perdu's pain-filled eyes as he begins to fade away, becoming one with his surroundings. My heart twists and aches as I watch him leave, knowing it wasn't really him.

"Tell me what the timer was for," I say.

Loralie glances at her hand, motioning for me to grab it, to trust her. She pulls me up once my hand is in hers.

"Evina, you poor girl. The timer represents the past. You had time to save him. You could've been there for him, to protect him and save his life. You didn't help him soon enough, did you?" Loralie allows her hand to graze my shoulders as her feet guide her body around me. My heart sinks in regret. The day we came back from Devil Oasis, Perdu came to me, his little sister, for help.

"Tell me about it," she whispers as she finishes her circle around me. "I'm your friend. I'm here to help you."

She's all I've had since Perdu died. She's all I have left now.

"He came to me. I rarely saw him cry, but there he was, standing in my doorway, tearstained face and bloodshot eyes. He asked me for help." I look at my feet and kick the dirt. She's right: his death was my fault. Perdu tried to get help. He tried, and I refused. I could've saved him that night. My chest tightens, and I drown in silent tears.

"Tell me what happened then, Evina."

"When . . . When he left, I never saw him again. Loralie, what was he afraid of? What was he running from?"

"I think he told you that night," she tells me, taking my hand in comfort "Evina, he was running from himself. Loneliness *is* suicide's most powerful weapon."

That word is like a stab to my heart. I've gone three years. Three years without ever calling his death that. Suicide. I know it was, but the thought scares me. Loralie's right: I had the time to save him. Time was ticking, and I refused to help him. What can I do now? How do I move on?

"Darling," Loralie whispers, wiping a tear from my cheek. "I'm here for you. Everything will be all right."

She wraps her arms around me and pulls me close to her. I close my eyes and sigh. She holds me like I'm precious to her, like I mean something. The way Mom used to before Perdu's death. I smile slightly, thankful I don't have to go through this alone.

Clair

I finally come out of the cemetery grounds, my heart racing and my lungs burning from the fear I felt while in there. But I'm safe, and it's time I find Evina. Quickly.

A loud bark suddenly breaks through the trees, and I snap my head to the right and reach for my knife. A rather large dog runs through the forest, coming directly for me. I crouch and prepare myself for the worst, but when the dog reaches me, she stops and tilts her head.

I've never seen a dog in the Oasis before, but there were plenty in Perdu's neighborhood when I was there a few years ago. This dog, however, is larger than most I've seen. Her shaggy fur is brown and white, and her eyes are as wide as they can get. She's asking me a question, and when she tilts her head, I know she's waiting for the answer.

I glance at her one more time, making sure she's not a threat, and then I start running through the trees again. I can figure that out later; right now I need to get to Evina.

The dog barks after me, but I ignore it.

Evina has to get out of here safely. If she is going to survive, this night has to play out differently than the others.

The dog dashes alongside me, and though I'm a quick runner, she's much faster than I could ever be. She stops in front of me, making me slam my feet into the ground to stop as well.

I try to step around her, and she blocks my path, whimpering.

"Move!" I shout at her. She whines again before barking at me. I yell into the forest and run my fingers through my hair. My voice echoes back at me through the endless trees. "I have to get to Evina. Do you not understand that?"

She barks again.

I can feel the desperation inside of Evina growing. I have to get to her before the twins' hold on her becomes too strong.

"Look, I would try to help you find your way home if Evina weren't here."

She barks again. The dog whines and lies on the ground, looking up at me with sad eyes. When I try to move around her again, she braces herself and growls.

"What?" I snap. "What the hell do you want from me?"

She suddenly breaks out into a sprint in one direction and then stops and looks at me.

"I can't follow you right now."

She runs in a circle whining and barking. She's pleading with me. This dog is panicking. Something is wrong. Finally, the loose piece falls into place in my mind. This must be Evina's dog, and she needs help.

She barks yet again.

"All right, all right, I'll follow you." I gesture into the forest. "Go, I'll follow you. Go on."

The dog walks briskly through the forest, and the air grows colder the more I struggle to keep up.

Chapter Fifty-Two

Evina

Loralie strokes my hair gently as I cry in her lap. The fabric of her dress is soft and silky against my tear-covered face. I grip her skirt tight in my hand, afraid to be without her. I hate being alone, and I've been so alone since I got here. When I'm not with Loralie, I'm all . . . all alone. A sudden thought makes me bolt up and search the trees.

"Marie?" I call. Where is she? My heart jumps into my throat, and an unsettling image of Marie lying dead somewhere flashes through my mind. What if an animal got her? When did I even lose her?

Think, Evina, think. When was the last time you saw her?

I . . . I don't know!

I stand up and start running in the direction we came. She has to be here somewhere.

"Evina?" Loralie asks as she stands up and runs after me. "Evina!"

I stop and snap my head to Loralie. "Marie. Where is she?" I'm out of breath, and each word is a small wheeze. Tears burn my eyes, and my hands are shaking. "I can't lose her, Loralie. Loralie, I can't lose her!" A sob breaks through my words as hot tears spill from my eyes.

"Evina." Loralie places a gentle hand on my shoulder. I fall into her arms impulsively and sob into her dress. "It's all right, Evina. Everything will be all right."

"She was *his* dog!" I pull myself away from her. "It's not 'all right.' "

When she looks at me, there's a sadness I can't quite place.

"I'm sorry," I whisper. "I shouldn't have snapped."

Another tear falls down my face as I scan the forest again. She's out there somewhere. Dead or alive, Perdu's dog is out there. And she's alone. I was so self-absorbed I hadn't even realized she was missing.

Loralie wraps her arms around me again, and I melt into her hug. She's so calming. Something about her is soothing in a seemingly unnatural way. She's like a breath of fresh air in a closed room. She's like the night sky, dark but glimmering with beautiful stars.

"Let's sit down," she says. "Marie is a smart dog—she'll find us. Right now you need to rest."

Loralie guides me to a tree, and we sit at the base. She puts an apple in my hand and closes my fingers around it.

"Eat," she whispers.

The apple is a deep red, like it's been dipped in blood. The gashes on Perdu's arms flicker in my memory, and I suddenly feel queasy. Biting into that apple would be like biting into human flesh. I drop it and watch it roll a few feet away.

"Do you think she's dead?"

Loralie sighs and shakes her head. She grabs the apple and bites into it, and I have to turn my eyes away. "Let's talk about something else," she says.

Chapter Fifty-Three

Loralie and I exchange stories for a while. All of my stories are embarrassing; all of Loralie's are adventurous. She's actually lived and done things and seen things. She makes her life seem so exciting.

"I was even engaged to a man once," she says, but her eyes stop sparkling when she mentions it.

"What happened?"

She shakes her head but doesn't answer.

The wind turns cold, and Loralie tenses next to me.

"I'm sorry. We don't have to talk about it."

She smiles, and I swear I see a spark of flames in her eyes. "The past has passed." She sighs.

"I've never been engaged." I cringe at my terrible attempt to change the subject. "I've never even had a boyfriend."

"Do you know Clair?" she asks, and something within her darkens and comes to life at the same time.

Clair. Perdu mentioned that name once, on the night he . . .

"No," I say.

"He and I were lovers once." She smiles. Something about Loralie seems off, like this conversation is . . . ungenuine. Like the real Loralie isn't here with me now. She's changed, and I don't like it. I shift uncomfortably next to her and keep my eyes on the ground.

The cold air begins to bite at my cheeks, and I shiver.

"It's cold," Loralie says quietly, keeping her eyes intently trained on the forest.

"Yes, it is."

The way she holds herself shifts. Loralie slowly cowers, though from what, I'm not sure. The emotion in her eyes flickers from nonexistent to overwhelming and back again. There's something between the trees, just out of sight, and it's messing with Loralie. She looks down at the palm of her hand before her eyes drift back to the bluish-gray forest.

"Loralie?" My voice is so quiet I wonder if she heard me.

"Not now, child." Her voice has an odd melody to it. "There are things at work greater than you."

Then she hums.

I shiver and clench the hem of my sweater.

Then, like she's not in control of herself, Loralie stands and grabs her skirt. Her movements are slow and airy, and she walks. Something is pulling her in, and I don't think she has the power to resist it.

Gentle sprinkles begin falling from the sky even though there's not a cloud in sight. Loralie turns to face the heavens, squinting to keep the water from her eyes.

"Dolion," she whispers.

Something moves in the forest again, and I suddenly feel like I am intruding, like whatever is about to happen isn't meant for me to see.

Pain blisters on the side of my face, pulling me out of the reverie as my cheek stings. I move my hand away from the spot and find blood on my fingers.

What the heck?

I scan the forest but find nothing. What hit me?

Another painful sting slices through my other cheek before a third takes a slash at my eyebrow.

The blood runs beside my eye and mixes with my fresh tears. "Loralie!" I cry out, my voice breaking. "What's happening?"

She holds out her hand before a drop of rain slices through her palm. No, not rain. These are shards of ice.

Loralie turns slowly to look at me, fear and terror strung through her face. "I'm sorry," she says. "He's angry at me. This is the only way."

"The only way to what?" I yell at her, attempting to be heard over the growing sound of the ice showering the forest.

"Communicate."

I have no idea what Loralie is talking about, but the blood flowing from her skin doesn't seem to bother her. She holds out her hands and welcomes the pain. Another ice shard hits me, this time on my wrist, and I instinctively pull it close to my chest for protection. Blood trickles from the small wound. I run toward the nearest tree and cling close to its base, hoping the branches will protect me.

But out in the killer storm, Loralie remains. She seems to be basking in it, in the pain, in the blood streaking down her ashy skin.

"Loralie!" I try to yell at her, but a dark figure in the trees holds her attention. All I can see is a silhouette, but it looks like a person. "Loralie!"

She doesn't turn away from the stranger in the forest. Panic grows in my chest as my heart slams against my ribs. The storm is going to kill her.

My only friend, the girl who's been there for me since Perdu's death, the only person I have left in this world is about to die. I clench my fists and prepare to make a run through the ice to drag her under the tree.

She isn't going to save herself. Someone has to do it.

But before I can, Loralie turns and faces me. My body freezes, and the air deflates from my chest as I stare at the horrific sight. The blood streaked down her face and the hopelessness shot through her drifting gaze cause me to pull my sleeves over my hands and curl back into the tree. I find myself wishing I could just open a window to get this fear to go away, like I've done with all my other fears.

Blood and death and terror.

"Dolion." Loralie's whisper somehow makes it to my ears. Something about her seems wrong. This isn't the Loralie I know. She smiles a wicked smile as she stares at me.

I scream.

My feet move almost as fast as my heart pounds into my chest. My own rib cage. My own bones.

Bones and blood and death.

Run, I mentally shout at myself as I sprint away from Loralie. The ice shards press in on me as they rain down, the way the walls would close in on me at home.

My lungs burn, and my feet ache. My knees weaken and threaten to give out. I step on a rock, and a shooting pain spikes up the side of my leg. I fall to the ground as tears spring to my eyes. My ankle is throbbing, but the pain of the intense fear in my chest is significantly stronger. I try to stand, but my ankle won't hold any weight, and I collapse back to the earth. I can feel death approaching as the figure Loralie saw in the trees steps closer to me. I didn't know he'd followed me.

"Help!" I call.

I'm struggling to see through my tears, but I claw my way forward, inching toward whatever hope I have left. My fingers dig into the cold dirt, and my good foot helps push me away from the monster behind me. The one who summoned this storm. The figure's shadow moves over me, and my entire body weakens as the adrenaline vanishes. It's over.

The sound of the figure shifting in the dirt behind me causes one last tear to fall down my trembling face. These are the last moments of my life. Never will I feel anything other than this terror again. I won't smile or laugh or cry or even miss Perdu *ever* again.

Then the forest quiets.

All sounds of life behind me disappear.

I turn my shaking body over to find that I'm alone. No Loralie, no mysterious figure, no more ice storm. No rain even. And the forest isn't wet.

It's just me, the trees, and the wind. My body shakes, and it feels like even my bones are vibrating in fear. My ankle throbs, but stretching it out slowly calms the sharp pains. I don't think it's broken or sprained, just sore. If it weren't for my boots, it would have been a lot worse. I sit on the ground, my body broken, my eyes filled with tears, and all the pain of the fear finally catches up to me. With the tight ache in my chest, the sharp pain in my muscles, and the loud ringing in my head, all I want is to sleep. I curl up in the dirt, folding my body in on itself until I feel some sort of comfort. And I lie there, staring off into nothing. My mind drifts to a very numb place. I think about everything and nothing, and yet somehow the nothingness overwhelms me more than any thought I could possibly have.

Blood and death and fear. It pressed in on me until I had no other option but to give in. And now I'm scared and cold and alone. Fog rolls between trees, and the light of the moon makes the forest gray.

Blood. On Perdu's arms in the vision. Running down Loralie's face. My own wounds no longer bleed, and that upsets me. Blood. It runs through my body, trapped inside the prison of flesh. I've been trapped before. Trapped inside a home with no air to inhale. Slowly, the oxygen was sucked out, and there was nothing left for my lungs to breathe. The walls closed in on me. All I needed was an opening. A door or a window. The blood trapped in my body is going to suffocate and die just like I almost did. And then I'll die. Never a release, never another breath.

I press my fingernails against my wrist. The blood needs a window. Just a little fresh air.

Chapter Fifty-Four

The small wound burns. All I could manage was just a scratch before the pain became too much and I pulled away. My light jeans are torn at the knees, and the sleeves of my cream sweater are brown with dirt. The only thing still holding up is my boots. My body is tired. I want to curl up in the dirt and sleep until the sun comes up.

I want to go home and be safe and warm in my own bed. Even the pressing walls of the house don't seem so bad now. I want my mom and my dad. I want my brother, and I want Marie. I don't want this anymore. I don't even want Loralie.

I'm worried about her though. Something bad was happening to her. I don't know what the figure did to her that made her act that way. I hope she is okay.

A small white flower sprout is nestled between tall green weeds. Something about the flower reminds me of what I've lost. Not my brother, not my family, and not Marie, but myself. The girl I used to be and was supposed to be. Evina Samantha Rose Witherite. I was innocent. I was young and naïve for my years. Mature in all the wrong ways and immature in all the right ones. I represented eternal youth of the mind. I was a little girl at heart despite my age. Darkness couldn't get to me—not the way it got to others. I'm not Evina anymore; I'm someone meant to entertain. Not a story that needs to be told. I was once this little flower, but I've been picked and grinded up until the gore and fear drowned out the simple girl I once was. My petals aren't white anymore—they're black.

I'm a broken flower lying on the forest floor. Alone. In the dark.

A dog barks off in the distance, and it makes me miss Marie. She reminded me of who I was supposed to be and who Perdu believed I was.

The dog barks again.

I reach out and touch the soft petals of the flower. *Evina* means life. That's who I am.

I close my eyes and listen to the sounds of the forest—the hum of the insects, the calming notes of the birds, the brush of the tree branches in the wind, and the barks of the dog, which have turned into quiet whimpers.

Suddenly, a wet nose presses against my cheek.

"Is she still alive?" a male voice asks.

The dog licks me, and I sit up to get away from the animal. The moonlight shines on her, making her fur appear glowing.

Marie!

She has never looked so beautiful, and I have never been so relieved to see her. She sits next to me, her tail wagging against the ground and her head high in the air, full of pride.

"You did it!" the man standing behind Marie exclaims. "You found her!"

He takes a step toward us, and I scramble in the dirt to back away from him. He stops moving when he sees how scared I am. Slowly, he reaches his hand down to Marie, and she lets him pet her; she even nudges his hand with her head.

"You don't have to trust me," he says to me. "After everything you've seen, I understand why you don't. But she does, and that should be enough for you to at least hear me out."

The man seems younger than I first thought he was. Blond hair, pale eyes, dressed in old worn clothes, a brown leather jacket keeping him warm in the spring mist, a white T-shirt underneath. There's a knife at his hip that makes me nervous, but he doesn't reach for it.

"Where did you find her?" I gesture to Marie. "I thought she was . . ." I can't finish my sentence, but I know he knows what I mean.

"She came to me," he says. "She knew you needed help, and she came to find me."

I look at Marie. She seems so sure of herself and the situation. She brought a strange man to me, and now I'm isolated in a dark forest with him. He could do anything he wanted to me and . . . Would anybody ever find out?

"Marie." I force my words out through the fear threatening to close my throat. "Come on. Now."

She steps closer to the man, rubbing against his leg.

"Marie," I say just a little louder. "Let's go. Please." The desperation in my voice makes me want to cry. I'm too weak to fight back if he decides to attack me, and for some reason, Marie seems to trust him. Would she protect me if something bad happened?

"Please just let me explain, Evina," the man says, reaching down to pet Marie again.

Fear spikes through my chest. It's so painful I can't breathe. He knows my name.

"Now, Marie." My voice shakes, and I know unless I run and leave Marie, this is the end. I'm crying now. I can't stop it. And my hands are trembling. I'm alone with this man.

"Evina—"

"No," I cry, surprised at myself for having the guts to interrupt him. "No."

"I knew your brother," he says.

Perdu only mentioned one person from this place in his letter. This has to be him.

"D-Dolion?"

"What?" the man says through a small chuckle. "No, not Dolion. My name is Clair. I live here." He smiles at me, showing dimples through his stubble.

Chapter Fifty-Five

"**I** wouldn't believe me in your situation either," Clair says. "But I promise you, Evina, I'm not going to hurt you."

"You knew Perdu?" My voice won't go louder than a whisper. Perdu did say something about him once, but I didn't know Clair had to do with this place. It's hard to imagine the man standing before me actually knew my brother. It's hard to imagine this is all reality and not some nightmare.

"I did." Clair gives a sad smile.

"Do you know Dolion?"

Clair nods slowly, like he's deciding if that's his actual answer. Then he looks me dead in the eye and says, "I guess you could say that."

Marie looks up at me, whimpering again, like she's pleading with me. To do what? Trust this man?

"Evina—"

"How do you know who I am?" My curiosity interrupts him.

"Perdu would talk about you."

"No, how do you know I am his sister and not someone else?"

"You look so much like him," Clair says. "You couldn't be anyone else."

Something about his answer seems off, like it's only part of the truth.

"You don't have to trust me," he repeats. "But will you let me show you something before you run from me?"

I glance down at his knife again. It wouldn't be hard for him to hurt me. *He's still a complete stranger, Evina*, I tell myself. *He could still hurt you.*

Clair sees what I'm looking at and reaches for his knife. I back away. He runs his fingers along the cotton-wrapped hilt like a painful war is raging in his head, then pulls it out of its sheath and extends it, handle pointing toward me.

"Take it," he says with an unsure voice. His eyes remain fixed on the knife. "I told you, I'm not here to hurt you."

I reach out and wrap my shaking fingers around the knife. When it leaves Clair's calloused hand, I can see a sort of fear in his eyes. I keep a firm hold on it and wait for Clair to say something, but all he does is watch the weapon.

"What did you want to show me?" I finally ask him, pointing my flashlight at him to get a better look.

He squints his eyes and blocks the light, and I immediately pull away, feeling bad.

"Follow me," Clair says as he slowly turns into the trees, running his fingers through the light hair he obviously cuts himself. It's kind of cute, oddly charming in a way, but definitely uneven. I follow behind him and listen to our feet navigate the ground. He's confident in the forest. He must have lived here for a long time.

After a couple minutes of walking, he looks back at me. "You know, the walk out is much easier with help."

What he said seems odd, but I stay silent as we continue walking. Eventually, he turns and makes his way up a hill. He watches his feet, careful not to step on any of the hundreds of flowers. The hill is covered in a symphony of color. Pinks, reds, oranges, yellows, purples, whites—anything and everything. I can't identify a single one, especially not in the dark. Each flower is unique. As we emerge at the top, I am surprised to see a very small graveyard. It has a certain feeling of terror to it that I've never felt before. Many of the wooden graves appear new. At the head of the path leading in is a small sign that reads *Edicius Hill.*

As my flashlight falls onto the graves, one catches my eye.

"Perdu."

Chapter Fifty-Six

Clair waits at the start of the small path as I walk over to Perdu. He's in the first row of graves. I reach my hand out, and my fingers graze the handmade board, proving this is in fact real. *Perdu*. His name is carved onto the surface. My finger, running along the rough wood, finds the word, tracing each letter of his name. This is my brother. I have visited the tree we buried him under many times, but I am always filled with memories and horror from the morning I found him. Now I almost feel like he is here, like this is where he belongs, like this is where I belong.

"What's this doing here?" I turn to Clair. It takes him a moment to pull his eyes from the grave.

"I couldn't forget him," Clair says. He looks at me, but his eyes are distant. "I couldn't act like I had never known him."

"You cared about him," I say.

He protected my brother's memory. Surprising him and surprising myself, I walk the few steps to Clair and wrap my arms under his. His muscles tense for a moment, but when they relax, I pull away, my face growing red from embarrassment. I look at my feet.

"Couldn't you have saved him?" I ask, looking up into his light eyes.

"I tried. I tried to save them all." He chokes slightly on his words.

I look around at the graves. Each one has a first name carved deep into the wood. Picked and planted flowers lie around the graves. Limited trees give the area great light, even at night. He tried to save them.

"They all died here? Did they all . . . kill themselves?"

Like Perdu, I think but can't say.

"Yes."

"How many are there?"

"Fifty-nine." He's so quiet I can hardly hear him.

I shake my head and pull on the sleeves of my sweater. It's all too much to think about. All of the families destroyed, just like my family. I give in to the exhaustion in my body and let my knees crumple to the ground. I sit at the top of the hill and stare out at the dark forest.

He sighs. The dirt next to me shuffles as he sits. I stiffen, not sure if I should move away or not. I choose to stay. He doesn't say anything for a while. When I look at Clair, he looks back at me. His diamond-colored eyes offer warmth. Something inside me longs to believe that he is good. That he really wants to help me.

"I'm here to listen," he says. "Or sit in silence if you'd prefer that."

"What is this place?" I ask him. "Honestly."

"Honestly?" he asks, and I nod in response. "This is the forest where I grew up." He says it simply, like that explains everything. "It's unlike any other place. It's . . . Well, it has a mind of its own. It knows what it wants, and it takes what it wants."

"What does it want?" My voice is shaking.

Even though I'm not looking at Clair, I can hear him shift in the dirt. "Right now? Right now it wants you."

Me.

"Because of my brother?"

Clair sighs, and his words are full of pain. "I don't know."

I should have asked Loralie why I'm here. Maybe she would have known. My eyes light up as recognition flares to life. He's Clair. Loralie talked about him.

"Loralie mentioned you," I say suddenly.

He scoffs. "I'm sure she did."

"She said . . ." Heat rushes to my face. "Well, she said that you two were together. Like, that you were her boyfriend or something."

His eyes suddenly light up, and he laughs like that's the funniest thing anyone has ever said. "She told you that? Of course she did."

"So, she was wrong?"

"Very."

I have never heard his voice so stern. His hand falls to his side.

"I'm a little worried about her," I admit. There has been a small breeze since I got to Devil Oasis, but it's finally warm instead of tainted with that frigid chill. I look out into the darkness to the trees and shadows of Devil Oasis. She's out there somewhere.

"Don't be." Clair's voice is emotionless.

"I haven't seen her since the ice storm. I'm worried something happened to her." I think of Loralie covered in blood and have to fight that memory out of my head.

Clair turns to look at me, the glow of the moon reflected in his eyes. His hand grips my arm. "What ice storm?"

"I don't know, but it hurt so bad. It felt like it was tearing shreds through my flesh." I focus hard to keep myself from crying. I have a sudden urge to grab Clair's hand and never let go. Reassurance that I'm not alone, that I'm safe.

Clair's hand tightens around my arm, and his eyes widen. "Evina, there was no storm."

"But . . . But that's impossible. I saw it. And so did Loralie." A new sort of fear shivers its way into my heart.

Clair's eyes darken in a way that causes new fear to take root. "Don't trust her, Evina."

"I *felt* the storm."

"She's trying to hurt you, just like she hurt Perdu and everyone else in this damn cemetery." There's a bite to his words. His hand flies out to gesture at the graves.

My heart gives a faint tremor. Loralie?

"Loralie is my friend. She cares about me. Dolion is the bad guy. Perdu said to blame him for what happened. Dolion, not Loralie."

"Dolion is Loralie's *brother*," Clair says. "You can't trust either of them."

"You don't know that," I say before I can think better of it. She's been my only friend since Perdu's death.

She said she doesn't have any siblings, I think. *Clair could be lying about it.*

"How could you . . . ?" I utter the words as my thoughts run frantic through my mind. Clenching my fists, I'm filled with a frustration and sense of betrayal I didn't expect. "She's my only friend, Clair. And she's been there for me much, *much* longer than you."

Fire flashes across Clair's eyes for a moment. His hand curls slowly into a tight fist as his other pulls at his hair. Then he closes his eyes and breathes deep. When his eyes open again, all of the fight I saw has disappeared.

"You have to listen to me, Evina." His voice is surprisingly calm.

"Marie, come." I glare at my dog, who has stayed by Clair's side. "Now."

She stays with Clair, and an intense anger floods through my veins.

"Fine," I snap. "Stay with him."

I tuck Clair's knife into my jeans and run down the hill, trampling the flowers on my way. My flashlight falls from my hand, and though it makes my heart turn, I leave it and keep running. I have to stay away from him, away from everyone. He tried to trick me. I can't trust him.

Can I trust anyone?

Loralie. I have to trust Loralie. She's always been there for me. There's a small voice in the back of my mind, though, that tells me Clair is right. Loralie isn't who she said she is.

Panic swells in my chest as a horrifyingly familiar feeling creeps its way in. The musty air, the silent scenery, the pit in my stomach. It's not a panic attack. It's her. This feeling is Loralie.

Evina, darling. Her voice echoes in my head. I avoid searching the trees around me for her. I don't want to see her. *Why are you running, dear?*

"Don't you trust me?" She appears in my path as her whispers become spoken words.

Chapter Fifty-Seven

The sight of Loralie standing in front of me makes me instantly wish I had stayed with Clair. She doesn't seem like the girl I knew before. Something about Clair felt right. It was a sort of comfort and security I haven't felt in a very long time. And I only now realize how cold Loralie is and how calculating her blue eyes are.

I take a step back, my shoulders folding forward as my body shrinks away from her.

"You needn't be afraid," Loralie says. "It's me. Would I ever hurt you?"

"Who's Dolion?" I ask her with a confidence I didn't think I had.

Loralie's eyes widen at first. Then she becomes . . . almost sad.

"Dolion?" Her voice is small when she says his name.

"Who is he?" I ask again.

"Dolion was my brother."

So, that's it. Clair is right.

Does that mean he's right about everything? I take another step away from Loralie, suddenly feeling her presence press into me like a room I can't escape. I have to get away from her. I need to be alone, away from everyone. Is there anyone I can trust? Loralie continues talking, saying something about how this means she understands me because she had a brother too. I'm not fully certain what she's saying though. I'm trying to figure out how to get away. Then she says something about Perdu's death, and I snap at her.

"Perdu didn't deserve to die. It should have been me, not him. I'm the one who turned him away when he needed help."

"It's not too late," Loralie says. "You could still get what you deserve. I can lead you to a better road, free of this guilt and shame you bear. I care about you, Evina. I've always cared about you."

Then she hugs me, the way she has so many times before. She wraps her arms around me and pulls me close to her. She's so familiar. Her scent of roses reminds me of the times I've cried into her shoulder, the hours she has spent listening to my pain. She knows me better than anyone. She knows why I'm in pain, knows the guilt I've felt for years. She knows me. Do I know her?

If I follow her, if I allow her to help me, where will I end up? If moving on were so easy, many people wouldn't have been strangled in this web.

"I'll be here with you, like always. Don't you want to know what type of pain your brother felt? I'm here, Evina, just like I've been here for you for years."

Of course I want to know what happened to him. I nod my head slowly. And I want Loralie to be the person I always believed she was. Maybe she is; Clair could still be lying.

Loralie pulls out a small blade, and slowly she slides it across her hand. Blood comes, dripping down her forearm to the fold of her elbow. I watch, almost feeling a sudden need to see my own blood, craving what she has, the pain, the beauty of the mark.

This is what happened to my brother.

"Loralie, I'm scared." My lips move, but no sound comes out. Still, she understands me.

"This will help you know what happened to him, Evina. All I want is for you to have the peace you deserve."

Sweat beads above my brow, and my knees feel broken and weak. Hands shaking, I reach for the silver blade.

"I'm here." Loralie places her hand on mine. I look to the only person who would ever be by my side long enough to support this, knowing I will be okay with her here. My heart chokes itself, afraid of the unknown, knowing I can never go back after this, not knowing what all it will change.

I cut once, drawing blood with the raw wound. I thought I would feel something—pain, pleasure, despair. Numb. I feel numb. The pain is there, I can feel it, but I don't register it. I see the pain occurring with each open slice. I know it's there. One after another, blood begins to pour. Each time I damage myself, Loralie's smile grows and her eyes brighten. Bringing the blade to my arm again, I prepare for another. Only God himself can stop me now. I look to Loralie for reassurance. She smiles, lowering her glare. Loralie is my comfort. She understands me. She knows how much I loved my brother. She wants what I want. She cares about me. She loves me. If she didn't, she wouldn't be here when I need her. Once again, I slit my arm. The blood surfaces and leaves trails behind each drop. I look up, wanting to see Loralie's satisfaction again only to be greeted by the trees and the wind.

"Loralie?" The ring of my small voice journeys into the void of the forest before me. "Where are you?" I look at my hands and arms, bloody and torn. Alone in the forest, I call out for help. The numbness fades.

My cuts burn. They sting and itch. Why wasn't I strong enough to leave the blade alone? It's all my fault. I can't blame anyone for this. Not Loralie, not Clair, not Mom or Dad. My heart is strangled by its own pain, pulling me deeper into the fear and hatred of my actions.

"What's happened to me?" The tears emerge as I curse myself into the night. Even the birds singing around me seem to be cursing my name, calling out to me as if I'm a witch or demon. Heartache. That's what follows the blood.

Give it a chance. Her voice plays through my mind. *Give it a chance, Evina. You'll learn to love the hatred.*

I look around for the girl, in need of her guidance. "Wh-where are you?" My voice bounces around in the trees and makes its way back to me. I sound weak and pitiful, my voice cracking, breaking, choking, and fading. Comparing that with how I feel would be a waste. How do I feel?

Feel.

Feel in my heart, mind, and body. How do I feel? Weak, scared, alone, broken, angry, foolish, ashamed—the list goes on and on. I hate being alone. *Please, someone come find me. Please.*

My thoughts transition to spoken mumbles. "Help me . . . Someone . . ." I stumble around the forest, thinking if I can just make it back to Clair, I will be fine.

"Please . . . Don't let me go through this alone . . ." How is there this much blood? Am I dying? This can't be right. "Help . . ."

Clair

I try to focus on something other than Evina alone in the dark woods as I quickly tie the board down over my window. Now my shack is secure and safe for the night. Safe for me to leave it alone while the twins are out.

Evina can't trust Loralie, but I misjudged Evina's loyalty to her, and I drove her away. Everything is failing. The twins have already had a chance to manipulate Evina, and so far they are succeeding.

I've always focused on the victim, on protecting them as much as possible. Maybe I need to cut it off at the root of the problem instead. To stop Dolion and Loralie from harming her, maybe we have to confront them instead of running from them.

"Stay here," I tell Marie as I go to close the door to my shack, that familiar pinch in my chest making me long to remain within the walls of my home. "You'll stay warm in here, and I'll be back soon, hopefully with Evina."

As if she understands, Marie lies on the floor by the fire and closes her eyes.

I shut the door and turn from my comforting home and into the dark forest.

As I walk, beginning what might be a long search for Evina, the events of the past day won't stop filtering through my head. The dream that's been on repeat for months now, years even, something I can't quite place nagging at the back of my mind like a warning, and Perdu's little sister coming into this death trap. There has to be a way to end this, a way to watch the rot that's built itself around my life die a violent death.

Stop Dolion and Loralie instead of trying to protect Evina from them, I remind myself. This has to play out differently than the last victims did if she is going to survive. But how do I do that?

Dolion and Loralie, though they don't know it, were originally meant to be one person before they were torn apart in their mother's womb. Which would explain why they are so desperate to be with each other again. And Loralie once said that the reason they are doing this to everyone *is* to be with each other again.

As I step over a large rock on the ground, my mind continues reeling. The thoughts run faster than my brain can comprehend as stress fills my body.

If I can figure out how to get them to be able to talk to each other and interact again, they will have no reason to go after Evina.

Looking out at the forest, I watch as the world continues to move on despite my presence. I want the pain to stop, I want Dolion and Loralie to stop, I want everyone to be safe, but I don't want to keep trying to save them anymore.

I don't think I can handle this right now. But, of course, I don't have a choice. I hold my hand out in front of me and watch as it trembles, the stress coursing through me.

My head hurts, but my heart is numb.

I want to run, but I can't. Running means abandoning. No one else will do this job. It has to be me.

I can't handle this right now . . . but I have to.

The world moves on around me as if I don't matter, as if my pain is invisible. Even when I cry, it's as if they're silent tears. I'm afraid of what will happen to me if I keep going like this, if I keep ignoring the weight that's crushing me. Maybe my heart isn't numb; maybe it hurts so bad it's been shocked into stillness. I don't think I'm strong enough to keep going.

So, what happens to me?

I keep moving forward anyway. I shut up and do my job.

Just keep smiling for them all, keep trying to fight back my anger so they feel safe, keep trying to befriend the ones who are about to die.

I don't want to do this anymore. I close my eyes and let the single tear fall. It's cold.

The forest stretches out around me, swallowing me in the isolation of my life.

I don't think I can keep going. I open my eyes and push the fear deeper inside me, stuffing it with every other emotion I can't afford.

Dolion and Loralie are my life.

Fuck Loralie.

I haven't even kissed her since Perdu's death, but the more I break inside, the more I crave her corruption.

Shaking my head, I breathe in, the air colder in my lungs than I expected. It takes all my strength to resist her and her darkness; every time I look at her, the lust is so powerful it nearly drives me mad. That's what she wants. I can't give in to her now.

CURSE RULE #4

No killing. In death, the twins will be capable of interacting with the physical world but will not harness the power to murder, only to manipulate the minds of their targets to encourage thoughts of suicide. This is the most powerful form of death; this is the death that must be achieved.

Chapter Fifty-Eight

Evina

"Help…" Curled under a tree, leaning on the base for support, I mumble the same words over and over. "I'm scared…Please …Anyone…Help…"

The wind picks up. My sweater, warm as it may be, has never been good to block out the air. The black trees towering over me and the tall grass make me feel small. To my relief, the blood on my arm is not what I saw before. It's not as bad as I made it out to be. The cuts seem smaller too. I can feel the anger from inside me spilling out through the self-made gashes. It is a release. But it's also a sponge. I can feel the negative energy that has been circling around me for years find its entrance in. This negative energy I've heard so many people call depression. Certain things you can only keep out for so long. Maybe I, with Loralie's help, have sent myself down the path I belong. If I am meant to follow Perdu, so be it.

The forest is beautiful. Rich in love. A love that's haunting and makes you wake up wishing you were dead. The type of love no one dares to live without but that chokes you with every breath. If you take one step without it on your own once you've promised yourself to it, it pounces and feasts on your heart. A forest overwhelming you with feelings of regret and longing. A forest promising a better day. Black trees darken the atmosphere but provide cover for the wounded. Grass reaching my torso brushes against the creatures passing through. Everything is graceful, everything is gentle. But as they say, it is the calm before the storm.

Here I sit, waiting. Waiting for life, waiting for death. Waiting for Clair, waiting for Loralie. I don't care what happens to me. I have no reason to. Maybe if this blood on my hands were only my own, maybe if I hadn't let temptation grab me and lead me, maybe if I could guarantee I'd be alive this time tomorrow, maybe if I could change, my life would be worth something. Anything. I don't cry because I feel the pain—I cry because I can't feel enough. My words mean nothing anymore if all I can do is beg and plea. My broken heart can't feel this loneliness any longer. In a single second, I mentally cracked, and with a knife to my arm, I picked at the crack until I split. If I could write my thoughts, I would burn them. If I could speak them to someone, I'd have to kill them. Get my thoughts out and let them die. How else can a person cope? Instead, they swim around inside, gambling with my sanity and peace. Tonight may be my time to rise and win the fight my brother lost. Burning the midnight oil means nothing when you can't tell time. Wait for morning to come, and darkness has to flee in fear. Ticktock. Each second brings you closer to your death. Ticktock. Each minute passes by your life. Ticktock. I think I'm going to die tonight.

Brush, brush, brush.

Something's rubbing against the grass. Someone is here, moving and walking about. Possibly looking for something. Possibly looking for me. I pull my feet toward my body, wrapping my arms around my legs. I stay small and hidden by the grass. It's Loralie. She's coming back for me. I've given her the smallest entrance, and now she thinks she owns me. Perhaps she does. Perhaps my thoughts will always be controlled by her. When I wind up dead tonight, I hope Clair buries me beside Perdu. Unless he's angry at me now.

The person walks closer to me, and I reach for Clair's knife, holding it tight in my unsteady hand. She can't have me. I try to make myself small, but my feet slip on the dirt. I stay still, my heart beating frantically, and hope Loralie didn't hear.

I jump when the person breaks through the veil of trees and comes into view. But it's not Loralie. Clair runs through the forest. With desperate breaths and an exhausted voice, he calls for me. I search, but Marie isn't with him. Is she okay?

"Evina!" he yells. "Evina, where are you? We have to talk."

For a second, I consider coming out of hiding, but I don't know Clair. I don't know if I can trust him or not. I push back into the tree and attempt to sink my body into the dirt.

The moment comes, the moment goes, and Clair is gone. His departure makes my heart drop. Maybe he was my only chance at getting out of here. Maybe I ruined everything. Maybe he needs me. I think I need him. I push off the ground, running in the direction he went.

"Clair!" I call after him just as he called for me. "I'm over here, Clair. I'm over here!"

It's been a while since I saw Clair, and I fear I might have lost him. The longer I walk, the farther I think I'm getting from him and the lonelier I feel. I should have come out of hiding when he was there. Being with a man I can't trust seems frightening, but as I venture deeper through the whistling winds of the forest, I know the most terrifying thing is being alone. I need Clair.

I journey through Devil Oasis at a slow speed, my tired mind and body limiting me, until I finally break out of the dark trees and onto the bank of the lake. The harrowing wind has calmed to a breeze, and my hair blows behind me gently. The water makes sounds of quiet peace. The air feels better here; I can breathe again, and it doesn't crush my heart anymore.

Scared bleats and whines come from my right, and I turn with caution. It might be a deer in distress. I remember them crying for help when I was younger. They would get trapped in the fence on our property. Mom and Dad told us to let them die; they said it was better for the deer and we could eat well that night. But I ran to Perdu's room, begging him to come help me. He always came.

Her body trembles slightly, like she's fighting the urge to give in to her inevitable death. I carefully step closer, not wanting to frighten her. Nestled between the vast lake and the all-consuming forest, this little deer seems tired, fragile, scared, and alone, a small insignificant blip in the endless cycle of the starless sky.

She struggles to lift her head as I kneel down beside the dying creature, but when her dark and tortured eyes meet mine, suddenly the world stops spinning and nothing else matters. In her pain and abandonment, in her eyes, I see myself. A creature awaiting death.

"What happened?" I ask her. Her back legs are broken, shifted up and to the left. I reach my hand out to her, and she checks my scent before allowing me to touch her head. "Good girl." I am shocked she lets me pet her, but I guess she's just as desperate as I feel I am. She can't eat, she can't drink. Who knows how long she's been like this.

I bring her water from the lake and watch as she takes a few licks, quenching some thirst if nothing else. The poor creature needs food. I gather various leaves, grasses, and plants. Mother Nature must love her deer—she provides food for them everywhere. The ground is flooded with anything and everything edible for the beautiful being. Above, there are leaves and flowers. If the deer is loved so much, how can she die like this?

I make my way back to the doe with her fresh salad. She eats it, thankful. I can't help her. I can't keep her alive. My best guess is she has only a few minutes left. Her legs have been broken and pushed into her ribs too far. I can't watch her die. Seeing her life drained far beyond her time would hurt too much. I make the decision to stand and leave. She probably needs someone to end things for her and make the pain disappear. I just . . . I don't think I am capable. As I walk away, she begins to bleat again, a loud and exasperated cry for help. I hear Perdu in her cries, begging me to stay with him that night. *I'm scared of being alone.*

"I can't stay with you," I tell her, feeling the tears fall from my cheeks once again. "I can't do it." I face away from her, not daring to look into her helpless eyes. I have to leave. I can't handle this pain. Perdu's face flashes through my thoughts. The fear, the pain, the guilt, that night—it hits me hard, and my hands shake. "I can't do this!" I yell into the darkness of the night. This throbbing pain in my chest has to stop. I can't breathe. My hands, still vibrating, come up to my temples, rubbing the pain in my head.

"Please, Evina. I'm afraid of being alone." Perdu's voice doesn't quit. It gets louder. If I leave this doe alone, I may as well be abandoning him all over again. I failed to save Perdu's life before, and I can't save this deer either. *"Don't leave me alone."* I may be able to keep her company. I can handle that. I try not to think about watching her death and just focus on the fact that she needs me now.

"You're a beautiful little doe, " I tell her, turning around and kneeling beside her. "I'm going to call you Daisy. It's a beautiful name."

I wipe my tears away, fighting back the remainder of my breakdown. Daisy sighs and nuzzles my leg. If she can go through this, I can too. We're in this together.

The slight breeze becomes a steady wind, and clouds start to cover the nighttime sky. Daisy doesn't panic about the weather; her heart doesn't quicken. She stays calm, looking to the clouds, swirling and gray. I can see it in her eyes—she's prepared for it. She's ready to embrace death. She breathes in, she breathes out, her eyes close, and she's gone.

Mother Nature cries for every child she loses. Every time one of her creations is taken from her world, she ignites a storm, bringing pain to the ones she blames. Raindrops begin falling as soon as Daisy's last breath is gone. It's simple, really: grief has to come. I think of Clair burying each of the victims he couldn't save. He gives them a grave with their name. He shows love to the ones who didn't believe they deserved it. I look to Daisy, thankful I had the opportunity to be a comfort to her. Clair would take care of her, wouldn't he? He wouldn't let her sit here in the rain and then get eaten by the next animal to pass.

I nod, knowing what I have to do. I begin digging. The dirt and rain wash away the blood on my arm. Once I'm done, mud covers me. My work has produced a hole large and deep enough for Daisy. I bury her, and each handful of dirt that covers her reminds me of my brother under the dirt on our property. I think back on the day we buried him under the tree. For the first time since my brother's death, I think back on that moment with peace and thankfulness I could be there to say goodbye instead of the awful guilt and reminder that he's gone. I close my eyes when Daisy's entire body has been covered. Lifting my face, I allow the rain to wash over me as the fresh air enters my lungs. Not all storms are painful. Not all winds bring suffering. Maybe I will be okay after all.

I sit in the weather for a while, staring out at the lake, watching waves and tides crash to the shore. I had forgotten how much I love the rain. Each drop hits my skin, cooling my inner steam. The rain glides down my face and arms. I am refreshed. Breathing in, the clarity of the moisture reaches my lungs. Breathing out, I feel my heartache depart. My eyes close, and I listen to the rain hitting the lake, adding to the beautiful water. The drops fall on dusty leaves, washing the forest clean. Cool mud slides between my fingers, and I long to feel this sensation on my toes. I force my shoes and my wool socks off. My feet slide into the mud before me, and for the first time in many years, I feel like I did when Perdu and I were kids: happy. My hair is drenched, along with my muddy sweater. I look at my arms and watch as the rain runs over my cuts, cleaning them and giving them beauty. Rinsing away the darkness and the pain. Then something happens, something I never thought I would experience again. I smile. I think a laugh might've escaped as well. There is always something to smile about if you look hard enough. Even in death. Even in rain.

In all this, I forgot something: Perdu's note in my pocket. I wipe my hands off on my pants and reach into the pocket, pulling out the paper, which is wet and falling apart. The words have all disappeared. Only one line can be read: *I believe in you. I love you.* The last words my brother ever said to me. He believes in me, and he loves me. I can do it. I look at the wounds on my arm. They show my weakness, but it's a weakness I overcame and have to continue to overcome if I want to make my brother proud.

"I love you too, Perdu," I whisper into the paper. I squeeze together the remains of his letter, then toss it into Halcyon Lake. "I love you."

Chapter Fifty-Nine

Clair

Clair. I know I once was him, but now I feel so distant from everything that once made me that man.

I squint into the rain, trying to fight the pull within my body to keep walking. My clothes are soaked, but the chill hasn't reached my bones. If it has, I haven't noticed. I can't tear my eyes away; I haven't been able to since I stopped running. I know what sits just beyond those trees.

This is where my search for Evina ends. I have to turn around—I know I do. But I swear I can feel the parts of me that I thought were gone forever sitting just out of reach. Just behind the trees.

Memories of a life I never got to live swirl inside me.

I try to pull my mind away. I have to find Evina. She needs to be my focus.

But I've lost myself as well, and I know that I am so close to finding it. Who I used to be is so close now. Everything that made me who I am isn't lost, is it?

Fuck, Clair, turn around, I try to urge myself. *Turn around.*

An escape is laid out before me, a way to go back. If only for a moment.

My mind is balancing on a very thin fence, and I know this moment will determine which side I succumb to. It's hard for me to care where I end up anymore; I just want the imbalance to stop.

I try to turn around, try to force myself to stay away from those tall dark trees, but the harder I try, the more it poisons my mind. I know what rests in there. I have to see it. Am I strong enough to resist?

No.

And so my feet guide me down a path I swore I would never walk again. With each step, excitement and fear find their way to the surface. I haven't seen it in five years. Is it still there? Of course it is. I can feel it.

I reach for my knife, but it's gone. Fear bolts through my body for a moment before I remember I gave it to Evina. Fuck.

"Evina needs you to be strong, Clair," I whisper to myself.

I have to fight this darkness. For a second I believe I have what it takes to pull away, to get out of here before it's too late, but when I see it between the trees, I know there is no going back.

It's nothing but broken and blackened wood now. The rain pours harder, nearly blocking it from my sight. Grandfather and I lived here for so many years. Here, in this shack, we were happy. Until I pushed him into the fire. Until I burned him alive and our home to the ground.

Misery chokes my heart and my lungs. I stand, staring at the place where my life ended, feeling the pain and anguish that stained itself into this land. The fire never spread past our home. The forest protects its own.

The roar of the rain beating down on the forest fills my ears, and I'm thankful for it. It keeps me from reliving Grandfather's cries as the fire consumed him. I can still smell the smoke and feel the heat as it pressed into my skin.

I changed that night. I became the man this life needs me to be, but I lost every part of who I wanted to become. So many memories flood my mind, memories I have shoved away for years. My grandfather, how happy we used to be, our old home, my old life, the fire, the cuts lining my arm where the scars sit now, Dolion and Loralie almost taking me. All of it. Memories of a different world. A world that existed fifty-nine lives ago.

Sixty. Grandfather. My first murder.

I want to get closer to my old home, but my feet won't let me. It's like they are protecting me from the things I would remember if I went there. All I can do is stare. Once, we were happy there. I was a child, and Grandfather was alive, and we actually had a life, something to live for. Now I've forgotten who I am beyond death and the twins.

A small pain tugs on my heart. Grief, something I'm all too familiar with. But this grief is different. It's not because of the loss of someone else—it's because of the loss of myself. Who have I become? Is this who I always will be?

My wet hair clings to my forehead like it's afraid to let go. The rain continues drowning me in the world I have tried to forget. I close my eyes, finally ripping myself away from the sight of . . . my home. I have to get out of here before I fall deeper into this darkness, this unbearably familiar dark oasis.

Electricity buzzes through my body, giving me the unexplainable urge to run, to get away from this all. I'm trapped in this forest, stuck because there are people here who need me. But I need help too, and I'm not sure what to do anymore. I have to go somewhere I can think clearly before I do something stupid. I open my eyes and sprint through the rain, desperate to make it to the calming waters of Lake Halcyon.

Chapter Sixty

Evina

I haven't left Halcyon yet. The sound of the rain pelting the lake and the feeling of it drenching my clothes keep me from leaving the peace of the water. Oddly enough, it feels as though someone is sitting here with me, listening to each breath I breathe. It doesn't feel like Loralie. No, it feels like someone who cares. Someone who understands.

I can't help but wish Clair were here. I know I can trust him now. He was right. Always right about Loralie and everything. And I know Perdu trusted him too. I'm not sure how I know, but that part of my heart that stopped beating after I lost Perdu comes to life again when I'm around Clair. Clair was important to my brother, and I pushed him away.

I hold Clair's knife out in front of me, studying the way the metal curves. My own reflection stares back at me on the blade. With my long hair drenched and my face pale from the cold, I look kind of sickly.

Like Loralie.

I decide to crawl over to a large tree and take shelter at its base. I can't force myself to let go of Clair's knife, so I just lean against the tree and keep it firmly in my grasp.

The sound of the consistent rain causes me to drift away every so often, a gentle sleep wanting to comfort me. Eventually, I'm far enough gone I can't tell if the sound of feet smacking into the mud and the broken yells that can barely be heard over the rain are real or only a part of my dreams.

When my mind starts to come out of a haze, something about the sounds seems not only real but familiar. My eyes flutter open, and I find a dark shape standing in the downpour. He's just a little taller than me. His white T-shirt and dark jeans are just as soaked as I am. He's facing the lake, yelling something I can barely hear.

It's Clair. My heart leaps in hope and excitement. Clair!

The world is okay again. I will be okay again. I am no longer alone. I push myself off the ground and take a step toward Clair, but then he falls to his knees in the mud, and I slink back under the tree. Something about him seems different, broken maybe. His body shakes, and his head is in his hands. I think he might be crying.

He's . . . upset? Is he in pain?

Clair seemed so . . . I don't know. Just the idea of him struggling seems so unnatural. He seemed so strong, so . . . untouchable.

If I were sitting alone in the rain crying, I would want someone to come see if I'm okay. I gather my courage and grip his knife for comfort. I can do this. I don't need to be nervous. He won't be mad at me for interrupting him. I know he won't.

I leave the shelter of the tree and run into the loud rain.

He's kneeling in the mud, his hands covered as he hits the ground repeatedly.

I can see he's yelling, but I can't hear it over the storm. Reminding myself to be brave, I slowly crouch to sit next to him. I place my hand on his shoulder, and he jumps and reaches for his knife as he turns to face me. But it isn't there, of course, because I have it.

Clair stares at me like I just hit him. I'm not sure why he is so shocked, but I can't bear the look on his face. He seems scared. His eyes are red and wide, and his hands shake as if the anger within him is too much to bear. He's small and broken, far different from the man I thought I knew. Maybe Clair isn't that different from me after all.

I don't know what I'm doing or how I think I can help, but the pain in my heart, pain for him, causes me to wrap my arms around his shoulders and pull him close to me.

"It's okay," I shout above the roar of the storm. "I promise you'll be okay."

He falls into me after I speak. To my surprise, he even wraps his arms around me, hugging me back. I think he might be crying again, but it's hard to tell. His head rests on my shoulder for a long time—long enough that the rain lightens up a little and the sound of his shallow breathing reaches my ears.

I don't know what's happening, I don't know why he is hurting or what happened to him, but I do know that I'm not scared and I'm not alone. I believe the words I spoke to him. It is okay.

After some time, he sits up, pulling away from me. The rain is quieter now, and I can see more than just a few feet ahead. The world doesn't seem so angry, only sad.

Clair looks out at the lake, his fingers fiddling with a small mud-covered stone.

Should I say something to him, or should I let him be? I don't want to annoy him, but I also don't want him to feel like I don't care.

"Do you want to talk about it?" As I say the words, I dig my fingernails into my palms, worried I shouldn't have asked. He turns his head up to the sky and then looks at me.

"We should get somewhere dry and warm," he says. His body is stiff, and he won't meet my eyes. He's clearly uncomfortable. It's my fault; I shouldn't have tried to push him.

Clair stands and reaches his hand down to me. I grab it, and he pulls me up.

"Are you ready?" he asks. "You got everything?"

I nod and tuck his knife back into my clothes. Before we turn into the forest, Clair takes one last look at the lake and nods like he is saying goodbye to an old friend.

Lady

A beautiful green leaf, separated from its branch before its time, drifts down to my waters until it rests upon my surface. It seems to float above the lake. Not even the raging storm can sink the small leaf. Something about it is comforting in this lonely world. I've been alone for so long.

Clair has been alone for so long too, fighting a silent battle the world will never be aware of. His pain is hidden because he knows he must be strong.

But today it is different.

Evina sees him in pain, and she hurts for him. She wants to help him. Her kindness toward him makes my heart hurt for her even more. She is so sweet, so pure. She does not deserve any of this. None of us do.

My waters ripple with the pain I feel for Evina, casting the small leaf farther away from the shore, further isolating it from anything it's ever known.

Through the rain that pelts my lake, I can sense Clair's unbearable emotions. His anger and pain are coming to a breaking point. One of these days something will destroy him, and he won't be able to remain strong.

Clair's shame at being so weak in front of Evina weighs on the little leaf. Though the leaf fights to remain above the surface, eventually the weight is too much to bear and it is pulled under. Clair didn't mean for Evina to see him so broken. He didn't mean to seem incapable in front of the girl who needs him to be strong. But he liked having someone to lean on for a change. Whether he realizes it or not, he needs that support. Just like everyone else.

Chapter Sixty-One

Evina

We step inside the shack, and the instant relief from the rain is calming. Clair heads over to the corner of the room and lights a fire where the remains of a previous one still smolders. He then pulls off his jacket and shirt, replacing it with a dry one and draping his jacket over the table. I haven't moved past the doorway, afraid I'll go somewhere he doesn't want me.

This is his home, I think. *This is where he lives.*

It's small, but the flickering light from the fire makes it feel homey. He has a cot near the fire and a modest table with some berries on the other side. There's a handwoven basket where he keeps his clothes and a little box that seems to hold miscellaneous personal items.

Clair looks in my direction. "You can come in."

"Oh." I shuffle forward. "Sorry."

"No need to be sorry. Here." He pulls out a wooden stool from the other side of the table. "It's a newer one, so you don't have to worry about a leg breaking."

I nod and sit on the stool. Clair's home smells like smoke, I'm assuming from the fire, and currently like wet forest.

"If you want anything to eat, I have some berries, and there are also nuts on the shelf over there. I haven't been able to go hunting recently, so that's all I really have."

I nod again. I've never been very good at going to other people's places. I've always been the awkward one, and Perdu was the one who wanted to make friends.

"Look." He sighs. "I'm sorry. About earlier. I was just having a bad moment, but I'm okay now."

I look at him. His swollen red eyes won't meet mine, his blond hair is at least three shades darker because of the rain, and his hands tremble like mine have been so much lately. Is he scared too? I wonder what he has to be scared of.

I shrug and make myself say something to him. "I didn't mind. Everyone cries."

"Yeah." He sits on his cot and rests his head in his hands. He looks tired.

"When I'm going through something hard, my dad likes to joke around. He tells the *worst* dad jokes."

He lifts his head and asks, "What's a dad joke?"

"You know, like a really stupid joke that nobody finds funny but everybody finds funny at the exact same time."

Clair looks like he doesn't understand.

"A dad joke, you know . . ." I continue. Does he really not know what I'm talking about? "Like the chicken and the road?"

He shakes his head.

"Okay, here's one. Tell me if it's funny or not. What's large and brown and deadly?"

He stares for a second and then asks, "Is that the joke?"

"No," I say, giggling. "Tell me you don't know, and then I'll get to the punchline."

"Okay . . ." he says, clearly unsure of where this is going. "I don't know what's large and brown and deadly."

"*Bear* with me," I say. "I'll think of it."

He pauses for a moment before chuckling. "That's not very funny," he says, though he can't help but smile.

"That's what I'm saying!" I smile at him, feeling accomplished. "My dad has been telling it for years, and he cracks up every time. I keep saying it's not funny."

"Bear with me," Clair repeats. "Not funny at all." His eyes shine with excitement. "I've got one."

"Okay, go for it."

"What's tall and green?" he asks with the most genuine smile I've ever seen from him.

"I don't know. What's tall and green?"

"A tree!"

I stare at Clair for a moment before laughing at his joke and making a mental note to reteach him how to tell one.

"A tree is tall and green," I say. I look up at him, and when I do, I see something I've never seen in anyone else: honesty and fire. He is strong, he is capable, and I am so thankful I'm not alone in this. "Do you feel better now?" I ask, watching the way the palms of his hands rub against his jeans.

"I do." He smiles. When he speaks, it's so genuine. "Thank you."

"Where's Marie?" I ask. "Is she okay?"

He moves his legs in response, and I find her curled up under his cot, sleeping peacefully.

"Marie!" I exclaim, falling out of my chair and onto my knees next to her. She opens her eyes when I pet her behind her ears. Her tongue pops out of her mouth in excitement. The floorboards squeak as Clair kneels next to me.

"She's missed you," he says.

I look at him, his eyes finally meeting mine for the first time since the lake.

"Thank you for taking care of him," I whisper.

His eyes sadden, and I know he knows I'm talking about Perdu.

"He loved you," Clair says, causing my heart to stop from surprise. Then he reaches over and grabs my hand, wrapping it in his.

I nod slowly, trying not to cry. "He loved a lot of people. And a lot of people loved him."

"You were different. He cared about you the most."

"He cared about Julie the most," I correct him, suddenly aware of the anger that still chokes my heart. "After all, he left me because of her, didn't he?" When Clair is silent, I explain. "Julie was his girlfriend."

"Yeah, I know." His voice is stiff, and his hand tightens around mine.

"Because he talked about her. Of course he did."

Clair shakes his head, keeping his eyes trained on the floor. "I knew her before I knew Perdu."

The heat from the fire is the only thing that makes me sure this is all real. Both of these people I have gone years without are suddenly in my life again through Clair. I never hated Julie—I even liked her when she and Perdu were together—but in the end, she took him from me.

"She was one of them. The graves where we saw Perdu. She's actually next to him." Clair lets go of my hand and shuffles his body away from mine slightly. "Dolion and Loralie got to her too. She was . . . my friend, like Perdu was."

He straightens his back and breathes in deep like he thinks it will get rid of the obvious emotions.

"They were very lucky to have a friend like you." I mean it. I'm lucky too.

"He still cared about you, Evina, in a way that he didn't care about Julie. You were his sister. No one could ever replace you."

I don't talk about Julie. Not because it hurts or anything that she's gone, but because it doesn't hurt. When I think of her, the only part of it that hurts is that my brother died because of her. He felt so broken because of her that he hung himself. When I think of Julie, that's all I think of.

"I guess," is all I can manage to say.

"You're mad at her, aren't you?"

"How could I not be?" I snap. "If she hadn't left him, he wouldn't have died."

"If she hadn't left him, if you'd been a better sister, if I hadn't fallen asleep—there are a million people we could blame, including ourselves. And we blame them because we don't want to blame the ones we care about and the ones we miss. The truth, Evina, is that Perdu took his own life."

I shake my head and face away from him as I fail to hold back my tears.

"Why would he do that? Because he didn't love me?" As soon as I whisper the wicked words, I regret them. I've turned Perdu's death, his pain, into a selfish thing. I've put myself at the center of it all.

"Evina." Clair turns me around to face him again, but I look past him at the fire, unable to meet his eyes. "Perdu never shut up about you. You were all he had left in life, and you were the only reason he was fighting so hard to survive his own mind."

I clench my teeth and shake my head as more hot tears burn my skin.

"I know it hurts—"

"You don't," I mutter. "Have you ever lost your brother?"

"I never had a brother." He sighs. Then his grip on my shoulders drops, and he shuts his eyes. His jaw tightens, and his head rests in his hands now as he pulls at his hair gently. "I only ever had one family member. And yes, I lost him. Five years ago."

Clair's breath is shaky, and he doesn't open his eyes.

"I'm sorry," I whisper, the guilt hitting me so hard I can feel the pain in my chest.

Chapter Sixty-Two

Clair

Evina is sitting in front of me, her legs crossed just like mine, with worry in her eyes. It makes me uncomfortable, knowing not only is all of her attention on me, but her pity is too. I'm not the one here who needs to be worried about—she is. Guilt rips through me when I think about how I want to tell her more about my life. And how I want her to listen.

I straighten my back again and shake my head, opening my eyes suddenly. It's time to move past all of that. Her emotions and her pain are what's at stake here. I'm sure this is exactly what Dolion and Loralie want—to watch me succumb to my own weaknesses until I'm useless and out of their way.

"Are you okay?" Evina asks. "I didn't mean to—"

"I'm fine," I say. Then I force a smile. "We'll have all the time in the world to talk about anything we'd like. But let's get you through this night first, okay?"

"Okay," she says. Then she reaches out and grabs my hand. "We'll do it together."

A slow knock comes from the door, and Evina's fingernails dig into my skin. Her eyes widen as she looks at me. Her hands start to shake, and her lips quiver.

"No," she whispers. "No, no, no."

I place my finger on my lips and reach for my knife. Damn it. A knife wouldn't kill Loralie anyway. I found that out years ago. I bring my feet under me and crouch on the floor. Squeezing Evina's hand before letting it go, I gesture for her to remain put and stay by Marie. Then I stand and make my way to the door.

Loralie is on the other side, as I expected.

"Give me the girl, Clair." She looks over my shoulder to Evina. I follow her eyes and see Evina shaking, holding Marie's paw in her hand. The firelight casts long shadows across her face. I step to the side to block Evina from Loralie's view.

I stare into Loralie's eyes, hoping she can feel every bit of anger and hatred I have for her through my glare.

"Get lost, Loralie." I start to close the door, but Loralie reaches out and places her hand firmly against the wood.

"Clair," she purrs, then bites her lip, looking up at me through her eyelashes. "Don't you miss me?" Her hand grazes my arm, and I'm overly aware that someone is watching us.

"Fuck you, Loralie," I say, knowing she has more control over me than I'd like. I step out into the light rain and close the door.

"There's so much left undone between us," she hums. The rain doesn't affect her at all. She's still perfectly dry. Her hand moves to my chest, slowly sliding lower. "I miss you. I know you miss me." She pouts as her hand reaches my waistband.

She's so magnetic. So all-consuming. I stare longingly into those beautiful eyes. She makes me weak, and she knows it.

She leans in close to me, her tempting lips only moments from connecting with mine, and I'm suddenly aware of how dry and cracked my own are. The smell of fresh flowers radiates off of her and cascades down my body, enveloping me in her trance. I try to remind myself I have to fight her temptations.

For Evina. I have to do it for Evina.

In the name of ending this, I have to resist Loralie.

"Go away." I put my hand on the doorknob. "And leave Perdu's sister alone."

Anger flashes across Loralie's eyes before she smiles again. "Don't turn me down, Clair. I'm warning you."

"And I'm warning you," I say, opening the door to my shack. "Leave before you really piss me off."

I step inside, leaving Loralie alone in the rain, where she belongs. I'm not scared of her—not anymore. But I am afraid of myself around her. I breathe in deep and try to focus my mind on what needs to be done. Evina will be different than the others. I know she will.

"Do you want to survive this?" I ask the girl curled up on the floor of my home. She nods. "Then we have to go over a few things. Are you going to listen to me?"

"Yes," she says, her voice still shaky. I sit next to her and place my hand on her shoulder.

"She's gone, Evina. You're okay."

For now.

Chapter Sixty-Three

Evina

Perdu's death. Loralie and Dolion. Devil Oasis.

Loralie is a temptress, and Dolion is a manipulator. They are dead. They want to be with each other again, and for some reason, they think the only way to do that is to feed the land the bodies of suicide victims. Julie came here in search of help, and Loralie got to her. Clair was here for that. Then Perdu, riddled with the pain of Julie's disappearance, fell victim to the twins as well. Clair also had to witness that.

He saw Perdu hanging from the tree, just like I did . . .

And now here I am, one of the many people Clair has tried to save from this curse.

"Has anyone survived them?" I ask through the silent tears I haven't been able to control.

Clair shakes his head, but it's clear he is lying when he looks down at his arm.

How did I not see them before? Perfect silver lines sit in a row down his arm. He was a victim once too.

"You survived?"

His voice is quiet. "Once, yes." Then he looks up at me, a new determination on his face. "And I'm hoping others in the past did too, before I was around to see it."

"Do you think that means I can survive?"

Clair looks into my eyes with an intensity I've never seen before. "I know you can." His voice is solid. "And you will."

Hope blossoms in my chest, and I can't help but smile.

"I promise you, Evina, you won't have to go through this alone if you don't want to."

I hug him, new tears starting to form. I hold on to Clair like letting go of him means death. In just a few hours I'll be home with Mom and Dad. I have to believe that.

"Don't leave me," I whisper.

He hugs me tighter.

"Do we have a plan?" I ask when I pull away and wipe my tears.

"I've been thinking about that." He stands and sits on his cot, leaning forward with his elbows on his knees. "In the past I've always either run or hidden, hoping we can stay away from Dolion and Loralie long enough for the sun to come up."

"When the sun rises, am I safe?"

A pained look strikes across Clair's face. "Safer, at least. Dolion and Loralie won't come for you after sunrise. They'll take a break, I think. But the thoughts they filled your head with might linger."

My mind feels like it's trying to stretch just to understand the little bit about this all that I do know. I can't even begin to imagine everything

I haven't yet learned. Maybe Clair and I will have to have a longer talk about this once we're safe. "So, if you don't want to run or hide anymore, what's the plan?"

"I need you to trust me, okay, Evina?"

"Okay," I say, unsure of where this is going.

"The only way to truly survive them isn't to last the night—it's to face them. It's to stand up to them and to the dark thoughts they've filled you with. We have to be the ones to go to them, Evina. Not sit around and wait for them to come to us."

"No," I say before I can stop myself. "Clair . . . Clair, I'm not going to willingly go to her."

Chapter Sixty - Four

I feel so silly, like a small little girl who is incapable of facing her fears on her own. But every time I try to convince myself to let go of his hand and show at least a little dignity, that pain in my chest returns. Clair is right. I knew as soon as he said it that hiding isn't going to do any good. I finally caved to what he was saying, and now here we are, walking toward the entrance gate of Devil Oasis.

Clair said if we can do this near the gate, then I can get out quickly when I've done what I need to do. He said it shouldn't be necessary, but it's a precaution worth taking.

"Do I have to do this alone?" I ask. It's the first thing either of us has said since we left his home.

I stare at his knife, now sheathed at his hip, and slightly regret giving it back to him. I have nothing left to defend myself.

He squeezes my hand gently before speaking. "I'll walk you to the gate, and I won't be too far from you once we separate, but I don't think Loralie's going to show herself to you if you aren't alone."

"Okay." I force the word out through shallow breaths. To say I'm afraid is an understatement. It feels as though Clair is my lifeline and tether to reality. He is warm and safe and comfortable. Leaving him worries me.

"You'll be okay, Evina." Clair looks ahead, his eyes on the gate that slowly comes into view. "And for what it's worth, you're handling Perdu's death better than I ever could. He'd be proud."

I laugh to myself and sigh. "Sure," I say, not knowing how to respond. I haven't handled it well; not a single part of what I've done since Perdu's death has been anything but destructive.

"I mean it."

"You wouldn't say that if you knew me."

"Then tell me about yourself." He turns and looks at me. "Try me."

I sigh. "I befriended Loralie, for one."

The birds' eerie whistles linger among the trees. My stomach turns at Clair's silence. Did I say something wrong? When I look over at him, his eyes connect with mine, and he's trying to force back a smile. Then Clair laughs like it's the funniest thing he's ever heard. And to my surprise, I find myself laughing as well.

"I *befriended Loralie*," I say again, and this time the humor in it makes me laugh harder. The one I'm running from, the one we are attempting to fight. I considered her a friend. I can't even place why the reality of the situation is funny to me; I only know that it feels better to laugh about it than to cry.

"I've done a lot worse," he says as his laugh dissipates.

"When did it all become such a mess?" I wipe tears from my eyes and look into Clair's again.

"I don't know." He sighs, the ghost of his smile still gracing his lips. "We're going to get you out of this, Evina. I promise."

"I know." I smile at him. "I trust you, Clair."

His hand tightens around mine, but he doesn't say anything. The wind rocks the trees and brushes against the grass.

"I've had a lot of anxiety since Perdu's death." I sigh and pull away from him the tiniest bit. He doesn't seem to notice. I've always been terrible at keeping things inside. An open book—that's what Perdu would call me. "My dad has taken me to a doctor for my panic attacks, but it doesn't seem to help. My mom doesn't realize any of it is even happening."

Clair doesn't say anything, but I know he's listening to me. His eyes are again facing the gate, which is hidden in shadows, and his hand grips mine with care.

"I can't be in closed spaces." My voice is a shaky whisper. Heat spreads slowly across my face, and I'm worried he'll think something's wrong with me. I look down at my feet and stop walking. "If there's no easy access to the outside and fresh air . . . I kind of freak out."

Clair stops walking as well and steps in front me, facing me. I can feel his eyes on me now, and I want to look up at him to see if he still cares for me.

"I'm not crazy," I say suddenly.

He lets go of my hand, and my heart drops. I pull the sleeves of my sweater over my fingers.

Then he unsheathes his knife. "You see this knife here?" His voice is calm and gentle, as if he's dealing with a small animal he doesn't want to spook. "Over the years it's become more a part of me than my left arm. I don't know who I am without this knife. Not anymore."

Guilt swims inside me when I remember he gave it to me and I kept it for myself. "I'm sorry."

"I wanted you to have it," he says. "I had hoped you would find the same sense of protection I felt from it. But what I'm saying is I have anxiety too. I like carrying a knife, and you need fresh air. There's nothing wrong with either of those things."

"Do you still think I'm handling Perdu's death well?"

"Better than I could ever." He smiles and puts his knife back at his hip. "Losing family is the hardest thing any human will ever go through, and even before it happens, we spend our lives fearing it. It's not easy, and you're doing great. Now"—he turns toward the gate—"let's get this over with and get you back home."

Chapter Sixty-Five

I wave at Clair as he disappears between the trees, and a new sense of dread settles into my stomach. The gate is so close to me now. I'm out of the trees, and all that stands between me and the exit is about twenty feet of a clearing. The wind beats against my hair lightly, and a new sense of loneliness hangs in the air. I look around the land and shiver. I'm so close to freedom, yet I know I can't run or they'll just follow me home. Like they did with Perdu.

The edge of the forest rises tall above me, like a monster ready to swallow its prey. Will this work? What if Loralie doesn't show up? And then if she does, what am I supposed to say? Clair said he can't tell me what to say because then it wouldn't be genuine.

Lean on your anger, Evina, I think. At least, that's what Clair said to do. Anger and fear—they'll drive me to push Loralie away.

A wave of nausea rolls over me, and I search the trees anxiously for any sign of Clair. This is it. I recognize this feeling. The heavy aged air, the silencing of nature, the stillness of time. I feel as though I'm stripped naked and given up entirely to the mercy of this monster. Loralie is close.

Separating from Clair was a stupid mistake. Where the heck is he?

He's not going to come back until this is over with. He can't if it's going to work. I hate my thoughts right now.

I face the gate and briefly consider running. Away from this fear and away from this pain. I pull the sleeves of my sweater over my hands and curl my arms into my chest.

Footsteps.

They're slow and steady, gradually making their way to me. I close my eyes in an attempt not to cry. Evil is creeping up behind me, and I somehow have to be strong enough to face it. I let out each shaky breath slowly, not wanting to show any signs of fear, but I know my body is trembling, and I'm sure Loralie can see it.

The footsteps inch closer at an unbearably slow pace. I'm caught in a moment of decision and fear. The terror that cracks through my heart like cold destruction drains my body and leaves me weak.

I really only have one option: Face this. Pull myself together and find what little courage I have left to finish this so I can go home.

My hair whips through the breeze, and I force myself to stand taller against the cold instead of folding in against it. I clutch my fists to keep them from shaking.

The world silences. Even the breeze becomes soundless. All except for the steps behind me and the steady cold breath on the back of my neck. A tear tracks my face, and my lips quiver. I have to fight every urge I have to fall to the ground in a fit of tears and curl up to hide from this nightmare. My body hurts with how bad it just wants to lie down and give in to the terror that slowly spreads like a fire through my soul.

"I am more than a weak little girl," I whisper to myself. "I am more than my fears."

I turn to face Loralie.

Surprised? His voice rings through my head, though his mouth isn't moving. A boy who looks exactly like Loralie stands before me smirking. His face is long, but his jaw is firm, and his black curls flick in the wind like tendrils of smoke. His blue eyes are identical to the ones that have been haunting me. The person in front of me is pale and skinny and sickly. His skin shines like he's coated in sweat. He makes me shudder and pull away. There's no mistaking this.

"Dolion."

He flashes a malicious grin, his crooked teeth showing through his split lips. He's proud of the fear I feel.

Were you not expecting me, Evina? He steps closer to me, and I back away.

"How are you doing that?" I ask, watching the way his mouth refuses to move with his words.

All I want is to play a game. He smiles again. *A game just like your brother and I played.*

The shock that has braided itself into my chest slowly begins to unwind as I process the situation. My eyes dart once again to the trees in hopes of seeing Clair.

"I'm not going to play a game with you," I snap, and the small amount of confidence I hear in my voice gives me hope.

I am greatly looking forward to proving you wrong. Dolion catches my eyes and glances behind him into the forest as well. *Hoping your friend will show up?*

"I'm not alone in this." I clench my teeth to keep my mouth from quivering.

You're still so naïve, Evina. Have you learned nothing? Dolion whips his head back to me and reaches out for my hand. Something about the sincerity in his eyes keeps me from pulling away. His hand is oddly damp to touch. And cold. Very, very cold. *Trust no one. Especially not Clair.*

He's messing with me. I know he is. Still, his hand tightens around mine, and I can't help but long to hear more.

"You don't know Clair." I fight for that confidence I had just moments ago. Somewhere in the past few minutes, the sounds of the forest came back to life. Birds caw as if it's the end of time, and the breeze rattles my ears. Somehow, I can even hear the waves at the lake lapping against the shore.

You *don't know Clair*, Dolion corrects me. *Clair has lied to you and kept secrets from you, Evina. He's not on the side you think he is.*

"No," I say, though my voice trembles, and I can't stop the silent tears that fall. "Please, no."

His words break into my mind like a crowbar on a jammed door. Each word he speaks drips with confusion and victory. I pull my hand away from his and back away from Loralie's brother.

Dolion. Blame him and that place. That's what Perdu wrote to me.

Blame Dolion.

Fear Dolion.

Run from Dolion.

I can show you, Dolion says before I can get away, and I pause.

"Show me what?" I approach the words cautiously, but Dolion smiles as if he knows he's got me.

I can show you the traitor Clair truly is.

My heart stands still, and in this moment, I question all I know about reality. I can trust Clair. I can. Right?

Don't you want to know the truth? Come with me. I'll show you. There is no need to be afraid. It's a harmless little game.

When Dolion walks, I follow. Maybe because I am spineless, maybe because all my strength has been drained, or maybe because I know, deep down in the truest crevices of my heart, Clair would never, ever betray me.

Chapter Sixty-Six

Clair

Evina waves at me just before she vanishes from my sight. Her wave is small and timid, but she has a look of hope in her eyes that I won't let go of. This will work. It has to.

I lean against a tree and fiddle with my knife, running my finger along the sharp edge of the blade. I'm here to watch and to wait, but Evina has to do this on her own. A string pulls at my heart, and it's all I can do to keep still. My hands shake, and I have to force myself to breathe.

She's got this.

I feel so helpless hidden here at the edge of the Oasis. I can't do anything more than hope now.

I think of Grandfather, and for the first time since his death, it doesn't cause a pain in my chest to remember him. I think of how he went through this too, countless times with kids I'll never know. Grandfather fought Dolion and Loralie, and that helps calm my mind as I feel close to him in a way that makes me smile. He knows what I'm going through; that tells me I will be okay eventually. I just have to keep fighting, even when I feel I have nothing left to give.

"Clair?" Her voice makes me jump, and I slash my knife in the air to my right. She's standing there, looking at me, tears filling her blue eyes, which seem to be dimmer than last time I saw her. She sniffles and says my name again. "Clair, I'm so scared."

Fuck.

"I don't have time for your games, Loralie." I pull my knife back toward myself and shift my eyes away from her.

"Clair." Her voice shakes, and her breathing is ragged. "It's not a game. Oh, they're so, so bad."

I have no idea what she's talking about.

She paces back and forth, biting at her nails, which are always so long and polished. When she stops pacing, she bites her thumbnail and looks at me. "Please, Clair. I need your help."

"No." I push myself off the tree and walk farther into the darkness of the forest. She follows, her small footsteps echoing behind me. I run my hand through my hair and pull until I feel the stress relief on my scalp. What could she possibly want now? I've gone through it before. I've jumped through her hoops, I've given in to her pull. There's nothing left she could want from me. I've given her everything that's mine to give.

"Clair—"

"What?" I spin around, hoping the anger is blazing in my eyes the way it burns under my skin.

"Something is wrong with the curse," she whispers. "I'm afraid."

"Fuck off." I grind my teeth as I walk away. My hand tightens around the hilt of my knife, and I have to reason with myself to not put it through her chest again. A waste of time—that's all that would be.

"I have no one else to go to."

She sniffs again, and I roll my eyes. There's no fucking way I'm going to believe this. Loralie and her brother are manipulators; that's all they know how to do. It's a trap.

"What the hell makes you think it's okay to come to me asking for help?" I keep walking.

"You're all I've got."

"No, Loralie. You have no one because you don't deserve anything but your miserable little death."

"Clair—"

"Shut the hell up, Loralie. You made your choices. You chose to be the villain here, and that's the life you deserve. Leave me alone or I swear I'll—"

"You'll what?" Her voice is steady for the first time since she approached me. "Kill me?"

I turn to face her, and she gives a weak smile.

"What will you do to me that you haven't done already, Clair? Treat me like I'm worthless? Like I'm less than you? Will you fight against me every waking moment of your pathetic life? Tell me what you'll do to me. You have nothing over me. You've tried everything. *I* am the one with power over *you*, but I am not the one you should be fighting. You think Dolion and I are the villains, but we aren't, Clair. And until you realize that, this will never end. Not for any of us."

Loralie leaves me speechless and mentally vulnerable. This is when she always gets me. Because she's right: I have nothing over her. I look into her eyes, and there's a mystery there I am desperate to solve.

"Until you realize that, this will never end. Not for any of us."

She acts as though this is something we are in together, a fight we must face together.

The sadness coating her eyes sparks something within. Something confusing yet hopeful.

"I'm not the villain." There is so much strength, so much passion, so much pleading in her voice that it scares me how much I long to believe her, but she is the reason Evina's life is at stake.

Evina is broken. Evina is hurt by the world, by Loralie, by so much more than anyone other than she could know. She's so broken that she has followed Loralie. She has followed her far into the dark, so far the light is nothing but a memory. She's followed Loralie into friendship, into the Oasis, and now I'm afraid she'll follow her to death.

Loralie turns to me. My heart races as I realize she can see me, all of me, for who I truly am. Her eyes lock with mine, and I'm surprised to find she's smiling. Loralie looks at me in a way that seems wrong for her.

Why does this all feel so familiar? Like I've lived it before?

She looks at me with fear, with sorrow, with pain, and with desperation.

And though she doesn't speak, I know what she wishes to say.

Help me, Clair. Please.

Over and over again, those words have filled my head, trying to break down some unknown wall that I built to keep myself from the truth. They kept causing an itch in my brain, raising questions that have been driving me mad, but now, because of Loralie, the wall finally breaks.

It's my dream.

Finally, the overwhelming questions fall into place as Loralie makes me see things her brother could not. There's so much more to this curse than I could ever realize. And after all these years, I think I'm starting to get it. We're all trapped. All of us.

Loralie leans in, and for the millionth time, she kisses me. I can't pull away. Not when this girl has given me the first ounce of hope I can cling to.

There is a way to end this curse—I know that now. And Dolion and Loralie aren't the enemy; they're the key.

Chapter Sixty - Seven

Evina

Clair has Loralie pinned against a tree. She's holding on to him like she needs him. And he's . . .

"He's kissing her," I whisper through the break in my voice.

Clair is lying to you, Evina. Dolion's voice is cold. *He's been lying to you since the beginning. He and Loralie* are *lovers, and he's never been on your side. He was part of the plan, just a tool meant to deceive you.*

"No." I can barely hear my own voice. "No, no, Clair wouldn't."

How much do you really know about Clair? How much of the truth has he told you?

"I know enough," I say, even though I am quickly doubting myself and doubting Clair.

Has he told you how his grandfather died?

"No . . ." My heart tightens as I fear the worst.

He killed him, Evina. Dolion places his hand on my shoulder, and though I want to pull away, I can't. *Clair killed the only family member he had. He's kept who he truly is from you. He's deceived you. He never cared about Perdu, and he never cared about you.*

The pain clenches my heart and strangles my lungs. Clair. The man who smiled at me, who held my hand. The man who loved Perdu just like I did. The man I had trusted and cared about.

"Clair." The tears track my face in a steady pattern. He pulls away from Loralie and turns to face me, panic in his eyes.

I told you. This time it's Loralie's voice in my head. *I didn't lie to you, Evina. I would never lie to you.*

She kisses Clair's neck as her words echo in my thoughts. Loralie did lie to me—she did. Just like Clair did. Suddenly, I feel trapped, isolated. Clair, Loralie, and Dolion suffocate my thoughts. I desperately gasp for each breath as my head begins spinning. I have to get out of here. I have to leave. Now.

"Evina." The desperation intoxicating Clair's voice makes me sick. "Evina, please." He pushes Loralie off of him, but she wraps her arms around his torso again, like a moth to a flame.

"Leave me alone!" I shout at Clair. "If you come near me, I'll scream."

"Fuck, I'm sorry, Evina. I never meant for—"

"For what? For me to find out?" My tears are hot now, and I'm filled with an explosive anger, something I have never experienced before. "Leave me alone, Clair."

I push past Dolion and run.

With my chest pounding, mind fluttering, palms sweaty, and face covered in violent tears, I fit right in with the sharp branches of the trees and the ugly color of the sky.

He betrayed me, I think. *Clair . . .*

He stayed by my side when I was hurting. He gave Perdu a grave to preserve his memory. He seemed so strong, so capable, so . . .

But he's one of them. The image of him kissing *Loralie* screams through my mind like an alarm. Clair has always been on their side.

The heat and shame flood my face like a prison I cannot escape. I trusted him. He must have been laughing at my foolishness from the day he met me. I fell for his trap.

I think of when I cried on his shoulder, when I told him about my anxieties, when I told him I trusted him, and it all makes me wish to cover my face and hide from the cruel world.

It was the perfect scheme, and it proves that I am no more than Perdu ever thought I was: a naïve little girl who needs protecting from the world.

I thought . . . I wipe at the tears streaming down my face and keep running. I thought he cared about me. I thought he understood me and I understood him.

I internally curse at myself for being so childish.

When I come to the large gate that leads out of Devil Oasis, wooden boards nailed together to create a large arch, I stop and stare at the tall structure. The way out of this cursed place.

Clair said leaving won't free you of the twins. But Clair could have been lying to me. He might have been lying to me about all of it or trying to mislead me.

I stare at the land beyond the gate, a land where life is different and fear isn't so strong. With longing, my eyes pass over the fields that roll across the small hills and the path that parts between the dry grasses whipping in the wind.

I gather my courage, promising myself I'm strong enough to do this, and step across the border of Devil Oasis.

Instantly, the air is different, and my heart feels lighter. Everything I experienced in the cemetery suddenly seems far away, like it was a dream or a story that happened to somebody else. I feel hopeful that this nightmare might end.

But that's when her voice, as calming as rain and as frightening as thunder, splits through the crevice in my wall of hope.

"Evina, darling." I turn to find Loralie standing below the arch. Her dress billows in the wind like a princess at war as fresh rain falls from the sky. "Betrayal and murder and fear. I know you're afraid, little one. I'm here for you."

"I'm not playing this game anymore, Loralie." In this moment, I see why Clair keeps his knife with him; having a weapon to clutch would calm the nerves making me nauseous. Clair. My chest tightens.

"Little Evina has grown a spine." I swear she giggles with her words. This isn't the Loralie I became friends with. She seems so lost now, like her grip on reality has faded. "Little Evina has forgotten she's mine."

I step away from Loralie. The raindrops, though nothing but sprinkles, are cold enough to soak into my bones.

"You needn't be afraid, dear Evina." Loralie reaches for me with her delicate hand, her finger grazing my cheek. "I am your friend, remember?"

"No, you're not my friend. You betrayed me, just like everyone else." A dark fog rolls in by my feet, covering the ground in a black as dark as the nighttime sky.

"Have you forgotten the nights I stayed up with you because you were afraid? Or the days you spent crying on my shoulder? You might not trust me, Evina, and I'm not saying you have to. But I am saying that I care for you, the way a little girl cares for her doll." Loralie's red lips seem to shine through the dark, but her blue eyes are duller than they once were.

"What do you want from me?"

Death, she hisses in my head. But out loud she smiles and whispers a word much less sinister. "Hope."

There's a conflict in my heart that makes me angry. Loralie has been my friend for so long, but friends can betray. Loralie never cared for me. I won't put myself through that again.

"Clair will stop at nothing to find you," she says.

"You're on his side!" I cry. "How am I supposed to trust anyone?"

"I'm using Clair, Evina. Nothing more and nothing less." She grins again like she remembered something wonderful.

I shake my head and turn away from the creature thirsty for my blood. "I want to go home."

"Home? You have no home. Perdu is gone, and your parents are shells of the people they once were. You have no home—not the one you're asking for, at least."

A small ache forms at the bottom of my heart, and I stare at Loralie, enthralled by her words.

"Your home hung from a tree three years ago. You may not trust me, but I know you, Evina. You cannot deny that." She steps closer to me, wrapping a long finger around a loose strand of my brown hair. Something inside me longs to cave and fall into Loralie's arms once more. "You want to go home, Evina? Truly go home? Wrapped in the arms of the only person you've ever felt like you belong with? I know the secret, the way to connect with the dead." Her smile splits across her face as lightning tears through the sky. "Perdu misses you too. I spend every night listening to his pain-filled cries as he begs for you."

Loralie moves her hand to wipe a tear from my face. When did I start crying? Did I ever stop?

Home.

Perdu.

Home.

Loralie.

"You know I know the way." Her voice is as soft as a kitten's purr.

"Death," I say. How dumb does she think I am?

"Mmm," she hums. "Death is nothing but another game to play."

"You're wasting your time with me," I say, though the temptation building within me is beginning to hurt.

"Your voice wavers with uncertainty, child."

Even the air I breathe seems to be filled with Loralie, her scent, dying roses, and the icy cold that radiates from her skin.

"There's a way less painful than a knife, less violent than a rope. No blood, no pain, no fear."

I shake my head. This shouldn't be enticing to me, but all I can see is Perdu, his lightly freckled suntanned face, those muddy eyes staring right into mine. He was strong and stable, everything you could want in a brother. He loved and was loved. He liked barbecues with the neighbors and doing chores around the farm. He liked playing games with Mom and Dad, and he loved me. He also loved Julie. Julie didn't make him leave me, just like Perdu didn't make me leave Mom and Dad. I have to remember that. Perdu loved her, meaning I have to love her in memory of him.

The image of his smiling face causes that broken part of my heart to finally give and crumble.

Without Perdu, I have no one. I've tried to hold on to Mom and Dad, but they're fading, and Clair . . . Clair. I look to my feet and shift uncomfortably under Loralie's stare.

Loralie was never my friend. Despite the longing in my chest for her, I know she has never cared for me.

Perdu, the memory of him, is all I have left. I've tried and I've fought for the other people in my life, but they never chose me. They never fought for me the way I fought for them.

Loralie wraps her arms around me and envelops me in her scent. She smells different now. Like the passing of ancient time. Must wafting in the breeze. She's so familiar—the girl who stayed up with me when I was afraid, who understood me for years. She may have lied to me about some things, but Loralie has always been there to care for me. She's always been patient with me and understood me. She's never made me feel like a burden. She may have tried to hurt me once, but really, if you think about it, it was out of love and care.

"I know you hurt, Evina. He's hurting too, without you. Brother and sister aren't meant to be torn apart." Loralie lifts my chin to look at her. "He needs you. He cries because he is afraid without you."

The pain I feel. Perdu has been feeling that too since we were separated. He needs me to have courage, but it isn't courage to survive; it's courage to find him again.

"How do I get to him, Loralie? What can I do to make this all go away?" The voice begging for Loralie's guidance doesn't sound like my own. I've become someone I never thought I would be.

"Here, child." Wilted in her hand, like death curling into death, is a flower. It's a deep purple so rich and devastating it beckons my heart to Loralie's whim. With black highlights that shine in the moonlight and dark green thorns cascading along the stem, this flower embodies everything Loralie is and can be. Gruesome beauty.

"Stop his pain, Evina. I can't listen to his heartbroken cries any longer. Join me on this side of death and go to him." She wraps my hand around the flower, the thorns biting into my palm.

In my hand is the way to my brother. Life has been so lonely without the conversations we used to have, the way we used to do our chores together or explore the neighborhood together. The pain Perdu is feeling burns bright in my chest, singeing a hole through my heart.

To be close to him. To be home.

The thorns dig deeper into my skin, drawing fresh tears from my eyes. I can almost hear his voice again. He sounded younger than he was, somehow, like that part of growing up never came for him. This flower has brought me closer to Perdu than I could have ever hoped for.

"Just one petal will do," Loralie whispers. "Then you will end both his and your suffering, Evina."

With a shaky hand, I pinch a soft petal between my fingers and separate it from the flower. I can feel death washing over me like a flood of nausea and fear and hope. Vile hope. The hope of death and the hope of the end of a life.

My grip tightens around the thorns, but I can't feel the pain anymore. The gentle sound of the rain rocks me into a peaceful trance.

"I'm so close, Perdu," I whisper.

The feeling of the petal between my lips is calming. It's like I can feel Perdu's arms around me. I bite into the petal, and an acidic taste floods my tongue.

Perdu died at the hands of Dolion. Now I will die at the hands of Loralie.

He left his family. Now I will leave mine.

He hurt me. Now I will hurt Mom and Dad.

Something small sinks inside my chest. The acid burns my mouth and makes my eyes water. Perdu wouldn't want me to hurt them, no matter how much he is hurting now. The burn of the flower trickles down my throat. He wouldn't want me to ruin our family more. He wouldn't want me to die.

Perdu wouldn't want this.

I won't live to see the sunrise, but I know you will. That's what he wrote to me. He wanted me to survive this. I lift my gaze, and through the stray wisps of my hair, I see light orange tinting the horizon.

I will live to see the sunrise, Perdu. I will.

I look up at Loralie slowly. The rain feels freeing as it hits my face. This isn't about my life—it never has been, not like they are trying to convince me it is. From the moment I entered this place, my life was never the one at stake. Somehow, it's still Perdu who is at risk. His memory. If I die, Mom and Dad won't remember him the way he deserves, and everything that matters will be gone.

Loralie is trying to convince me my struggle is whether or not to end my own life, but the struggle has always been and always will be grieving my brother. Learning how to move on from that morning but not forgetting what made Perdu who he was.

It has never been about me.

It's been about who I can become if I don't let grief consume me.

I drop Loralie's flower into the mud as the acid turns cold in my stomach.

"You can't control me, Loralie. You can't manipulate me anymore." My voice is surprisingly calm and steady compared to the rage boiling within. The rain falls down around us but never touches Loralie.

"My child, if that were true, I wouldn't be here and that acid wouldn't be burning a hole in your stomach." Though she attempts to say it with confidence, her voice wavers. "It's over, Evina. And Clair has lost, just like he always does."

Clair?

"No," I say, my voice so quiet even I can hardly hear. I will keep going, I will keep fighting. For Perdu, for Dad, even for Mom. I raise my voice as I speak. "No, you can't do this, Loralie." I hate the tears that fall from my eyes. "You were supposed to be my friend, you were supposed to care about me, but you're evil. And manipulative. You deserve whatever hell you are in for doing this to me and to my brother."

And to Clair, I want to add, but I stop myself. I have to fight the urge to trust him again.

"Evina—"

"No," I snap. "You don't get to speak—not anymore. This is *over*. You *cannot* manipulate me any longer." As I say it, I feel a solid wall building itself between me and Loralie in my mind. She once was a friend, and watching the unexpected sadness in her eyes hurts me and confuses me.

She was my friend . . .

I shake my head and lower my gaze, determined to hold true to what I know.

"This is over, Loralie."

She doesn't try to speak as she slowly backs away from me. She wipes a tear from her eye, and I have to remind myself she isn't actually sad. *Loralie does not care.*

The world around me seems to darken as the sun comes up, and it confuses me. Then Loralie's sad face morphs into a grin just as the first rays of sunlight sparkle on the ground.

I don't feel death coming, I just cease to exist. One moment I'm staring at the sun Perdu knew I would see, and the next moment I'm nothing but a memory to everyone who knew me.

Chapter Sixty-Eight

Clair

I'm not strong enough to resist Loralie.

"Dammit," I mutter as I dash through the trees. Where is Evina? She has to be here somewhere. The panic that fills me makes my legs threaten to give out. "Evina!"

She doesn't answer.

I finally break the clearing and see the gate a ways ahead. A small figure stands by the entrance. Loralie. And she's alone.

No, no, no. Fuck. She's not alone. A body lies on the ground by her feet.

"If you touched her!" I shout as I run up to Loralie. The anger pounding in my chest ignites a wave of hatred, all directed toward Loralie.

"Once again, Clair, your threats mean nothing to me." She smiles as she turns to face me. "You can't touch me."

Evina lies behind Loralie, her body enveloped slowly by the mud.

Another person gone, another child lost, and the small glimpse of hope I saw when Evina entered the Oasis flickers out as her light fades.

Gone.

Loralie vanishes into the rain, and I am left alone with Perdu's little sister.

So, she's dead. The last hope, the last light in the Oasis, is dead. I should be sad. I should kneel over her and cry for hours because she's gone. But the truth is, of course she's dead. There isn't another possible ending, is there? It always goes the same way.

I stand up and turn to face the forest that I hate, the forest I despise, the thief, the monster, my nightmare . . . my home.

"Is this what you want?" I throw my hands out as I yell into the trees. "Does this make you happy?"

My throat burns, but I keep screaming into the night. "Go fuck yourself, Loralie! Telling me you *fucking* need me." I grab my knife and throw it into the dark. Regret instantly fills me.

I walk toward Evina's body before turning back to the Oasis. "You know what?" I shout. "You've won. I'm done. How's that? I don't care anymore. Do whatever the hell you want."

I rub my shaking hand over my mouth. What do I do now?

I can feel my heart shutting down and my mind turning off. I can't keep going, and now there's no more reason to fight. She didn't survive. Clearly, I'm doing something wrong.

I can't handle this anymore.

I'm done.

"Go fuck yourself," I mutter, turning away from the forest. After a moment of silence, I whip my body around again and continue shouting. "Are you just going to let me go? I could leave, walk out of this forest forever, and it doesn't matter to you, does it?" Who am I talking to? Loralie? Or am I talking to Devil Oasis itself? "All these years I've been a part of this, and it wouldn't even matter if I just left."

I sit next to Evina and hit the ground repeatedly.

"Help me, Clair . . ." Loralie's voice drifts through the morning air. "Please . . ."

I bury my head in my hands and try to block her out.

Chapter Sixty - Nine

Evina

Gone. That's what happens when a person leaves this earth. They are gone. They leave everyone and everything that was important. When a person dies, it's a loss that hurts the people they loved. When a person dies at their own hand, it's a loss that kills those people. The thing is, hurt is real. Pain is real. And sometimes you don't want that hurt anymore. Your heart has been beaten so many times that it can't stand under the weight any longer. And when that happens, Dolion and Loralie have been given access to your heart. This, this moment right here, is when you have to decide if your life is worth fighting for.

A soft breeze whistles as it rushes past my ear. My stomach lurches suddenly, and burning acid climbs my throat. There's a reason my body is in pain right now. What is it?

I open my eyes slowly. The bright sky and a few white clouds look down at me, and I can't help but feel protected under their care. Why am I outside? I close my eyes again and listen for more sounds. A tree in the breeze . . . I must be in the front yard. Maybe I fell asleep while Perdu and I were playing hide-and-seek. That's happened before . . . right? Yes, when we were kids.

The gentle sound of a lapping lake reminds me we aren't kids any longer—not really. I snap my eyes open and stare at a small cloud next to the blinding sun. My stomach tightens before rolling as reality sinks in. Perdu and I aren't kids, and we aren't playing a game. Perdu is gone. Devil Oasis surrounds me. And Loralie wanted me dead.

I roll over just in time for the acid to blister my throat and mouth before I vomit a dark goo into the dirt beneath me. It sizzles as it settles into the ground. My stomach tightens, and tears come to my eyes as I clutch my neck, praying for the burning to cease. My insides stir again, and I move to my knees before once again hurling the burning poison. My arms shake, fighting to hold me up as the rest of the poison leaves my body. When I sit back, I'm trembling and crying and cold.

A man kneels next to me. I notice him now. Clair. I know I can trust him; the pull in my heart tells me this man is a victim just like I am and no more.

"Evina?" Clair wipes his nose with the back of his hand and blocks his eyes from the light reflecting off the lake. "You're alive . . ."

His voice is weak, and his body trembles faintly.

"You're alive," he says again, reaching out for me. Before his hand touches my face, he pulls away, staring at me with eyes that look as though they're lost somewhere in darkness.

I look away from him. Heat rushes into my cheeks and forehead at the humiliation of puking in front of Clair. All I can do is nod my head, staring at my mud-covered boots.

"I carried you over to the lake, so you're safe now. It's all going to be okay," he says, still sounding as though he is in shock. "How do you feel?"

I feel like puking out my insides again and curling up in the sunlight until I fall asleep.

"What happened?" my small, weak voice croaks. Each sound I make feels like dragging a knife through my sore throat.

"Loralie," Clair answers, a hint of anger breaking through his voice. "She got you to poison yourself."

Yes. That's it. I remember the panic once I knew it was over. I'd already eaten the flower, and it was too late.

"How did I survive?" I clutch my stomach, afraid I might throw up again.

"Did you eat the entire petal?" He asks it calmly, but the look in his eye tells me his mind is anything but calm.

I shake my head.

"You don't get to speak—not anymore." Those are the words I said when I fought back; that's when I took back my own life. And it worked because I meant what I was saying. That's the difference. *"This is* over. *You* cannot *manipulate me any longer."*

I ate enough to poison me, but not to kill me before I stood up for my life. Because in the end, I am strong enough.

"I know this isn't my place to say anymore, but your brother would be very proud of you."

The sun behind Clair blinds out most of his features. His square jaw and his messy hair are outlined in the light. The light! How did I not notice it before? I sit back slowly but with excitement, looking at the bright sky. The sun is coming up. It's . . . It's sunrise. I did it? I'm here? I look over at the lake, which is reflecting colors of red, orange, and pink.

Everything that happened in the night comes back to me. The fear, the pain . . . the betrayal. Clair kissing Loralie, the one who wanted me dead.

"You kissed her," I say.

"I did." He runs his fingers through his hair and looks at the ground.

"Why?"

He shrugs and says, "Because I'm weak. Because she has a hold over me and has for many years."

I shrug. When he speaks, I know I can trust him, because I understand. "You're not weak," I say. "She tricked me the same way. She made me believe she was my friend."

"I'm really sorry, Evina." He finally turns to face me, his light eyes full of emotion. "I'm sorry I wasn't honest with you. I'm sorry I'm this way."

"I'm sorry I'm this way too." I turn away from Clair and watch the peace of the morning lake.

Clair places his hand on my shoulder. "Are you okay?" he asks.

Other than the pain in my stomach, throat, and mouth, I believe I am. I nod, looking at the man from the cemetery. His eyes are red and puffy, his cheeks are tearstained, and his hands shake slightly. He looks tired.

"Are *you* okay?" I ask him.

He seems shocked at first and then looks to the ground as if searching for the answer before he slowly lifts his head, eyes connecting with mine. "You survived," he says, nodding, his voice faltering. "I was starting to think it was impossible to survive."

I smile softly. Birds fly over the lake in the sun, chirping morning songs.

He sits beside me. I lean over the water, looking at my own reflection: green eyes, tangled brown hair, my face tired and covered in tears. Even so, I'm free of Loralie. My arms and wrists are still cut, and I'm still bruised, broken, and hurt, but I'm free of the heart-wrenching fear that I may never live to see the sunrise again. I can breathe, and it doesn't hurt. I can think and not risk the danger of death. I understand now what happened to my brother. I get it. I can't explain it, but I understand. My heart hurts for him. I wish he'd had the strength to survive. I wish I had known and could've helped him.

I lean back again, sitting with Clair as the sun continues to rise. I once again surprise myself when I nearly fall onto him, burying my face in his shoulder. His sleeve is soon wet with my tears. I can't speak; I struggle at the moment to breathe.

His arms wrap around me as he comforts me. "I know," he says in a quiet voice, nearly a whisper. "I know better than most."

As he holds me, I see the lines, the scars, that run up the inside of his arm. He does know. He's like me. I turn my arm around to see my own cuts. They will be scars one day too.

I pull away, sniffling a couple times. The tears have dried on my cheeks. I watch as the water sends small waves to our feet, the birds fly in the air, and the sky begins to turn bright blue. I allow a large smile to spread across my face.

"I did it," I say.

"Yes, you did."

I look at Clair. He returns my smile, his crooked teeth and deep dimples giving him a boyish charm, but there's something about him that's sadder than he used to be.

"You should leave with me," I tell him. "You shouldn't have to stay here any longer."

"This is my home," he says. "It always has been."

"Don't you want to go somewhere else? Somewhere you can have a life?"

He looks out at the water, his eyes sparkling in the sun. "I've lived here my whole life. This is where I belong. This is where I have always belonged."

"That doesn't mean you can't find a new belonging," I tell him. "I'll help you, like you helped me."

"I guess . . ." He looks out over the water, the soft wind blowing through his blond hair. "I guess all I've done is fail. I haven't been able to help anyone."

"So, what am I?" I grab his hand, smiling. I feel unusually comfortable with him, like I've known him a long time. "I wouldn't be here if not for you. So, thank you."

He looks at me, then back to the water. "You were capable of fighting the battle on your own."

"Yes," I say. "But you were right: the walk out was much easier with help." I lean my head back against his shoulder. "If you want to stay, I understand. If you want to get out, you have a place to go. This land is a nightmare anyway. Guess I should've gotten that before though; it is called Devil Oasis."

"True," Clair says. "But *devil* spelled backward is *lived*."

Lived. I lived. Not everything is black-and-white. Not everything is exactly how it seems. Devil Oasis is an evil place. But it's also a place of peace and victory; you just have to be willing to see it. Now, after facing the darkest thing I've been through, I am safe, not afraid, and not alone.

I escaped Loralie. I am a survivor. I lived past her temptations. I personified my dark thoughts without passing that knowledge onto myself and without knowing that I was my own hunter. I have scars from my journey that I may regret, but I'll never forget. When I look at my arm, yes, I am reminded of the battles I forced myself to fight, but I am always reminded of the battles I had the courage to win. If she ever comes back for me, she'd better be prepared for a long fight. My life is mine, and I deserve the right to keep it. No one, not even I, can take that right away.

I was the victim. I was the villain. And now I am the victor.

"You're right," Clair says. "I want a life. I want to leave Devil Oasis."

Epilogue

Lady

Fish cluster in the shallow water near the shore as I watch another sunrise.

The air feels different these days. It's like death has settled deep within every crevice of the land. The trees have become taller, thicker, darker. With each death, the forest grows impatient, like it's waiting for something it isn't being given. The story isn't over. The curse is becoming darker, still hungry for children, still hungry for death.

I will spend eternity attempting to forget the bloodstains from the countless deaths I wish I hadn't been forced to witness.

Without a caretaker, a guardian to guide the others out, a hole has been left in the forest—a hole I fear will soon be filled with something so vile the light will be choked out before anything can stop it. Every dark living thing within the land stirs, chirps, and chatters in anticipation of what is to come.

The water I've become feels like a curse all on its own, like shackles forcing me to watch as Devil Oasis drives Dolion and Loralie, manipulates them, and uses them as its pawn. Each child, each slaughter, I am forced to relive, trapped in my prison, unable to do anything to help them. Karl was only nineteen, still so young, so innocent. And they took him. They took my child like they have taken so many others.

My dead body lies at the bottom of the lake, and for the first time in decades, I can feel it pull to me. The mud laces between its toes. The long hair floats in the water, reaching toward the shore I am forbidden to walk upon.

"Karl was so young," I whisper, wishing my ties to the water did not leave me incapable of crying. "They were all so young."

But the light has not yet lost—I have to remember that. Clair is safe. The last of my family has left the Oasis. He's safe now. It's over.

He'll be back, the Oasis whispers in the wind. *He is a boy of the Oasis. He will always come back to me.*

CURSE RULE #5...

The twins were born from the curse; they were created from the power of the land. Therefore, they alone are the sole force capable of destroying the forest. Divided they are unable to achieve their full strength. In order to be stronger than Devil Oasis, the twins must unite and turn against the land as one.

Did you love this book? Would you like to support me as an author?

Leave a review on Amazon or Goodreads!

Newsletter

For access to early releases, giveaways, and insider information on the Dark Oasis trilogy as well as my other releases, sign up for my newsletter! Links can be found on my Instagram page @jacieneher. Thank you for reading this book and supporting my career as an author!

Turn the page for more...

- A bonus chapter from Loralie's POV

- A sneak peek into book 3

- Bloopers

- Acknowledgments

- About the author

And content exclusive to the hardcover edition including

- A letter from Emmeline to Arron

- A short story about Karl and Edmund's life

- Author Q&A

- Character art of Marie the dog

Loralie POV

1941

Shortly after Loralie gave birth

The wind beats against the house, causing the shutters to knock clumsily against the wooden trim. When I look down at the child I gave birth to, his scared eyes meet mine. I focus my gaze forward and fight against the strength of the storm. The closer I get to the house the less painful the rain drops become, and my sore, achey skin is thankful for it. It feels as though it's been hours since I left Karl's house, though I know in reality it hasn't been. I have to get rid of this baby before the sun comes up, if I don't do this while Dolion is asleep it won't happen. He would force me to keep the child.

My dress is wet and heavy, but at least the dirt is washed out and the colors are bright again. I have to walk carefully to keep from tripping on my weighed down dress, the child in my arms keeps me from pulling the skirt above my feet. This baby will be Mother's problem, not mine. She deserves the chains a child brings.

The baby watches me with hopeful eyes, and it makes me angry.

"I'm not here to protect you," I snap. His small, dark eyes continue staring at me as though I am someone he loves. I clench my jaw and try to keep myself from dropping the child here and being done with him.

"We're close now." When I speak the baby reaches up and wraps his small hand around a curl of my drenched hair. He tugs a little. My eyes widen slightly at the familiar feeling. Dolion used to do that when we were kids and he wanted my attention. I would always ignore him.

I shake my head and pull my hair away from the baby's hand. I can finally see the front door.

The wind picks up and I have to brace myself against the storm to keep moving forward.

Finally we climb the steps to the porch. I suck in a deep breath, aware that I am willingly walking back to Mother and Emile. Back to the darkness they bring. I knock.

A light flickers on inside the house, shining through the living room window. Hope springs to life within my chest, growing lighter when there's quick movement from inside. I stand and wait in the shelter of the house.

Maybe it'll be different now. Dolion was always the one she truly hated after all. I stiffen as I realize what I am thinking. Who the hell cares if Mother thinks differently of me when Dolion is not around. I don't need her.

I shake off the thoughts but can't help the hint of a smile that rests on my face. I wait, holding the child in my arms. Soon they're going to open the door for me and Mother will realize that she missed me. I was her prized child after all. *I* was the one she carted around to present to her friends. *I* was allowed to go to the parties. Soon the door will open.

Soon.

My smile fades as doubt rings in my head with each passing second. I shift on my feet and adjust the baby in my hands.

Soon.

But when the light inside flickers off my chest tightens.

"Mother?" The word is barely a whisper. "Mother, please. I need you."

I stare at the closed door, my eyes sting but I'm unable to blink. The patterns in the wood slowly bleed together as my mind drifts further from reality. I want to turn and run away, I want to hide like I did so many times as a small child, but I can't.

Then my lips curl into a sudden smile as tears burn trails down my cheeks. An abrupt laugh comes from somewhere deep inside me, followed by the crack of thunder as lightning rips through the sky, illuminating the porch, casting my thin shadow against the door that won't open for me.

The baby starts crying.

"Shut *up!*" I yell at him.

I'm alone and cold. I'm probably going to be sick. How could Mother do this to me?

My teeth grind against each other and my jaw ticks.

Fuck her.

I pound against the door with a new sense of urgency.

"Let us in!" I yell loud enough I know they can hear. "You hear me? Let us the fuck inside this damned house right now!"

Everything remains perfectly still within the silent home.

Hot tears burn my eyes. What the *hell* is so wrong with me she won't help me when I need her? No, it's not what's wrong with me, it's what's wrong with *her.*

This baby, this prison I can't escape, pulls at my hair again and I fight every urge to throw him off the porch.

My hair blows in the harsh wind. I look up at the window next to the door, a new fire awakening in me.

"It's funny, really!" I shout at the woman I know is inside. "You raised me but you were always afraid of me. I know you were!"

I sit the baby on the floor and turn back toward the window. My fists are clenched by my sides and there's so much pressure on my jaw that my teeth ache.

I close my eyes and listen to the chaos of the world around me. The thunder rolling through the clouds, the wind whipping branches, the rain pelting the house. I breathe in the cool air and open my eyes, excitement sparking through my chest.

I grab a rock and the child starts crying again as soon as the sound of the shattering glass drowns out the storm.

All I am is anger. It pulses through me, it corrupts my mind, it drives my arms and legs, pushing me to move past the pain of recent childbirth to be able to carry out my mission. I grab a hammer that was leaning against the side railing and pull back, thrusting the weapon through the wall of Mother's precious home, the house she has taken pride in for so long. The anger shocks me with adrenaline like it's electricity flooding through my veins.

I step in front of the door and hold the hammer above me.

"You will take this child!" I yell so loud my voice breaks. "You can't hide from your fate!" Then I bring the hammer down on the door and the rough edge of the handle slices open the tip of my finger. A loud crack comes from the wood. I swing the hammer back again, the weight pulling at my arms slightly. I lean into the weight and use it to propel the hammer forward, driving it further into the front door.

"Don't." I slam the hammer against the door again. *Bang!* "Treat." *Bang!* "Your." *Bang!* "Children." *Bang!* "Like." *Bang!* "Shit!" *Bang!* Breathing heavy, I pull away from the sight of the mutilated door, the handle hanging limp from part of the split wood. I smile slowly. In the darkness of the night I see destruction and it gives me hope. Hope that someone as evil, as vile as my mother, may one day get what they deserve. I toss the hammer to the side as lightning strikes the sky again. The cut on my finger stings and fresh blood runs down my hand. I love it.

"What the hell?" Emile roars from inside. The sound of his voice makes the baby cry louder.

I gather my skirt and sprint through the pouring rain until I'm hidden in the darkness. Mother's precious home has been destroyed, and now she has another fucking baby to hate. That's what she deserves. A fate worse than death, a fate chained to that sickness I grew within my stomach.

I look up at the night sky and panic. Morning is close. I have to get back before Dolion wakes.

Arron,

I know you don't wish to hear from me, but I couldn't leave it the way we did. I love you, Arron. I've loved you since we were kids. I made a mistake, and I don't deserve to have your love another day in my life. I'm not asking for what I don't deserve, I simply want to leave things better than... than that awful look on your face when you saw me with him. I'm so sorry. I know what I did was monstrous, he's your brother for goodness sake! My mother had just died, I wasn't thinking well. I just need you to know I love you. I have always loved you, and I always will.

With love,
Emmeline

KARL AND EDMUND

A DARK OASIS SHORT STORY

JACIE NEHER

Cover design: Jacie Neher

Instead of a full story, with a beginning, middle, end, and climax, this is really just glimpses into moments of Karl and Edmund's lives. It shows what growing up had been like for them after their grandfather was killed, and it shows aspects of how Edmund became the person we knew him to be in Dark Oasis. Each section is a time jump, and it's all a small portion of their true story. I had a very hard time writing this, as its structure is abnormal and covers a very large period of time. I hope you can take this moment to connect with Karl and Edmund as characters, and I hope you enjoy this little peek into what their lives had been like.

~Jacie

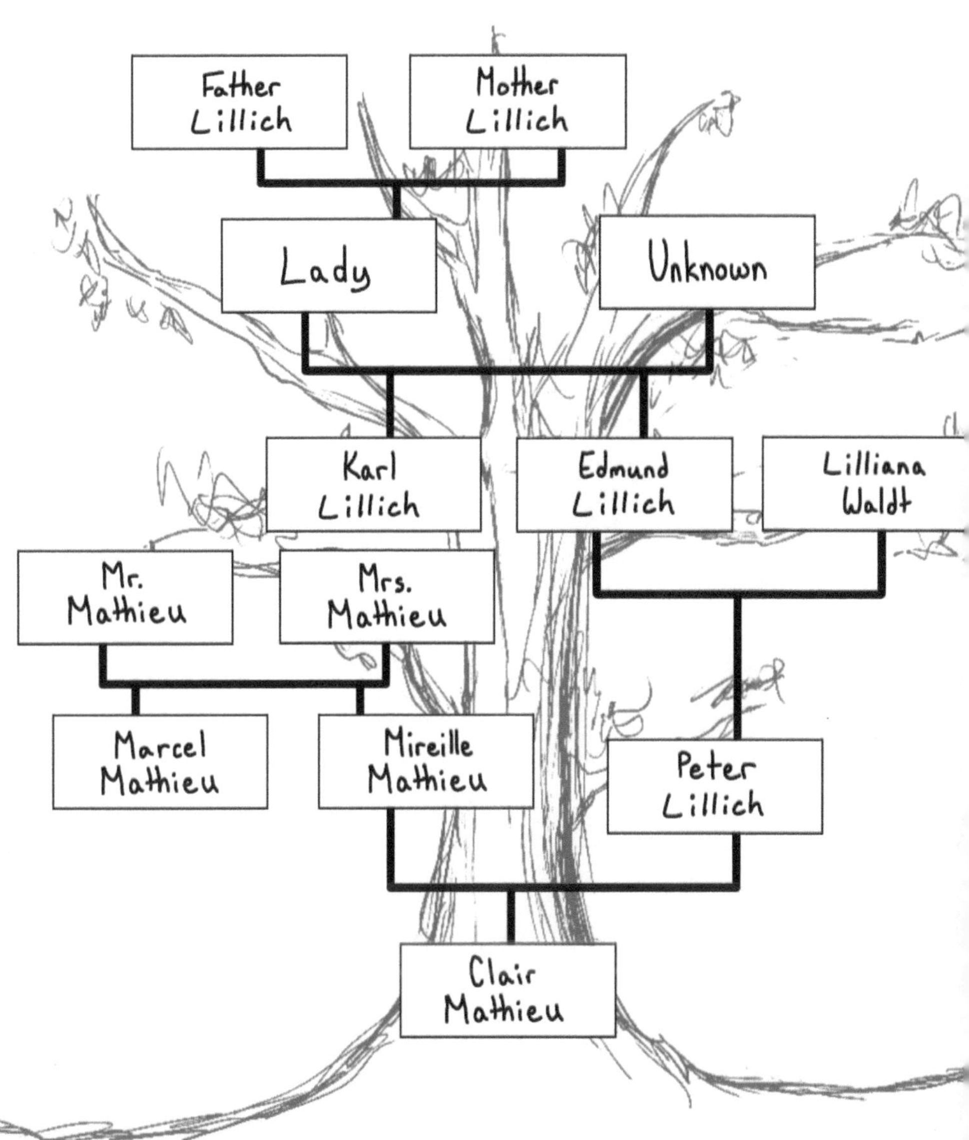

Father Lillich
Mother Lillich
Lady
Unknown
Karl Lillich
Edmund Lillich
Lilliana Waldt
Mr. Mathieu
Mrs. Mathieu
Marcel Mathieu
Mireille Mathieu
Peter Lillich
Clair Mathieu

"Without you here, I'm so alone. But I will fight 'til my last breath, 'cause you are the compass that beats in my chest."

Compass, Sail North

1941–1958

Karl

1941

An hour after Dolion and Loralie's deaths

I unknowingly befriended the one person I could never be friends with, who is more connected to the curse than I, and now our grandfather is gone, and Edmund and I are alone.

The wind rages on as the tree above me and my brother thrashes its branches against the roars of thunder. Edmund cries in my arms and I rock him. My body trembles, but I don't let my arms weaken; my mind breaks, but I won't let myself cave. I look down at this child and in him I see everything I felt in myself the day our mother left us. He is scared and alone and confused because he is so young. I think of the way our grandfather had become our only light in life. He watched over us and shielded us from the world when Mother went to be with the lake. Now I must do that for Edmund.

The blood that is splattered across Edmund's clothes causes the image of our grandfather, skull cracked and eyes permanently open, laying on the ground in front of our home, to flicker in my mind. I hold Edmund closer to me.

I may be ten years old in body, but I'm not a child anymore. I've been alive for almost three times my physical age and I am old enough to understand the situation Edmund and I are in.

Our mother left us nearly two decades ago because she had to protect us from a coming curse, a curse that Dolion and Loralie's deaths have brought upon us. What happens now that the curse has started is still a mystery to me, Grandfather never explained that far into the future. Mother leaving gives me and my brother a shot at survival because she will always be in the lake to watch over us. Or at least that's what Grandfather told me. When she died, mine and Edmund's ages were frozen in time because that was the deal our mother made with the curse, but now we will begin aging again.

Our mother had become the lake this land thrives off of. The lake that's only a couple hundred yards away.

My little brother cries again when the thunder cracks.

"Mother," I whisper to the lake but stop myself before I say anymore. I don't need her. She left me and Edmund years ago, and whether it truly was to protect us or not, she abandoned us. Left us confused and hurt. I don't need her help to protect my brother the way she never could.

Edmund clutches at my shirt, his pale blond fuzzy hair flicking in the wind. He looks so much like Mother did.

I curl him into my chest and brace myself against the bitter wind. I could feel the moment the curse began; thunder ripped through the sky and hasn't stopped for the past hour. Grandfather warned me this day would come, and now it's upon us and he's not here to guide me. It's Edmund and me against the world.

Karl

1946

Five years after Dolion and Loralie's deaths

The rain starts pouring as Edmund tramples inside. He looks up at me, the water from the rain drenching his pale hair and dirty clothes. The rain came out of nowhere, as it usually does here.

Edmund shouts something at me but the sound of the downpour keeps me from understanding.

"What?" I yell back at him, stepping close and leaning down to my brother.

"Leaking again!" he shouts in my ear and I barely hear him above the rain. He's been using English words instead of German lately, and there's only one place he could be hearing English from. Dolion and Loralie are communicating with him somehow. I know a few English words from the days before Dolion's death, when I foolishly considered him a friend. But in the past few months, I've been learning more and more from Edmund and it's making me uneasy. I'm about to scold him for using English again, but before I do, I realize what Edmund is saying.

I look up to the branches above us. Damn it! I hadn't made it into town before the storm. Water is pouring through our torn roof.

"Hide the clothes and anything else we want to keep dry!" I exit our shelter as Edmund nods his little head firmly at me before carrying out the task assigned to him.

Then I begin the climb I've grown to despise. Branches. So many branches.

Something ripped a gash in our tarp last week. I had feared we'd get a storm like this before I got a new tarp from town, but I had hoped the weather would hold off. Damn hope.

"Shit," I mutter as I lose footing. I cling tightly to the branch I'm holding, causing the bark to dig into my skin. When I regain steadiness, I pull myself upward.

As I climb, I don't miss the distant glow of unmistakable blue eyes watching me.

We aren't alone in this forest, the forest that has seemed to grow from nothing in the last five years. Other than the tall grass between the trees, there is no trace of the empty field this land used to be. Every so often I'll hear a ghostly hum float through the branches, or the creak of decaying bones as someone wanders through the woods. My brother thinks they are his friends, and he pretends to talk to the apparitions regularly. That's why I never let Edmund out of my sight and make him sleep beside me at night. If my brother leaves my side, even for a second, I dart awake and scan the dark for him. Because I know the truth about the noises I hear. They belong to the ones who killed our grandfather.

Dolion and Loralie haunt this forest, and I may not know all of the rules to their curse, but I know for a fact that they will come for me and Edmund one day. According to Grandfather, they crave our deaths because of our blood. We are connected to Edith, and any blood relatives of hers are unwillingly tied to the twins.

Why? I don't know. That devil, Loralie, killed my grandfather before he could tell me.

The rain pushes against me and I fight to get higher in the tree. My clothes weigh me down as the rain soaks through them, forcing me to strip my shirt to finish the climb.

I finally reach about ten feet above ground and lean back on a solid branch, eyeing the pool the rain has created in the tarp, and the gash the rain water is forcing its way through. I'm sure it's pouring on Edmund right now. I've got to get this fixed.

With what? I left the sewing kit in the shelter.

That's all right, I tell myself. *Just ask Edmund. He knows where you keep it.*

I carefully find my footing on the corner of our shelter, an area where tarp drapes over a large tree branch. As long as I keep my feet steady, the structure will support me. I had to make sure it would hold once I realized repairs on the roof would be a regular thing and I would be spending a lot of time up here. Step to the right, duck under the hanging branch, don't slip in the rain. I've got this.

Finally, I make it to the tear in the tarp and shout down at my brother.

"Edmund!" In seconds his little head appears below me, with his hand above his eyes to block the spray of water. "I need…" My words get lost in the roar of the storm.

I hold onto the wobbling structure below as a harsh wind picks up, threatening to push me over the edge of mine and Edmund's home.

"I need rope and one of those wooden needles!" I shout, now that I'm confident he'll be able to hear me. "The ones I made last summer!"

He nods and ducks out of view. I shiver as I wait for him to come back. The wind and rain are starting to reach my bones and I'm afraid I'll catch a cold soon.

"Get a fire going inside!" I tell him as he stretches as high as he can to hand the supplies to me.

Fear glints in his eyes, and for a moment, I remember my brother is only five. He's so young, but I know he is brave. He's older than I could ever understand behind those glassy eyes that reveal nothing. He's so closed off. I think he got that from the woman we called our mother. The woman who left us to suffer in this position, who left me to deal with all of this. Edith, that was her name. Edith.

"Edmund, I need you to get the fire going or we'll get sick. Be careful, I've shown you how to do it before. Remember what I told you and I promise the fire won't hurt you."

The fear in his gaze begins to shift to determination and my heart swells with pride at the courage my little brother shows. He's always been so afraid of flames.

The rope fits in the large wooden needle perfectly, just as I made it to do, and after a few seconds of forcing, the tip of the needle breaks through the tarp. I overlap the two sides of the gash to keep as much water as possible from leaking through the roof again before I continue binding it together. Once I'm confident it'll keep us mostly dry, I climb down the tree and rush back inside the small shelter—made from branches, leaves, and a giant tarp—that me and my brother call home.

Before I duck inside the shelter, I scan the young trees again for those blue eyes. Some nights the twins are active, and some they aren't. I'm not sure what decides it, but I fear one night my nightmare will come true and Edmund will follow the song of his supposed friend and fall right into Loralie's hands.

Edmund

1949

Eight years after Dolion and Loralie's deaths

Her name is Lilliana. She is a girl who lives near the rapidly-growing forest Karl forces me to grow up in. She says kids outside of this forest are happy. Karl isn't happy, he's stressed all the time and he never smiles. Lilliana says that he's not a kid anymore. Karl is eighteen and she says that doesn't count.

"But you and me, Eddie, we're still kids." She leans over and whispers the next part. "That means we're still fun."

Karl doesn't know about Lilliana. Karl won't let me have friends.

Karl

1950

Nine years after Dolion and Loralie's deaths

The sound of the rough wood smoothing out under my hand echoes through our small home as my brother assembles his new cot. Soon this table I'm building will be finished and Edmund and I can stop eating meals on the floor.

Loralie has started whispering my name when it's late at night, long after Edmund has fallen to sleep. Something about her calls are enchanting and alluring and so very, very tempting. I never see her though, only hear her. Dolion, however...I can feel him watching me and Edmund far past the earliest hours of the morning. A growing sadness pierces my chest each time his gaze settles in on me. The boy who was my friend. The boy who fell prey to his sister's cruelty.

If I were to die... maybe Dolion and I could be friends again. When I realize what I just thought, I snap myself out of the daze I was caught in and force myself to keep sanding the table. What the hell was that about?

I'm nineteen now. Certainly much older than the boy I was when they killed my grandfather. But still, I feel my old self longing to be friends with Dolion again. He was kind, he was thoughtful and patient and brave. Loralie corrupted him, the same way she corrupts anyone who comes across her. He cared more about Loralie than he did about anything else, and that, in the end, is what ruined him.

I can't let myself think about Dolion for too long though. I have to cut every emotional tie I have to the twins before they become my weakness.

Edmund moves his cot against the wall and stands back, looking at it with pride.

"Did you see that, Karl? I carried it all the way from town myself." His little chest puffs up and he turns to look at me with a shine in his eye. Of course he didn't actually do it by himself, but I'll let him have this moment.

"Well done, Edmund. Go fetch us some wood and we'll make a fire." Brief fear flashes through Edmund's eyes before he scampers out quickly as I finish the long process of making a table for mine and Edmund's new home. This table has taken me three weeks, and I've only been able to work on it in the evenings when we aren't busy making runs into town. Now, running my hands over the freshly sanded lump of wood, I've never felt more accomplished in my life. I made this. It makes me excited to make many more things for our little home here in the woods. I've put off making a permanent place for us for years, I've always been so convinced our time here was temporary. But lately, well, I've started to feel so connected to this place. Like this is where I belong.

I know this is where I belong... I need the comfort the darkness brings...

So I built a shack for us. A home.

The idea of leaving this continuously growing forest scares me... I belong here. I know I do.

Karl

1950

Nine years after Dolion and Loralie's deaths

My muscles tighten as I stare through the dark at the ceiling of our home. Edmund is asleep beside me, breathing peacefully. Good. Tonight is not the night she will get him.

She doesn't speak, but I feel her presence calling to me all the same. She paces around the outside of our home, trailing her finger along the wooden walls as she walks. I hear each breath as if it were a symphony calling to me. It takes everything I am not to give in and go outside, allowing myself to be full of her presence.

What's happening to me? The older I get, the less human I feel. I'm becoming nothing but another wild animal that roams these woods. I hunt, I eat, I sleep, then I do it all again. There's no point to life. At least, not my life. But Loralie... Dolion... this forest... There's something about it all that seems to pump life back into my veins. All of the dread and the inescapable weight I carry seems to go away when I immerse myself into this world.

Before I think better of it, I crawl out from under my covers, the cold air prickling my skin slightly, and shuffle across the floor, careful not to wake Edmund. When I open the door and finally step outside, I'm surprised to find an empty forest. No Dolion... no Loralie.

I shiver and wish I brought a jacket. The forest is unusually cold for this time of the year, and the sky looks as though it may rain. Angry... the sky looks angry. Every inch of this forest is full of emotion. It's such a curious thing to me. Sometimes I wonder, though I won't ever say it out loud, if this forest is more than just land. Something about it seems to be alive. Is it alive?

Suddenly, I realize I'm lost. I don't know where I am, or how I got here. Trees rise tall on either side of me, stretching so high I can't see them anymore. Wasn't I just standing outside of our home? Or was that a while ago now? Have I wandered into the forest and gotten lost?

Nothing feels right anymore. I have to try to find my way home.

Each gentle thump in my chest guides me in the right direction. I am alive, that means I have to be here for Edmund. I know he needs me.

Is that why Loralie wants me to die? Do they somehow need better access to Edmund? I don't understand anything, but maybe if I did, it would be easier to navigate this. Our blood. It has to do with our blood, right?

The forest stretches up all around me, tall and unfamiliar. I don't know where I am or where I'm going. Edmund is out there, somewhere, hopefully tucked safe inside our little home. I have to get back to him. How long have I been gone? I'm so confused.

Thunder cracks and the wind whips around me.

Home.

I need to get home.

"Karl, Karl, Karl." Loralie's figure appears before me, black against the lightning streaked sky. "What are you running from? We're old friends... remember?"

"We were never friends, Loralie."

"Any friend of Dolion's belongs to me as well." Her smile flashes through my mind. Her bright white teeth, her glossy red lips, as if they are covered in blood. She feasts on the living and the dead. She is a monster.

Dolion is behind her, watching the situation. It's so strange seeing him again. It almost feels as though we've gone back in time, to when I was just a boy wanting a friend, and he was just a boy wanting his sister. But, this isn't back then, it's a different, more complicated time. He doesn't speak and he hardly makes eye contact with me. There's so much pain there, I almost want to feel bad for him. I mean, he had been my friend at one point, hadn't he?

"I have to get home," I say to Loralie, though my eyes don't leave Dolion. He stares at his feet as they shuffle in the dirt.

"Do you?" She hums.

I nod and grip my hand into a fist.

"Let me ask you a question, Karl." Loralie tucks a loose curl behind her ear and stares at me innocently. She then gestures toward the exit of the land and asks, "Why not leave? Why not take your little brother away from this place and move on?"

The wind suddenly shifts directions and blows toward the exit gate, as if it were attempting to guide me away from here.

Why not leave? I've been asking myself that for a while now. This place is poison and rot. All it does is make me sick. Why not take Edmund away so he can live a happier life?

"I-"

"Why not do something worthwhile for once?"

Dolion's eyes harden, laced with a clear warning. He's looking at Loralie as though he wants to say something, but for some reason, he can't.

Ignore her. I'm shocked to hear Dolion's voice in my head. He's still not looking at me.

Loralie, however, has her blue eyes locked firmly on mine. "Why..." Her mouth curls into a smile. "Not..." There's something about her that makes me shudder with fear. "Leave...?" Her smile grows wider.

Why not leave?

Out there, things could be different for us. So why haven't I left?

I look at Dolion and then at Loralie. Then I look at the forest all around us.

This place is death, but it's also life. Who would I be without the rot that fills this land? I am trauma, I am tragedy... who would I be without this peaceful darkness?

I am nothing without this place.

Nothing.

Every time I think of leaving, I hear a low, quiet voice in the back of my mind laugh at me. I'll never leave. Because, if I'm being honest with myself, I'm obsessed with this place. There's something about it I long to be filled with. Anything I have promised Edmund about leaving someday is a lie. There is something about Devil Oasis I can't live without.

There is no escape. As long as I am alive, Devil Oasis will torture me.

Edmund

1950

Nine years after Dolion and Loralie's deaths

Karl has been leaving a lot at night. He doesn't know I notice but I'm nine and half, I'm not just a child anymore, like he thinks I am.

I'm worried about him. I told Lilliana about how he disappears after dark and she said her brother used to do that when he turned nineteen too. She says older people just don't like to be around their families much anymore. I think it's more than that. Karl wouldn't just abandon me, he's always been too scared to leave me alone in the middle of the night. I used to hear giggles and voices in the forest, and I would follow them because Karl didn't let me have friends and it sounded like they were having fun.

But since Karl started acting weird, I've stayed away from the voices. I'm afraid they have something to do with the way Karl has been behaving. Maybe he started listening to the voices, too.

It also makes me nervous to think that Karl is like Lilliana's brother. He died when he was nineteen. What if the same thing happens to my brother?

Karl

1950

Nine years after Dolion and Loralie's deaths

"We need food, Karl," Edmund whines again. "It's been days."

He grabs my wrist and pulls at me lightly.

My body is heavy, and every time I try to get up, everything hurts. It's just too much.

"Please, Karl," Edmund begs. "We'll die if we don't do something."

I have to hold back a laugh. There's nothing funny about death. Nothing funny at all. Yet, the sickness festering in my mind says otherwise.

When I finally lift my head to look at my brother, I find his red, sleepless eyes full of tears.

"I've been trying," he whispers. He's been hunting. I told him not to go into town without me, and he took it seriously. But soon, I'm sure he'll leave without me. "But, I can't catch anything. I'm not as good as you. Please..."

Why not leave? Loralie's words haven't left me. Why not give Edmund a better life? I shake my head. The thought of leaving scares me. I belong here.

"You have to lift the bow," Edmund says. I look down at my little brother, shocked to see we are now outside, and there's a bow and arrow in my hand. When did that happen? How did we get out here?

Edmund places his hand on mine and looks ahead, at the target I'm sure he's hoping will be his next meal. "We have to do this, Karl. We can't go on like this any longer."

The roots of the trees twist under my feet, forming large knots and trapping plants that grew in their path. Sometimes I feel as though the roots have weeded their way into my mind as well, trapping me in this darkness. There's no way out. Even if somehow I were actually able to get myself to leave this forest, it would always be a part of me. It would always fester in my mind.

Edmund shakes his head angrily and grabs the bow from my hand. It shocks me and confuses me. Why is he so upset?

He points the bow at the deer, and, even though the weapon is way too large for him, he shoots. And misses. He does, however, spook the deer, and she runs away.

Edmund throws the bow on the ground and shouts. "Why won't you help me, Karl? What's happening to you?"

What's happening to me? Nothing feels wrong. In fact, everything feels perfectly fine. I'm here, in this forest... I'm home. What more could I want?

No, there *is* something wrong. Everyone wants me to leave this place. *Why not leave?*

I can't leave. But, I'm keeping Edmund here, aren't I?

I'm scared, confused, and alone, but there is one thing I know to be true. I don't want to leave this place. Ever. And, it's time I do something to make sure I never leave.

Karl

1950

Nine years after Dolion and Loralie's deaths

I need to be close to the earth, I need to feel its pulsing life in my body, I need to be here, where I am home, forever. The rope is the only way to never have to live without this land, I see that now.

Death. Death is life... It's an escape. Maybe Edith got something right after all.

Edmund

1950

Nine years after Dolion and Loralie's deaths...
3 hours after Karl's death

Another splinter drives into my finger, but I keep going, keep shaping, keep carving.

I was younger then, hours ago, when I still had my brother with me. He was asleep right next to me, like every night. Then, like he has so many nights lately, he left in the quiet darkness. I'm sure he had no idea I was awake too. The door to our home shut behind him, and I was left all alone to face the sudden emptiness. That was then.

This is now.

I've had to make this grave with a branch, so it's not the best, but still, I think Karl would be proud. It's small, it's uneven, but it's meant for Karl, so it's perfect.

Karl.

I saw him.

His swinging body, his haunted face. The birds had already gotten to him. I yelled at them, hot tears streaming down my cheeks as I beat the birds away from my brother's body. Death crept up my spine and poisoned my own body as I touched my brother and pulled him down to hold him.

I shake my head, new tears forming as I think about it all. I try not to cry, I must be strong for Karl. But I am incapable of holding back my tears.

The ground I buried him beneath is only feet away. His body... my brother.

Keep working, I tell myself. *Karl wouldn't want you to be weak.*

The board is finished, now for the most important part. I steady my brother's knife over the wooden board and slowly, carefully, carve his name in the surprisingly soft wood.

Karl... Did he have a last name? Do I have a last name?

Karl. That's all I carve into his board. That and a small number *19* below his name to remember the age he died. I wipe away the tears that have fallen, but more take their place.

I feel as though I've mentally aged at least a decade tonight and I hate it. I'm scared, and there's no one here to help me, to be with me.

That's not entirely true...

I glare at the blue eyes drifting through the first rays of sunlight. They are here, they are always watching.

I don't trust them, not anymore. I don't know how they are connected, but they took my brother from me. Somehow, I know it's their fault.

I dig the board into the ground above Karl's body and stand back to look at it. One last tear falls down my face as I stare at the sloppy grave.

"I'm sorry," I whisper to my brother. I wipe the tears from my face and set my gaze hard. Karl will now expect me to be strong, to fill the role he had to play for so many years. Karl needs me, and I will not let him down.

I make the vow within myself to never shed a tear again, to never let my weakness show, to be the man Karl needs me to be, not the boy I've always been.

Edmund

1950

Nine years after Dolion and Loralie's deaths...
Five hours after Karl's death

Something is wrong with Devil Oasis, Karl's hanging body convinced me of that. I shove my belongings into a small bag as my heart races frantically.

Leave.

I have to leave.

Or I might end up just like Karl.

Sick images of darkness and death fill my mind, and though I don't know what the cause is, I know it won't go away until I've left this land.

My hands shake as I pick up my bag and pull it onto my shoulder. Lilliana said I could stay at her house for a while. Her parents like me, she said. She's told them about me.

I walk out of the shack, the only home I've known besides our tarp and branch shelter a few years back, and leave Devil Oasis and its dark and twisted trees behind.

Edmund

1955

**Fourteen years after Dolion and Loralie's deaths...
Five years after Karl's death**

I pull at my hair as I stare at the newspaper for the millionth time. There's got to be something here that can help.

I may have left Devil Oasis five years ago, but Devil Oasis has never left me. Every night, I'm flooded with dreams of darkness and terror and horror. A boy and a girl only a few years older than me whisper to me in my dreams, telling me things I wish I didn't have to know.

Each death is on your hands, each death is because you aren't here... Over and over again their voices drive me insane, it's gotten so bad lately I swear I've started hearing them while I'm awake too.

Each death is on my hands. I didn't know what that meant for years. Not until one morning when Lilliana's father huffed deeply as he slammed the morning paper on the kitchen table and exclaimed in anger that another child had gone missing and was presumed dead. *Another child.* He said it like there has been many more before that one. So I started collecting the newspapers to read myself.

At least once every few months, if not more often, a child is reported to go missing. There appears to be no pattern to the disappearances, but there's one thing everyone around me seems blind to, like some sort of spell was placed on them to keep them oblivious to it all. Every child who disappears is nineteen.

With every disappearance I read about, I become more and more certain whatever happened to these kids is exactly what happened to my brother. I would bet anything it's also the same thing that happened to Lilliana's brother. And I know Devil Oasis, it's sick and vile rot, is responsible for it all.

Edmund

1957

**Sixteen years after Dolion and Loralie's deaths...
Seven years after Karl's death**

I smack the table and stand from my seat, pacing my room. There has to be something here. A clue or *something* that will help me figure out what's going on.

The newspapers that litter my room overwhelm me. It feels as though each one of them is a death begging to be solved. Not a single article, not one, mentions Devil Oasis. Is the world fucking blind? It's so obvious! The forest has something to do with this!

Yet nobody sees. I tried to tell them, but they wouldn't believe me. Then, because of how strongly I voiced my opinion, the public started to suspect me and Lilliana's family. Everyone is so damn blind.

A surge of anger bursts through me and I kick my trash can. The contents spill across the floor. Crumpled paper and failed ideas I had thrown in the garbage now stare back at me.

I slump to the floor amongst the mess.

I'm a failure...

"I'm sorry, Karl. I really thought I could do it." My eyes start to water and I panic, quickly standing and rubbing my palms on my pants. Everything is all right. It has to be all right. I haven't cried since the night of Karl's death, and I'm not about to now.

A small knock comes from the door.

"Edmund?" It's Lilliana's sweet voice. She opens the door and when she sees me, lost to this world of madness, her eyes soften with sorrow. "Come out for a little. I made you some food. It would be good for you to eat."

She walks to me and places her hand on my back. She's too good to me, too kind. I don't deserve the way she treats me. I'm too cold and hard. I know that, and I know she knows it too.

"People are dying, Lilliana. I can't just take a break. For all I know we are hours away from another death. If I just figure out what's going on, maybe I can stop it. Don't you see why this is important?"

"This doesn't have anything to do with you." Though she speaks softly, her words anger me.

"It has *everything* to do with me. It killed my brother. And yours too! Have you forgotten about him?"

"Of course I haven't forgotten!" Lilliana pulls away from me. "But you've created a whole conspiracy out of their deaths when there isn't one there. And it's ruining you, Edmund Lillich. Can't you see that?"

I discovered my last name during all of my research. Now Lilliana loves using it when she's mad at me.

"This is real, Lil, and I am so sick of you not believing me." I turn away from her, back toward my papers and newspaper clippings.

"This isn't who you are," she says. When I don't reply, I hear the door to the room close. And just like that, I'm alone again.

This is real... I know it's real. Karl would have believed me.

Edmund

1958

**Seventeen years after Dolion and Loralie's deaths...
Eight years after Karl's death**

"I'm going!" I shout at her again.

"Edmund." She breathes deep and calms herself as she stares into my eyes. She has the most beautiful brown eyes. "Please don't, please stay here."

"I'm tired of having this argument with you." I close my eyes and fight to stay as calm as she is. "The people in Devil Oasis need me. I've told you what's going on there, Lilliana. How can you expect me to stay here and not do anything?"

"You've told me your *theory*, Edmund. That's all it is."

"A theory I've been studying and researching for *years*." How can she not see how big this all is? Devil Oasis, the land that took Karl, is ripping other families apart as well. "I know what's happening. How can I not do something about it?"

"Please, Edmund. This doesn't have to involve you."

"It's involved me since the day I was born, Lil. It will corrupt me, drive me to insanity, if I don't do something."

She looks at me with fear in her eyes, and with a look so heartbreaking I have to look away. "It already has," she whispers.

Those three words ignite something within me. A fire, a swirling rage of anger. "It took everyone I love, Lilliana!" I shout at her. She flinches, tears filling her beautiful eyes.

"Well *I* love *you*, you idiot!" I pause as I realize the mistake I made. Damn.

Devil Oasis.

It drove Karl mad. It feasted on him. I will not let that happen to more families.

"I'm sorry," I tell her, shaking my head. I grab the bag I've kept packed every day I've been here and the knife I've grown accustomed to carrying around. "I'm leaving. Do not try to stop me or follow me."

And she didn't. That broke my heart more than anything else she could have.

1998-2003

Edmund

1998

**Fifty-seven years after Dolion and Loralie's deaths...
Forty-eight years after Karl's death**

"I'm not happy about this, you know. Neither of them would have wanted this."

I stare into the man's eyes and force my face to stay set hard. He will not make me lose my temper. That's all he wants, to prove that they were right about me.

He shakes his head and hands the sleeping child to me. I cradle him in my arms. "How old is he?" I ask, ignoring his last words.

"If you had been a good father and grandfather, you would know how old your grandson is."

"Damn it, Marcel, tell me how old he is." I bite the inside of my cheek and curse myself. *Just get past this and then you won't have to deal with this anymore. Your life can be your life, alone and right again.*

"He's three months old, Edmund." Marcel looks just like her, his sister. The French woman my son ran off with years ago. "He was with me and my wife when his parents were in the accident."

"What's his name?" I hold the baby closer to myself. I didn't do things right with my son, this baby's father. I understand that. But this forest and the children within it, they need me. I knew Peter would be safe with his mother and I didn't want this curse's poison to infect him. Not like it had with Karl. Not like it has with me.

So I stayed away. I was an absent father.

And now my son is gone and I can never fix my mistakes.

The baby in my arms opens his eyes and looks intently at me. I'm surprised he's not crying.

"Clair," Marcel says. "His name is Clair Mathieu."

"That's French." Marcel nods at my words. "His mother's last name?"

"They didn't want him associated with you." Marcel looks me up and down, his eyes catch for a moment on my mud covered boots. "Peter wanted to pretend he had never been your son. He had wanted to protect his own son from you."

I keep my face steady despite the pain that shutters through me. My jaw clenches and I hold the baby tighter.

"If I could take him and keep him away from you, I would. But you're who the state sought out. Good luck, Edmund. I'll be here to pick up your slack when you inevitably fail."

Marcel then leaves. And I'm left alone, standing in this forest with my only remaining family in my hands. I lean my head back to the sky and close my eyes.

"What do I do now, Karl?" I ask my brother.

I know, if he were still alive, he'd tell me to protect this boy the way he protected me. He needs me. I hold Clair close to my chest and step into the small shack Karl and I had lived in together many years ago.

"Hello, Clair." I lay him on the cot and swaddle him in extra blankets. "I'm your grandfather."

As I carefully light a fire, very aware of how the flames seem to be getting closer to me, as if they want me, I think about the small boy laying on the cot. Maybe I need him too.

Edmund

2003

Sixty-two years after Dolion and Loralie's deaths...
Fifty-three years after Karl's death

Clair runs through the trees of Devil Oasis, much like I had when I was his age, only five years old. And I watch over him as he plays, just as Karl did for me back then.

I've only left the forest a few times since I left Lilliana's house. My mission has been clear to me since I figured out what happened to my brother. I have protected as many kids from Dolion and Loralie as I possibly can, and I will do so until the day I die.

I eye my grandson as guilt washes through me. I'm subjecting him to this nightmare. But, I've been able to save over thirty children since I started this. I know when the time comes, I can save Clair, too.

Clair looks at a small bug in frustration. He had told the bug to hop into his hand so they could go on a hike together. The bug did not listen. In many ways, Clair reminds me of my older brother. Karl would be proud of him. So would Lilliana.

Author Q&A

Have these books gone down the road you expected when you started writing?

No. Not at all. When I started this series I was in the middle of another series that I have yet to publish. It was, at the time, the largest project I had attempted to take on and so I needed a break. I wanted to write a short story, my hope was a novella, something that would be easier to write and edit. Spoiler alert: it's nearly four years later and I am still in the middle of that "little" project that ended up turning into one of the hardest things I've ever done.

When I first came up with the idea for this story, this is what it looked like. It was going to be a standalone novella about a girl named Evina who lost her brother Ehno to suicide a few years back. She ended up going into a nearby cemetery called Devil Oasis in an attempt to discover what had happened to him. There, a girl named Loralie who was about Evina's age, nineteen, formed from Evina's own mind and attempted to convince Evina to kill herself. Along the way Evina met an old man, the cemetery caretaker, who went by the name of Mr. Clair. Evina eventually discovered that Loralie was never a separate person, she was actually another part of Evina's mind. A side of her thoughts that she had personified into a girl named Loralie.

Obviously the story has grown a lot over time, but you can see where it started. That was my vision for the book in the beginning, and along the way it grew into something much bigger and greater than I could have ever imagined.

Which was more challenging to write? Dark Oasis or Vile Hope?

This is an interesting question. I think Vile Hope was harder for one reason: Dolion and Loralie's story. Dolion and Loralie's story is easily the most challenging thing I have ever written, and I think a lot of that has to do with the psychology of it all. I spent hours researching topics that were hard to read about, and I drew from aspects of my childhood for their home life that was emotionally difficult to think back on. I knew I had to get Dolion and Loralie's story exactly right, I knew I needed to tell the truth about who they were and are, but I got so lost along the way and it seemed like the end was never in sight. At one point Dolion and Loralie's story had strayed so far from the truth of what happened to these characters, it all became so muddled and messy within my own mind that I ended up having a massive breakdown. Thankfully though, the best breakdowns are always accompanied by a breakthrough.

Dark Oasis was absolutely hard to write, but Vile Hope was just so different, something about it was deeper and darker, and I think it had to be that way to do Dolion and Loralie justice.

What has been the process for writing this series?

It's all been one huge mess. I started with Evina's part and that was meant to be the entire story. But it kept growing. I wrote half of Evina's story before I took a break to write the entirety of Dolion and Loralie's story. After that I either finished Evina's story or drafted Clair's, I don't remember which came first. And then after all of that was written I wrote Perdu's story.

After I had written all of those my plan was, at that point, for it to all be one book. It was going to be in the same order it is now, Clair, Perdu, Dolion and Loralie, and Evina, but instead of being spread across two books, all four stories were in one and it was going to be a standalone titled Silent Chaos. As I was editing I could tell that something was off. I tried multiple ways to resolve the issue, including drafting a second book that took place maybe twenty or so years after the events of the first book. That's a complicated topic though that I'll probably get into in the Q&A in book 3's hardcover, since the two new characters in book 3 originate from that non-existent book that I had started writing. Needless to say, that book was scrapped and I went back to having just the one book. But still, something was missing. There was so much to the story I knew I hadn't explored. I ended up deciding the answer was in the epilogue. So I tried multiple variants of the epilogue but it felt like I was trying to cram an entire book of information into just a few pages. Which I was. Finally, I made the decision to listen to what the story was telling me to do, and I made the series a trilogy. The book had been growing so much at that point that I either had to start suffocating the story that wanted to be told, or give in and let it flourish. So I separated the book into two books, Dark Oasis and Vile Hope, and made the epilogue an entire third book instead of trying to stifle the information. I still remember that day, sitting in my room at the secretary my grandfather had built, staring at all of my notes and my screen. I even talked it over with my mom, as I often do with everything writing related, and I finally accepted that this story is a series, not just a standalone.

Do you have any regrets with the series so far?

In Clair's story in Dark Oasis, during one of Lady's first chapters when she is saying goodbye to Karl and Edmund, she mentioned something about how they will not age again until Dolion and Loralie die. Even though I didn't change that aspect of the story, I did cut out her mentioning that in book 1 and I do regret it. It has made it a little harder to explain in book 2 why Karl and Edmund don't age, and that part doesn't flow through the series as effortlessly as it could have.

Other than that it would be really easy to say that I regret things like how much money I spent on unnecessary things to publish Dark Oasis or things like that, and I do have days where I wish I was smarter with my money back then, but I learned a lot of valuable lessons from all of that, and even though a lot of it wasn't needed, Dark Oasis wouldn't be what it is without all of that and I really love that book.

How has the process for writing Vile Hope differed from writing Dark Oasis?

Well, the first part of editing Dark Oasis and Vile Hope were done at the same time and the process was the same since it was only one book at that point. Other than that, even though they have taken different routes, they've both mostly just been me floundering around randomly and attempting to get something right. They were both a lot of failed attempts, a lot of anxiety, late nights, early mornings, stress, fear, and complete messes.

What is your favorite scene in the book?

As much as I absolutely hate the scene where Annalise burns Dolion—I've literally cried because of it before—that is the scene that I always come away from feeling like I nailed it. I'm very proud of it. So even though I hate it, if we're looking at it strictly from a writing perspective and not a story perspective, it is my favorite.

How did you come up with the titles for your series?

So, as I've already explained, at the very beginning, when it was just Evina's story and nothing else, the book was called Evina Means Life. That's the reason I chose Evina's name, because it means life, so I thought it was a good fit. After I added Clair's story, Perdu's story, and Dolion and Loralie's story, that title just didn't work anymore. I spent eight months trying to come up with a new title. I went through *so* many cringy and terrible titles. I tried a bunch of different techniques and watched several videos on how to title your book, until eventually I wrote down a bunch of words that had to do with the book and started pairing them together to create dozens of different titles. Then I picked my favorite ones (probably eight or so) and posted them to a writers subreddit I was involved with at the time, asking everyone to pick their favorites. Silent Chaos was among them, and that title won. I decided to go with Silent Chaos. But then the book became a trilogy, meaning I had to rename *again*. I decided I wanted to keep Silent Chaos, but I knew that title didn't fit the first or second books anymore. But it did fit the third. So I named the third book in the series before I named the first two. From there I believe I named Dark Oasis next, but I might be wrong. Either way, as I approached naming the first two books, I knew I wanted the title to be uniform with Silent Chaos, and I decided that I wanted all of the titles to be two words, both of the words contradicting each other, and I wanted each title to be a mental state or mindset that the characters have during the story.

With Dark Oasis I loved the idea of having the word *oasis* in the title, since it's such a beautiful word and has such a strong meaning, so I knew I needed to find a word that was contradictory to *oasis* and explained what my characters were going through internally. The word *dark* kept coming back to mind. I was worried, though, that having the title of the book be Dark Oasis when the name of the forest is Devil Oasis would be confusing. I got several people's opinions on it and thankfully they all said they don't think that it's an issue.

Vile Hope took me a while to name. I was constantly keeping an eye out for words that would be perfect for the title and one day while I was reading a book the word *vile* was used and I was so intrigued by it. I ended up looking up the meaning and decided it was perfect. I honestly don't really remember when or how I decided *hope* would be the other half of the title, but either way, I love it. For me it represents those moments in life when you get your hopes up and you're let down. When it begins to happen so often that you start to view hope as more of a painful thing than a good thing.

What's one thing you learned through the process of this book?

Only one thing? Okay, let's see if I can narrow it down. I think the most valuable thing I have learned while writing Vile Hope is that, even when it feels like you've lost a very important part of yourself, it's never truly gone, just hidden. Throughout the last half of writing Vile Hope I lost my love and passion for writing for a while and that was difficult and scary. But I got it back, and now I'm as in love with my stories as ever.

Another thing I learned with Vile Hope is to listen closely to my characters. They are always in the loudest corner of my mind, attempting to tell me their story. Instead of fighting against them, I need to listen to them. But that's two things, so I should stop talking or I'll keep going.

Which character is most like you?

Well, in the Q&A in Dark Oasis I talked more in depth about what parts of me I see in each of the characters, because small parts of who I am is in each of them, so I won't go too into detail with that so I don't repeat myself. But the character I see myself in the *most* is both Clair and Evina. Clair is very similar to the adult version of myself. He's who I have become through years of heartache and pain. Evina was very heavily written for my child self. Not just inspired by who I was back then, but she was actually written for who I was about ten years ago, as a way to preserve the type of person I had been. So I look at Evina with a sort of nostalgic love.

Do you have a routine or a process that you use to write?

No (I wish I could add a laughing emoji to this), my writing "process" or lack thereof, is really just one massive scramble to get the book out on time. It's so random and chaotic, and there is no way I could ever repeat the same process twice.

There were some new characters added to this book. Who do you love? Who do you hate?

I love the majority of the characters that were added to the series. Keep in mind that, even though for you guys they are new characters, to me because of the order I wrote these books in, they've been around much longer than some of the characters in book 1. Jonny and Emile's characters existed long before Perdu was a developed character, so to me they're not new, they're just... original I guess. Marie is probably my favorite of the characters that were added in book 2. Yes, she was mentioned in book 1, but she didn't really have much of her own page time. She's inspired a lot by my mom, she was even named after my mom. I love how loyal she is, and how protective she is over Evina. When Perdu died she really stepped up. I like Jonny too. He's a complex character who didn't get much time on page to really be explored. Who knows, maybe we'll get to learn more about him in the future. I'm not a fan of Emile at all, I don't really like Charles or his family (besides Arron), and Annalise still remains as one of my least favorites. Arron was a character that I loved to write, and I really hope I get the chance in the future, whether through short stories or another way, to explore him deeper. His relationship with Emmeline is so intriguing to me, even though it was only brought up maybe twice in the entire book. I want to learn more about that and I'm hoping an opportunity will present itself at some point.

What were the biggest differences between book 1 and book 2 for you?

The biggest difference between the two was really just my personal life. A lot has changed from when I started writing the series, and who I am as a person has changed a lot too. My life circumstances between the two books were just very different. For Dark Oasis I was incredibly focused on the story and regularly spent eight to twelve hour days working on the book. With Vile Hope I just didn't have that type of time anymore and I had to learn how to make time. That was a very interesting change of pace for me to learn to work with.

For book 1 it was anything but straightforward. I had hired a cover designer way back when the series was still one book (which was *way* too early to be knee deep in cover design) and after getting a good way through it my cover designer disappeared for about six months. I couldn't get a hold of her and I definitely started to panic. I had paid her a portion of the money already so I couldn't really afford to start designing a new cover with a new artist until I knew what was going on with that situation. Eventually she got back in touch with me, explained what happened and apologized, and she refunded me the money. It worked out because I wasn't as ready to design the cover as I thought I was and the story changed a lot since then and that cover wouldn't have gone with the story as well as the one I have now, but it was a stressful experience. I learned two important things from that time. Don't start cover design before you know for a fact what your story is going to need, but start the process as early as possible in case something goes wrong and you need the time to reassess and recover (no pun intended) the situation.

I looked through a *ton* of cover designers and artists trying to find the right one to do my cover, and after quite a few struggles, I finally found the very talented artist who did the covers for Dark Oasis and Vile Hope. I'm hoping to hire her for Silent Chaos as well. I have had a lot of anxiety over the design process for both covers, but as long as you hire a designer you know you can trust, everything will work out for the best in the end. I think my biggest fear with cover design so far is that I will never find the perfect cover to be obsessed with. I've had multiple covers designed at this point and I can safely say I am obsessed with all of them.

How did Lady come to be?

Lady really started as a convenient tool for me to use to explain things the characters couldn't explain to the readers, but as time has gone on she's become the unofficial narrator of the story. She's woven herself into the story to a point that now even the curse wouldn't be what it is without Lady. She's a role model to me, and she reminds me a lot of my mom. A lot of inspiration for her has come from the person my mom is.

In the original (deleted) version of the prologue for book 1, we saw Annalise give birth to Dolion and Loralie. And this random lady kind of came out of the lake (if I am remembering correctly) and spoke some sort of prophecy about the twins to Annalise and Henry. That was Lady's first appearance in the story, and that's all it was originally meant to be. But over time her character evolved and became something much different than what I originally had in store for her. At the beginning she wasn't even Karl and Edmund's mother. She wasn't really anybody.

Marie (art by MacKenzie Neher):

Keep reading for a sneak peek of book 3!

Chapter One

Lady

When my head finally breaks the surface, I sharply inhale, a cold pain running through my chest. My hair falls heavy and wet on top of my head, the ends still floating carelessly in the water. It's a strange sensation, one I haven't felt in so long. My vision is blurry as I look through wet eyelashes. My body aches but is numb at the same time. The water splashes around me as I move, my joints throbbing. My body has awoken. I can finally walk on land once again.

I had forgotten what pain felt like. I had forgotten what it felt like to be constricted by my own body.

Somehow, I end up on the shore, my toes buried soothingly in the mud as I pull my body out of the water, instantly becoming heavy without the force of the lake surrounding me. My soaked and dripping dress hangs from my shoulders, clung tightly to my skin as I continue stepping forward. The gentle wind sends shivers through me. The bottom of my dress drags in the sand, collecting grains of the fine dirt. I blink a few times slowly, my eyes coming into focus on the forest standing tall before me.

Large, dark, dense trees line the edge of the lake. Long dry grass blows in the wind below, creating a soft brushing melody throughout the forest. The air smells faintly like fresh mint and a cool summer breeze. So this is the forest I have been feeling and watching as it has grown into something greater all these years. This was once the field where my children would play. This is where the twins had died. This is where everything happened.

The rush of the waves causes me to turn my head, laying eyes on my lake for the first time ever. I knew it was growing worse. I knew the life in this once beautiful water was fading, but when I see what it has become, I'm nearly sick. It's dirty, it's intoxicated. Halcyon Lake does not look like the beauty and peace it is meant to provide. Not anymore. Not since Clair left and all of the light and hope faded. Just like the rest of the forest, it has become darker since then, darker with each death that passes through.

"I'm sorry," I whisper to my home.

Then I turn my back on the water, facing the dark forest again.

Things are changing once more, Devil Oasis is breaking rules. It's time I break some rules myself. I am sick of watching people die and doing nothing about it, so I force my feet forward, digging into the muddy dirt below as I take step after step toward the exit gate of Devil Oasis.

Want to continue reading? Book 3 releases 2025...

Would you like to know more?

**Follow Jacie Neher on Instagram @jacieneher or keep reading for
a couple fun questions about book 3!**

Which characters is book 3 about?

Part One of Book 3 follows Lady's POV as we learn more about her and
her previous life. Part Two follows everyone as the finale unfolds. Clair,
Evina, Dolion, Loralie, Lady, and two new characters fight against Devil
Oasis in an attempt to end the cycle once and for all.

When does this book take place?

Book 3 takes place after the events of Evina's story!

Bloopers!

This page contains some of my favorite typos from the editing process.

- Karl was still so young, so innocefinent. And they took him.

- My lungs burn and my feet ache, my knees weaken and threaten to fall apart.

- I can feel deat45h approaching, his claws preparing to dig into my back. (I had a cat on my lap. Also, I don't think this scene necessarily exists anymore.)

- I look at me feet.

- In a flinker of an instant my chest tightens and my arms want to move to hug her.

- The mubble of the townsfolk continues behind us as we come to a stop.

- I find myself slightly jealous, wishish I had grown up this way.

- And we actually had a life, smething to live for.

- Goosebumps creep up my spink and my muscles stiffen.

- Even though I'm not looking at Clair I can hear him shift in the dift.

Acknowledgments

Here we go again, writing the acknowledgements. This might be my favorite part of writing a book. I always save the acknowledgements so it's one of the very last things I write. That way I can take this moment to reflect on the journey this book has been. And my, what a journey Vile Hope has taken me on. It's so surreal to think that this book is done and my time with this story is almost over. There's only one book left in this series now. I guess we'd better get on with the acknowledgments before I get too emotional.

First, as always, Mom. You continue to be my biggest supporter and my greatest encouragement. Without your love, support, and the years you spent raising me and teaching me I never would have become the woman I am today. I love you, more than life itself. More than I love this series (and that really says something). Pieces of who you are have been braided into this book because you inspire me and I look up to you. Clair has your heart, how much you care for other people. Marie has the comfort and peace I always feel around you. And Lady, well her character is special. She was inspired almost entirely by you. By the type of mother you have always been to me and my sisters. She was inspired by your bravery and your strength. Everything I love about Lady I love about you. Thank you for being you, don't ever stop. We got this.

Next, Lily. You read this book way back when it wasn't a series, only a standalone. You gave me some of the first feedback that made me feel like I can do this, like maybe it really is a good story. For so many years you have been one of my very best friends, and I love seeing things about you shine through this book. Your drawings for the page numbers are, as always, amazing. The way the three of our relationships as sisters has grown and changed has inspired my love for writing close siblings like Evina and Perdu or even Dolion and Loralie. I love that Dolion and Loralie's appearance was inspired by you and how truly beautiful you are. I am so proud of the person you are becoming. You are so strong and capable, and I look forward to seeing where you go from here. I love you.

Kenzie. You have spent so many hours with me working out massive plot problems and publishing struggles. This book wouldn't be where it is if it weren't for you. You are a beautiful, bright, and talented person, and I am so thankful I get to call you my sister. So many elements of this story has been inspired by you, by the struggles you have faced and overcome. I love that I can see pieces of who you are in this book, even just in the way that Clair's freckles were inspired by yours. Your art for the hardcover edition is amazing and I can't wait to see what the next book looks like. You've grown up so much even just in the last year. I am so proud of you and everything you are. Keep smiling. I promise everything will be okay. I love you.

As you, the reader, can probably see at this point, the most important thing to me about my books is forever keeping a part of my loved ones close in the form of my writing. I love etching who they are into my books and filling my work with reminders of the people and places I hold closest. As the list continues, remember how much I value every one of you, and how much you have impacted my books and my career.

Thank you to my beta readers, who I really took on a wild ride this time around. It was a chaotic one! As always your feedback has brought this story to a point where it can really shine and I am so thankful for all of your help.

To everyone who participated in bringing the physical book to life, thank you for making this book the beauty it is. Lexie from Selkkie Designs outdid herself with the cover art once again. Daphne Paige's art for Karl and Edmund's short story in the hardcover edition as well as the page breaks are as beautiful as ever. Lily's art is absolutely stunning, and Kenzie's drawing of Marie in the hardcover edition is gorgeous.

To everyone who supported and inspired me, Miranda, Grandma Carolyn, BroPa, Jon, Daphne, Deani Driver, and many, many more, thank you for everything you've done for me.

To the characters of this story who have always had my back and been there for me, Clair, Evina, Perdu, Julie, Marie, Dolion, Karl, Edmund, and yes, even you, Loralie, I hope I have done your story justice and I am so thankful we still have one more book together. You guys have changed me, and I will forever hold you close to my heart.

To my readers, the love and support my characters and story has received has been a dream come true. I am so grateful for a community like you all, and I only hope this story stays with you throughout your life. I hope you remember that you are never alone, even when it feels like nobody cares or understands. You are not alone in what you are going through. I promise.

Lastly, I owe a huge thank you to myself. This book was *rough* to write, and I am so thankful I had the determination to stick with it. I am so thankful I never gave up.

As this adventure closes, the next one begins. On to the next book!

Jacie Neher started writing when she was ten years old. Her first book was about a boy trapped on an island. The story was pretty dark considering the author was so young. Since then, she's been obsessed with stories, and when she finally started drafting the Dark Oasis trilogy at the age of seventeen, something just clicked. She knew it was the story she was meant to tell. She's changed a lot since the beginning of the series, but she knows no matter what happens, the Dark Oasis trilogy will always be at the heart of who she is.

During the summer, she's probably at the Renaissance Festival, and in the cold months she's out enjoying the snow.

To learn more about Jacie, follow her on Instagram @jacieneher